T0308987

LEGEND OF THE GALACTIC HEROES

VOLUME 8
DESOLATION

YOSHIKI TANAKA

HAIKA SORU

SAN FRANCISCO

LEGEND OF THE GALACTIC HEROES

VOLUME 8
DESOLATION

WRITTEN BY
YOSHIKI TANAKA

Translated by Matt Treyvaud

Legend of the Galactic Heroes, Volume 8: Desolation
GINGA EIYU DENSETSU Vol. 8
© 1987 by Yoshiki TANAKA
Cover Illustration © 2008 Yukinobu Hoshino.
All rights reserved.

English translation © 2018 VIZ Media, LLC .
Cover and interior design by Fawn Lau and Alice Lewis

No portion of this book may be reproduced or transmitted in any form or
by any means without written permission from the copyright holders.

HAIKASORU
Published by VIZ Media, LLC
P.O. Box 77010
San Francisco, CA 94107

www.haikasoru.com

Library of Congress Cataloging-in-Publication Data

Names: Tanaka, Yoshiki, 1952- author. | Huddleston, Daniel, translator.
Title: Legend of the galactic heroes / written by Yoshiki Tanaka ; translated
    by Daniel Huddleston and Tyran Grillo and Matt Treyvaud
Other titles: Ginga eiyu densetsu
Description: San Francisco : Haikasoru, [2016]
Identifiers: LCCN 2015044444| ISBN 9781421584942 (v. 1: paperback) | ISBN
    9781421584959 (v. 2: paperback) | ISBN 9781421584966 (v. 3: paperback) | ISBN
    9781421584973 (v. 4: paperback) | ISBN 9781421584980 (v. 5: paperback) | ISBN
    9781421584997 (v. 6: paperback) | ISBN 9781421585291 (v. 7: paperback) | ISBN
    9781421585017 (v. 8: paperback)
    v. 1. Dawn -- v. 2. Ambition -- v. 3. Endurance -- v. 4. Stratagem -- v. 5. Mobilization --
    v. 6. Flight -- v. 7. Tempest -- v. 8. Desolation
Subjects: LCSH: Science fiction. | War stories. | BISAC: FICTION / Science
    Fiction / Space Opera. | FICTION / Science Fiction / Military. | FICTION /
    Science Fiction / Adventure.
Classification: LCC PL862.A5343 G5513 2016 | DDC 895.63/5--dc23
LC record available at http://lccn.loc.gov/2015044444

Printed in the U.S.A.
First printing, December 2018

MAJOR CHARACTERS

GALACTIC EMPIRE

REINHARD VON LOHENGRAMM
Kaiser.

PAUL VON OBERSTEIN
Minister of military affairs. Marshal.

WOLFGANG MITTERMEIER
Commander in chief of the Imperial Space Armada. Marshal. Known as the "Gale Wolf."

OSKAR VON REUENTAHL
Secretary-general of Supreme Command Headquarters. Marshal. Has heterochromiac eyes.

FRITZ JOSEF WITTENFELD
Commander of the Schwarz Lanzenreiter fleet. Senior admiral.

ERNEST MECKLINGER
Rear supreme commander. Senior admiral. Known as the "Artist-Admiral."

ULRICH KESSLER
Commissioner of military police and commander of imperial capital defenses. Senior admiral.

AUGUST SAMUEL WAHLEN
Fleet commander. Senior admiral.

KORNELIAS LUTZ
Fleet commander. Senior admiral.

ARTHUR VON STREIT
Senior imperial aide. Vice admiral.

HILDEGARD VON MARIENDORF
Chief imperial secretary. Often called "Hilda."

FRANZ VON MARIENDORF
Minister of domestic affairs. Hilda's father.

GÜNTER KISSLING
Head of the imperial guard. Commodore.

HEIDRICH LANG
Chief of the Domestic Safety Security Bureau.

ANNEROSE VON GRÜNEWALD
Reinhard's elder sister. Countess von Grünewald. Archduchess.

RUDOLF VON GOLDENBAUM
Founder of the Galactic Empire's Goldenbaum Dynasty.

DECEASED

SIEGFRIED KIRCHEIS
Died living up to the faith Annerose placed in him.

FREE PLANETS ALLIANCE

YANG WEN-LI
Commander of Iserlohn Fortress. Commander of Iserlohn Patrol Fleet. Marshal. Retired.

JULIAN MINTZ
Yang's ward. Sublieutenant.

FREDERICA GREENHILL YANG
Yang's aide and wife. Lieutenant commander.

ALEX CASELNES
Acting general manager of rear services. Vice admiral.

WALTER VON SCHÖNKOPF
Commander of fortress defenses. Vice admiral. Retired.

EDWIN FISCHER
Vice commander of Iserlohn Patrol Fleet. Master of fleet operations. Temporarily relieved of duty.

MURAI
Chief of staff. Vice admiral. Temporarily relieved of duty.

FYODOR PATRICHEV
Deputy chief of staff. Rear admiral. Temporarily relieved of duty.

DUSTY ATTENBOROUGH
Division commander within the Iserlohn Patrol Fleet. Yang's underclassman. Vice admiral. Retired.

OLIVIER POPLIN
Captain of the First Spaceborne Division at Iserlohn Fortress. Commander.

LOUIS MACHUNGO
Julian's security guard. Ensign.

KATEROSE VON KREUTZER
Corporal. Often called "Karin."

WILIABARD JOACHIM MERKATZ
Veteran admiral. Commander of the Yang Fleet's remaining troops.

BERNARD VON SCHNEIDER
Merkatz's aide. Commander.

DECEASED

ALEXANDOR BUCOCK
Died as the last great admiral of the Alliance Armed Forces.

CHUNG WU-CHEN
General chief of staff. Died in battle with his commander.

FORMER PHEZZAN DOMINION

ADRIAN RUBINSKY
The fifth landesherr. Known as the "Black Fox of Phezzan."

DOMINIQUE SAINT-PIERRE
Rubinsky's mistress.

NICOLAS BOLTEC
Acting governor-general.

BORIS KONEV
Independent merchant. Old acquaintance of Yang's. Captain of the merchant ship *Beryozka*.

ARCHBISHOP DE VILLIERS
Secretary-general of the Church of Terra.

*Titles and ranks correspond to each character's status at the end of *Tempest* or their first appearance in *Desolation*.

TABLE OF CONTENTS

CHAPTER 1:

I
STARS LIKE SHATTERED CRYSTAL shone upon the golden-haired young man who stepped out of the landcar. The assembled crowd of soldiers roared, and his fair locks seemed to gleam all the brighter with the ring of their cry: *Sieg Kaiser!* Reinhard von Lohengramm raised his hand to acknowledge the crowd, which roared again. The boy once dismissed as "that golden brat" by the nobles who opposed him was now hailed as the "golden lion." And just as Reinhard never tired of gazing at the stars, his loyal soldiers would have happily basked in the aura of their youthful emperor forever.

It was April 2, SE 800, year 2 of the New Imperial Calendar. The twenty-four-year-old kaiser was preparing to leave the planet Heinessen, former capital of the now-defeated Free Planets Alliance, for the next destination on his journey of conquest: Iserlohn Corridor. He already held the better part of the galaxy in his porcelain-white palm. He had usurped the Galactic Empire, annexed the Phezzan Dominion, and crushed the alliance utterly. Only a few grains of stardust had slipped through his slender fingers—but those grains were now the last redoubt of the political force that had controlled half the galaxy for 250 years. As long as they remained outside his control, Reinhard lacked the last piece of the puzzle that must be completed to fulfill his staggering ambition of conquering the entire galaxy.

Reinhard accepted the reverent salute of Commodore Seidlitz, captain of the Imperial Navy fleet flagship *Brünhild*, and stepped aboard. He was followed by his staff officers from imperial headquarters—around twenty in all, including Marshal Oskar von Reuentahl, secretary-general of Supreme Command Headquarters—and his personal bodyguard Emil von Selle.

"Fräulein von Mariendorf!" said Reinhard.

A young woman stepped forward. Hildegard von Mariendorf was the daughter of Minister of Domestic Affairs Count Franz von Mariendorf and chief secretary to the kaiser in her own right. She was a year younger than Reinhard, and kept her dark-blond hair closely cropped, giving her the mien of a lively, perceptive, and beautiful young boy.

"Yes, Your Highness?"

"Has that matter we discussed been taken care of? I forgot to check for myself."

The young countess did not seek clarification of Reinhard's vague inquiry. Not for nothing was her ingenuity said to be worth more than a fleet of warships.

"Your wishes have been conveyed to the relevant parties, Your Highness. You may rest assured that you will not encounter that displeasing sight again."

Reinhard nodded in satisfaction. On the occasion of his departure from Heinessen, he had ordered the destruction of just one nonmilitary structure: the great bronze statue of Ahle Heinessen, founding father of the Free Planets Alliance.

This was not mere conqueror's hubris. The main memorial to Heinessen, as well as his tomb, had been left untouched. The statue was targeted partly for political reasons and partly out of a cynical solicitude for the reputation of the man it depicted. Reinhard had never suffered from the psychic illness that drove some to assert power and authority with outsized effigies, and his imperial edict on the topic had made his position on the matter clear to the entire galaxy. For as long as the Lohengramm Dynasty survived, no one would be permitted to erect a statue to any emperor less than ten years after their death, or in any case larger than life.

"If Heinessen was worthy of the esteem in which the people of the alliance hold him, he would surely have backed my decision," Reinhard said to Hildegard. "No statue, however imposing, can stand against a righteous man."

Hildegard nodded, and Reinhard switched the channel of his thoughts from planetside matters to the stars.

Senior Admirals Fritz Josef Wittenfeld and Adalbert Fahrenheit had left the planet in advance of Reinhard and were currently leading their respective fleets toward Iserlohn Corridor. Both were fearless commanders always eager to go on the offensive, but Wittenfeld in particular was known for his valiant leadership of the Schwarz Lanzenreiter fleet. He had been at the vanguard of Reinhard's expeditionary force since its departure last year. His military record was formidable, and he was so well-known that his name had a destructive power all its own.

There was an anecdote about Wittenfeld's fearlessness in which one staff officer asked "Is Wittenfeld at the front?" and another replied "*At* the front? Wittenfeld *is* the front." According to Marshal Wolfgang Mittermeier, commander in chief of the Imperial Space Armada, Wittenfeld had spread this story himself, but no one could deny that it captured him well.

Mittermeier himself was with Reinhard, preparing to depart Heinessen with him alongside the admirals Neidhart Müller and Ernst von Eisenach. On the way to Iserlohn Corridor, they would also rendezvous with Admiral Karl Robert Steinmetz.

Admiral August Samuel Wahlen, too, had left Odin, the Galactic Empire's nominal capital, and was hurrying through the distant Phezzan Corridor to join them at Iserlohn. The task of guarding the Phezzan Corridor had been left to Admiral Kornelias Lutz and his soldiers, but even without them the sheer size of the force that would gather at Iserlohn was prodigious.

Heinessen itself would be under the protection of Admiral Alfred Grillparzer. Grillparzer had formerly served under the now-deceased Helmut Lennenkamp, sent to the planet as high commissioner. The kaiser had warned him on the occasion of his promotion to be fair and magnanimous, and Grillparzer had meekly agreed, vowing to keep Heinessen safe until Admiral von Reuentahl arrived to relieve him.

Von Reuentahl was currently secretary-general of Supreme Command Headquarters, but once Iserlohn Corridor was conquered he was to take command of the entire former Free Planets Alliance territory as its new landesherr. At thirty-three, he was nine years older than the kaiser, and would rule more than half the Neue Reich in His Majesty's name. Von Reuentahl's record of feeding the kaiser's boundless appetite for conquest and dominion was near-flawless, but once the galaxy had been unified, administering this colossal domain would put him to the test on a new front. Of course, no one doubted that he would rise to the challenge.

Admiral Ernest Mecklinger's fleet was stationed at the other end of Iserlohn Corridor to harass the enemy from the rear. A vast net encircling the corridor at both ends was almost complete.

It was fair to say that this vast concentration of force had been mustered to subjugate a single man: Yang Wen-li, former marshal of the Free Planets Alliance, now commander of Iserlohn Fortress and the Iserlohn Patrol Fleet. In the last days of the alliance, the Imperial Navy admiralty had almost come to see Yang as its personification, and begrudging admiration for him drifted both above and below the surface of their psyches. It was difficult to believe how many defeats this single man had handed so many veteran imperial commanders.

Put less charitably, a galaxy-spanning empire was devoting its entire military to defeating a single man. Officially, this was not only to ensure that unification was completed, but also to prevent Yang Wen-li from becoming the core of an anti-imperial movement.

In Reinhard's office on *Brünhild*, effectively the mobile headquarters of the Imperial Navy, the kaiser was considering some specific future maneuvers when his ice-blue eyes suddenly rose to meet those of his secretary Hilda's.

"Tell me, Fräulein von Mariendorf," he said. "Do you remain opposed to my leading this expedition personally?"

Hildegard's opposition to Reinhard's personal involvement in the operation against Yang Wen-li's forces was well-known. There was a roguish twinkle in the smile the kaiser now directed at his beautiful and sagacious secretary, but his object was not to intimidate her. On the contrary—he hoped that she would argue with him.

Hildegard knew this, and obliged him willingly. "If I may speak freely, Your Highness, yes. I do."

The handsome young conqueror's words were evidence that his biorhythms were rising, his psychic energy putting forth new shoots in search of an outlet.

"You are surprisingly stubborn, fräulein," said Reinhard, laughing merrily despite the irony of a man of his personality criticizing her on those grounds in particular.

Hildegard blushed lightly for reasons unclear even to her. "I was under the impression you were already quite familiar with my personality, Your Highness," she said.

And that isn't entirely fair, either, she thought to herself. She opposed Reinhard's involvement not on political or military grounds, but because she knew that his true motivation was personal pride and sheer competitive spirit. To this might be added respect for, and high expectations of, his enemy. If Yang Wen-li were to abandon all resistance and kneel meekly before him, what would Reinhard's reaction be? Disappointment, Hilda suspected, notwithstanding the fact that Yang's defeat had been the kaiser's object since the previous year. Reinhard viewed Yang first and foremost as a worthy opponent, and intended to engage him with the highest of honors—along with impeccable strategy and overwhelming force.

How would Yang react to the Imperial Navy's movement toward Iserlohn? Would he fortify his position in the impregnable Iserlohn Fortress? Would he advance to El Facil at the corridor's exit for a fleet-to-fleet battle? It was impossible to say.

II

The front lines of the Imperial Navy at that moment arced through inhabited space as a vast dragon of light, one well over ten thousand light-years long. The dragon's head was pointed at the former territory of the Free Planets Alliance at one end of Iserlohn Corridor, and its tail reached the worlds of the old empire at the other. If Iserlohn Fortress fell to the Imperial Navy, the dragon would swallow its tail and form a loop drawn tight around humanity's galactic footprint.

In principle, military science frowned on such lengthy lines of battle, but the strategic balance between the two sides was so uneven that it seemed unlikely to become a liability. Yang Wen-li was in Iserlohn Fortress, restricted in his ability to make bold maneuvers. The Imperial Navy might be stretched thin, but he had no way to strike at their flank. Beside that galaxy-spanning dragon of light, Iserlohn Fortress was a bird's egg at best. The strategic inequality between the two sides was staggering, and a tactical victory was Yang's only hope of overturning it. His position was as difficult as it had been before the Vermillion War. But Reinhard knew that using mere strategic leverage to corner and extinguish Yang would not satisfy the ferocious lion stirring now within him.

"Whatever fantastic maneuvers Yang may be considering, ultimately he has just two choices remaining: advance and attack, or retreat and defend. The question of which he will choose—how he will seek to stop me—is a most interesting one."

Reinhard moved according to the whims of the conquering spirit within him. His strategic superiority guaranteed freedom of action. His decision to pin Yang down and wait for his counteroffensive had only been possible because he had already conquered the other 99 percent of the galaxy.

However, Reinhard did not hold all the cards necessary to move history and the people who made it. And the same, of course, could be said of his formidable opponent.

It was April 19 when ill tidings arrived on seismic waves from Phezzan. Terrorists had bombed the residence of the planet's acting secretary-general. Secretary of Works Bruno von Silberberg had been killed. Marshal Paul von Oberstein had been wounded, along with Nicolas Boltec, acting secretary-general, and Senior Admiral Kornelias Lutz, fleet commander for the Phezzan region. Forty-one other casualties had been recorded. Already embarked on his expedition of conquest, the golden-haired kaiser was silent as the news arrived by FTL transmission. His ice-blue eyes glittered with a dark intensity.

The details of the terrorist attack that threatened to contain Reinhard's single-minded advance with filthy, unseen shackles soon became clear.

On April 12, Senior Admiral Wahlen had landed on Phezzan en route to Iserlohn and had been temporarily reunited with Lutz. The two men had served as Siegfried Kircheis's right and left hands during the Lippstadt War, playing no small part in the empire's victory, but now Wahlen was to continue on to Iserlohn to join the fray while his spirits and sense of fulfillment were high, while Lutz would be forced to stay planetside, still smarting from his defeat.

As the newly appointed fleet commander for the Phezzan region, Lutz was responsible for the security of one of the new empire's largest transportation, distribution, and communication routes. The appointment was not ignominious by any means, but, as a warrior, Lutz sorely rued his withdrawal from the front lines just before the final clash with Yang Wen-li. He would have no opportunity to regain the honor he had lost in allowing Yang to recapture Iserlohn Fortress through trickery. His liege and fellow officers would clean up after that mistake in his stead.

Wahlen could not banish the sympathy he felt for his friend. He shared Lutz's humiliation at having fallen for Yang's ruse, which had undone everything they had achieved on the battlefield. To openly express that sympathy would only risk wounding Lutz more deeply, but Wahlen had accepted Boltec's proposal—despite his distaste for its open flattery—and agreed to attend a joint welcome and farewell gathering for the two of them because it had seemed an opportunity to offer at least some comfort to his friend. The party began at 1930 hours, but Wahlen was having trouble with his artificial hand that evening, and by the time he had made the necessary adjustments to his prosthesis and arrived at the venue, it was 1955.

The military-grade high explosives had detonated just five minutes earlier. In a sense, Wahlen's hand had saved him from martyrdom at the hands of the terrorists. Going further back, an observer might give that credit to the fanatic who had wounded Wahlen with a poisoned blade during the subjugation of the Church of Terra's headquarters the previous year.

In any case, Wahlen arrived at the horrific scene five minutes after the explosion and immediately set about giving orders to the shocked and dazed survivors, successfully keeping the situation from sliding into panic as it had threatened to moments earlier. To the terrified crowd, the miraculously unharmed admiral must have seemed like the only thing they could rely on.

Von Silberberg had been taken to the hospital immediately, but with severe blood loss and shrapnel impacted in his skull, he failed to regain consciousness and his heart stopped at 2340 hours.

The Lohengramm Dynasty had lost one of its top technocrats to this act of terrorism. Von Silberberg's ambition had been twofold. First, he had intended to perfectly balance the social capital and economic foundation of the new dynasty and usher in an age of economic construction to follow the conquest. Second, he had intended to place himself at the center of the technocracy overseeing that construction and one day rise to the position of chancellor.

"Hardly an outrageous dream," he would say, brimming with confidence, and, indeed, his goals were far from unrealistic. But now that ambition, along with the man who had harbored it, had vanished from the face of the planet.

The assassination prompted Wahlen to delay his date of departure from Phezzan so that he could, after reporting the situation to Reinhard, organize a makeshift memorial service for von Silberberg and direct the search for the terrorists responsible.

If those incompetent assassins had to murder someone, they could have at least made it von Oberstein. They might even have attracted some sympathizers there.

Although Wahlen did not voice these thoughts aloud, there was an unmistakable difference in his attitude toward Lutz and the two other officials. He visited von Oberstein in the hospital, affording the marshal the respect due a superior, but—partly on doctor's orders—left immediately. His visit to Boltec he had an aide perform on his behalf while he headed for Lutz's ward instead. Lutz had no serious internal injuries, as if to demonstrate that his fate lines were on an upward trajectory, and the doctors expected to discharge him in two weeks. If anything, he was in higher spirits than before, despite being in a hospital bed. "Die before von Oberstein?" he said. "Never! I've only made it this far, through all those battles, by looking forward to mouthing an insincere eulogy at his funeral while my soul dances on his grave."

Not a very popular man, our minister of military affairs, thought Wahlen, his own opinion of the man notwithstanding. He well understood how Lutz felt, of course. The man's anguish over the death of Siegfried Kircheis three years before had become an arrow aimed at von Oberstein's back.

One week later, Wahlen finally departed Phezzan. On Reinhard's orders, protection of the planet and the hunt for the perpetrator had both been delegated to Lutz's lieutenant, Vice Admiral Holzbauer. Von Oberstein and Lutz would, no doubt, be pleased to take over this responsibility themselves once they had recovered completely.

"Church of Terra diehards, no doubt," was Holzbauer's frowning assessment. "Or loyalists to the former landesherr Rubinsky, perhaps, gone to ground. How dare they trouble His Majesty the Kaiser's thoughts at such an important juncture?"

Of course, it was precisely because things were at "such an important juncture" that the perpetrators had sought to throw the Imperial Navy off-balance by striking at them from behind. At this goal, however, they could only be said to have failed. The true target of their murderous designs had surely been the three top navy officials rather than von Silberberg, but von Oberstein and Lutz had sustained only light wounds, while Wahlen was entirely unharmed.

Kaiser Reinhard regretted the death of the priceless human resources he had appointed, but did not delay the progress of his fleet toward Iserlohn for a moment. He simply instructed Hildegard von Mariendorf to announce a day of mourning along with the promotion of Undersecretary Gluck to acting secretary of works.

"After Iserlohn Fortress falls, von Silberberg will be granted a state funeral. Until then, Wahlen's memorial service will have to do."

Reinhard explained this to Hilda, but it was not the entire truth. Certain details of the bombing—von Oberstein and Lutz escaping with light wounds, Wahlen delaying his departure in response, Reinhard's refusal to interrupt his journey of conquest—invited speculation regarding the perpetrators, and the possibility of a second attack was something the kaiser clearly foresaw, or even anticipated. He knew that he could rely on von Oberstein and Lutz to demonstrate the skill and composure necessary to deal with that eventuality. If circumstances on Phezzan deteriorated to the point of rebellion rather than terrorism, he would send Wahlen back with his fleet to quell the uprising. If even Wahlen could not contain the situation, Reinhard would be required for the first time to decide how to react. Until things reached that point, however, Reinhard had absolutely no intention of turning *Brünhild's* bow from its course.

As Reinhard's secretary, Hilda saw no reason to object to these conclusions. She did, however, urge him to spare a thought for von Silberberg's family.

Reinhard misread her expression slightly—or perhaps only pretended to, in order to provoke her into revealing her strategic judgment clearly.

"You seem to have something you wish to say to me, Fräulein von Mariendorf," he said.

As he spoke, she realized that she did, in fact, want to draw his attention to a certain matter. "Your Majesty," she said, "what if Yang Wen-li sorties from Iserlohn Fortress into imperial territory? If he breaks through Admiral Mecklinger's defensive line, nothing but uninhabited space will lie between him and Hauptplanet Odin."

"An interesting idea. Yang Wen-li might indeed hit upon such an idea, but at present he lacks the resources to carry it out successfully. How unfortunate that the skill of a great general should be restrained by mere circumstance!"

Reinhard's elegant lips curved wryly upward. It was not clear who his sarcasm was aimed at—for who, after all, had engendered the harsh conditions that now hemmed Yang in?

"I almost feel like giving him half a dozen battalions to play with, and seeing what magic he works with them. Now *that* would be interesting!"

"Your Majesty…"

"Fräulein, I cannot rest until my score with Yang Wen-li is settled in full. Once I have his submission and the galaxy is unified, that will mark the true beginning for me."

In the face of this masterfully crafted remonstration, Hilda fell silent.

"And even that prospect does not satisfy me," Reinhard continued. "Would that I might face that magician on equal strategic ground!"

Hilda offered her first counterargument. "In that case, Your Majesty," she said, "I beg you, do not bring the battle to him just yet. Return to Phezzan, and then to Odin. Allow Yang to grow strong, and challenge him for supremacy once his power is greater. There is no need to fight him now, when he is at the end of his options."

Reinhard did not reply. He simply toyed with the pendant on his breast, as if to help him endure the sting of her reproach.

III

Marshal Wolfgang Mittermeier's lively gray eyes shone with a rather complex quicksilver brilliance. It was in his nature to favor action, agile and swift. To pause for thought in the shadow of unease went against his inclinations. He *had* agonized at length before seeking the hand of his wife Evangeline in marriage, but the unease he felt now was of a different quality.

His reaction to the tragic incident on Phezzan was caustic in the extreme. "So von Oberstein didn't die?" he said. "Pity—it would have been an excellent way to prove that he was human. Well, at least Lutz wasn't badly hurt."

Mittermeier's friend Oskar von Reuentahl was even more biting. "Von Oberstein is a walking disease. Speculating purely on the possibilities, if he turned out to have arranged the whole thing for some nefarious purpose, I wouldn't be a bit surprised. And, if so, a second act is coming."

The malevolence of this slander left even Mittermeier speechless.

Mittermeier's loathing of von Oberstein was a matter of temperament. He knew that the minister of military affairs, he of the white-streaked hair and cybernetic eyes, had valid reasons for his behavior, and important responsibilities to fulfill. But Mittermeier could not smother his own tastes and principles, and he had no interest in harmonizing his own worldview with the other man's.

He suspected, however, that von Reuentahl's animosity toward von Oberstein was somewhat different in nature. After all, were the two men not fighting over the same jewel? Both of them expected Kaiser Reinhard to embody their own ideals perfectly—and if those ideals were different in tone, was not a clash between the two inevitable?

Mittermeier was perceptive enough to realize all this, but he recognized with gloom that the truth of his insight was incompatible with its utility. He could share his thoughts with von Reuentahl, but he doubted the other man would accept his conclusions without argument. To von Oberstein he felt no desire to convey anything. It was clear to him that von Oberstein rejected any prospect of compromise or change in his relationship with von Reuentahl, despite understanding well the meaning of the conflict between them. If so, it was perfectly natural, if not inevitable, that von Oberstein should attract misunderstanding and hostility. And what about von Reuentahl? Mittermeier was confident that his friend's sagacity surpassed his own, but he also had the strong suspicion that von Reuentahl was suppressing his thoughtful side intentionally and letting the flow of events take him where it would. Even though the end of that flow was likely a waterfall plunging into the abyss…

"It felt like a much longer battle than it was," said Mittermeier. "In any case, this will put an end to it."

"A desirable end for us, I hope," said von Reuentahl.

This exchange marked the conclusion of the strategy discussion between the two men aboard von Reuentahl's flagship, *Tristan*. It was not that they were tired of fighting. In fact, it was precisely because their energies were not exhausted that they could not stop their thoughts from racing ahead to what would come afterward. Of course, their focus was slightly different from their young ruler's.

Hesitantly, Mittermeier asked, "By the way, whatever happened to…?"

Von Reuentahl turned his infamous heterochromiac eyes directly on his friend. "No idea," he said, somewhere between spiteful and indifferent. "Nor do I care to find out. You have some interest in the woman?"

"What interests me is how you have dealt with her."

The two fell silent, both thinking of Elfriede von Kohlrausch, the woman who was reportedly pregnant with von Reuentahl's child. Pushing further in this direction seemed unlikely to lead to anything but fruitless argument. Von Reuentahl had no interest in children, while Mittermeier and his wife were childless. Neither could help feeling injured in his own way at the injustice of the situation.

On April 20, Senior Admiral Fritz Josef Wittenfeld held a meeting aboard his flagship, *Königs Tiger*. Under his command, the vanguard of the Imperial Navy had almost reached Iserlohn Corridor. The enemy was within hailing distance. At some point they would have to halt their advance and await Kaiser Reinhard's arrival from Heinessen, so it was necessary to ensure that the entire fleet was of one will.

One of the officers at the meeting made a sly proposal. "Suppose we offer peace terms to Yang," he said. "Guarantee safe passage for his men if he swears allegiance to His Majesty the Kaiser and surrenders Iserlohn Fortress as an offering. We could even throw in recognition of the right to self-governance on El Facil or somewhere—say that we'll permit a republic to exist there within the bounds of the empire."

Wittenfeld frowned silently. Deputy commander Admiral Halberstadt and chief of staff Admiral Gräbner conducted a furtive, wordless conversation with their facial expressions.

"It doesn't matter what conditions we offer, because we won't have to follow through with them," the officer continued. "Once Yang strolls out of the fortress for peace talks, visions of sweet success already starting to give him psychic toothache, we simply capture him. His Majesty takes possession of the entire galaxy without spilling a single drop of blood. How does that strategy sound?"

"You want my answer to that question."

"Yes, sir, of course."

Wittenfeld bellowed loud enough to empty his lungs. "I never want to hear such idiocy from you again! If the kaiser had the slightest interest in deceitful scheming of that nature, he would have had Yang Wen-li executed at their meeting after the Vermillion War and been done with it! His Majesty wants to defeat that impudent magician on the battlefield, not force his submission by any means available!"

The fierce, orange-haired general's overwhelming glare bore into the officer.

"If His Majesty were to dismiss me as incompetent, that I could bear. But were he to castigate me as a coward, it would render all of my service before that day meaningless. Is even that beyond your feeble understanding?"

Scoured by Wittenfeld's vituperation, the officer left the room a half-dead wreck. As Wittenfeld struggled to steady his breathing, Halberstadt and Gräber exchanged a look of shared understanding: *Thus always with our commander.*

The meeting finally adjourned without any original ideas being given voice. Of course, Wittenfeld had not been granted full strategic discretion in any case. As much as it went against his own temperament, it seemed they could do nothing but quietly fortify the front lines until new orders arrived from the kaiser.

During his regular comm channel conversation with his friend and fellow senior admiral Adalbert Fahrenheit, Wittenfeld joked about the tedium at the front and asked if there wasn't anything the two of them could do about it. "If only the enemy would attack first, we could start the war without waiting for the kaiser to arrive," he said wistfully.

Fahrenheit did not immediately reply. Like Wittenfeld, he was an aggressive tactician, but he was older than the other commanders and understood the authority that had been vested in him in the kaiser's absence. He would have to rein in Wittenfeld's restless spirit and ensure that no grave errors were committed before Kaiser Reinhard's arrival. To the staunch blue-eyed general, this duty was also a way of keeping his own spirit under control.

Eventually Fahrenheit made a proposal: they would urge Yang Wen-li to capitulate. Yang would never agree, of course, but there was no need to waste the time remaining before the kaiser's arrival, even if combat itself was out of the question. It was worth making the attempt to probe their enemy's inner emotions.

In truth, Fahrenheit had not made this suggestion with any great enthusiasm. He himself was distracted by the countless scout ships that needed to be dispatched to their intended battlefield. The Dagon Stellar Region, where the Imperial Navy had suffered an ignominious defeat a century and a half ago, was close to their route, and its name aroused his interest in the task of battlefield reconnaissance.

Accordingly, when Wittenfeld actually put the proposal into action, Fahrenheit was as surprised as anyone else. And there was certainly no way he could have foreseen the remarkable events that would be set in motion as a result.

I

IN THE WORDS OF DUSTY ATTENBOROUGH, Iserlohn

Fortress was filled with festive anticipation for the "riotous Rite of Spring" to come.

As of April 20, there were 28,840 ships and 2,547,400 officers and men gathered under Yang Wen-li at anti-imperial headquarters. In purely numerical terms, it was the largest force that Yang had ever commanded. But just under 30 percent of the fleet was in need of repairs, and over 20 percent of the troops were either recruits from the last days of the alliance or new conscripts, and would need training before they could bear arms. What was more, the sudden expansion in the fleet's military resources following their merger with the Revolutionary Government of El Facil had necessitated a restructuring of the entire military organization. Alex Caselnes had remained acting general manager of rear services even after his reinstatement as administrative director of Iserlohn Fortress. Had anyone sliced open his neural circuits, they would have drowned in the sea of figures and charts that burst forth.

When Wittenfeld's communiqué arrived from the Imperial Navy, Yang was taking breakfast in the mess with Julian Mintz. Along with the usual tea and toast, the menu also featured a country omelet, thick pea soup, and yogurt. Julian gravely signaled his approval to his hazel-eyed culinary apprentice, Yang's aide and wife Frederica Greenhill Yang, who stood beaming beside them. She seemed the happiest of all of them that her hard work and careful planning had paid off, and Yang prayed silently to the goddess of cooking, for her sake and his own, that her success had been no coincidence.

The arrival of Wittenfeld's message was reported to Yang by Attenborough, who had grown comfortably into his role as lieutenant commander in the Revolutionary Reserve Force and would one day write a chronicle of the events then taking place. He appeared on the visiphone, still holding a haphazardly assembled ham, egg, and lettuce sandwich, to give Yang the news. Yang appeared to ascribe no more importance to the message than Wittenfeld had himself.

"Would you at least like to see it, sir?" asked Attenborough.

"I may as well give it a once-over," Yang said. "Forward it to my screen."

Without straying beyond the bounds of protocol, Wittenfeld's missive was acerbic in the extreme.

To Yang Wen-li, greatest commander of the former Alliance Armed Forces and only commander in what remains of the republican faction, my greetings from within the Imperial Navy. As I am sure is clear to a man of your perspicacity, further resistance to peace and unification would be not only morally bankrupt but tactically unfeasible and strategically impossible. I offer this sincere counsel: if you hope to preserve your life and some measure of your honor, lower the standard of rebellion and throw yourself on the mercy of the kaiser. I would be happy to act as your intermediary in this matter. I earnestly await your rational reply.

"Admiral Wittenfeld has quite a talent for high-stakes provocation, it seems," said the golden-brown-haired Frederica. "A pity he was not born to the alliance. He would have made a fine politician."

"A fine sparring partner for Job Trünicht, you mean?"

Musing that he would probably root for Wittenfeld in that case, Yang changed the subject.

"Admiral Attenborough, as one of our other 'only commanders,' what do you make of this?"

"Utterly devoid of literary sensibility, I fear, sir."

"That isn't what I meant…"

Yang took a sip from his second cup of the tea Frederica had brewed. It sat pleasantly enough on the palate, perhaps second cousin to the tea Julian made. This might have been an illusion, of course, but when happiness was dominant, susceptibility to such illusions was inevitable.

"I'm asking *why* you think Wittenfeld would send me a message like this."

"I doubt it means anything in particular. Perhaps if it had come from the kaiser himself, but this is Admiral Wittenfeld, after all. If he hopes to bring the full force of the Black Lancers to bear in seeking revenge for the Battle of Amritsar, it would be neither surprising nor out of character."

Yang was in agreement with this observation and conclusion. However, all of his strategy and tactics were constructed with Reinhard's intellect and will in mind. If Wittenfeld slipped out from under the kaiser's direct command and began to act independently, not only would Yang be forced to modify his immediate response, but corrections to his long-term plans might also be required.

"Shall we send a reply, Your Excellency?" asked Frederica. She had a knack for addressing her husband with formality when others were present without sounding unnatural.

"Hmm…" Yang said. "What do you think, Julian?"

His youthful ward brushed back flaxen bangs. Julian was eighteen this year, fifteen years junior to Yang himself. One description of him preserved for the ages said, "His slender, proportionate form and sensitive, translucent features put one in mind of a young unicorn."

"I see no great danger in ignoring it," Julian said. "But perhaps the bare minimum of a reply is in order, for protocol's sake if nothing else."

"That sounds about right," Yang said with a nod, although it did not seem to the other three present that he had yet made his final decision.

●

"Without enough men to staff even a single one of the former navy's fleets, he was preparing to wage war against nine-tenths of the galaxy. At such an extreme of tension and fear, an outbreak of madness would have been far from mysterious. But no man betrayed such symptoms. For—"

"'They were all quite mad already,'" declaimed Commander Olivier Poplin, striding into the senior officer's library.

Attenborough turned from the notebook in which he was scribbling a draft of his so-called *Memoirs of the Revolutionary War* to cast a dirty look over his shoulder.

"If your writing's too predictable, your publisher will complain long before your readers have a chance to get bored," Poplin continued. "You need something fresher, more stimulating."

"Just what I needed, advice from the self-proclaimed ace of the fleet. How about attending to your own literary endeavors before you start criticizing mine? Weren't you supposed to think up a comeback to the Imperial Navy's 'Sieg kaiser!' cheer?"

Attenborough was in a bad mood after recalling an encounter several days earlier in which Poplin had prevented him from butting in on a gathering of younger officers. "No over-thirties!" the other man had insisted. Youngest commander in the former Alliance Navy though Attenborough was, he would still be thirty-one this year.

He had spent the night before his last birthday railing against the injustice of it all. "Why should I be condemned to turn thirty?" he had demanded, somewhere between despondency and outrage. "I've done nothing wrong, unlike Admiral von Schönkopf."

Von Schönkopf, singled out as a living injustice in this way, had stroked his slightly pointed chin. "Don't ask me," he said, serenely unbothered. "As far as I'm concerned, incompetent good-for-nothings who've never done anything wrong have no business turning thirty anyway."

Back in the library, Poplin met Attenborough's challenge with a cheerful nod. "Yes, the response has been decided," he said. "It's 'Viva democracy!'"

"That's what you ended up choosing? I thought you said it 'lacked grandeur.'"

"There is one more, actually."

"Let's hear it."

" 'Damn the kaiser!' "

"That's much better." The future historian offered a brief appreciation of the second option, praising its richness in "republican expressive power" and other dubious concepts he invented on the spot, and then grimaced bitterly. "Still, though—can't we come up with a single cheer that doesn't invoke the kaiser by name? It leaves a bad taste in the mouth. Are we nothing but linguistic parasites?"

As Attenborough and Poplin sparred, a more serious and significantly darker discussion was quietly underway within the Revolutionary Government of El Facil. Their chairman, Dr. Francesk Romsky, had been in regular contact with the Revolutionary Reserve Force's headquarters as he scrambled for a response to the looming threat of an all-fronts imperial invasion. Now an official from the government steering committee had brought him a new proposal. Its argument went roughly as follows:

However brilliant and eccentric a strategist Yang Wen-li might be, in the face of overwhelming numerical superiority even his defeat was assured. When that happened, El Facil would share his fate. Was it not time to choose between their revolutionary government and Yang's faction? Why not surrender Yang and his followers to the Imperial Navy, along with Iserlohn Fortress itself, in exchange for a guarantee of self-governance? The first step would be to lure Yang out of Iserlohn Fortress on the pretext that the empire had offered to recognize his faction's right to govern itself. Once he was captured, Iserlohn Fortress would be powerless. They could then negotiate at their leisure with the Imperial Navy...

It was the same basic idea that Wittenfeld had flatly rejected in the imperial camp. A certain bitter humor may be found in the fact that low-level schemers from both sides had identified the same weaknesses in Yang's political designs. Recognizing that his ultimate goal was peace and coexistence with the empire, they surmised that he would be unable to refuse such an offer.

Dr. Romsky stared at the representative from the steering committee, half-stunned. It took the better part of a minute before his rationality climbed back up to the top of the cliff.

"Absolutely not," he said at last, shaking his head vigorously. "Marshal Yang originally came here at our invitation. We have enjoyed the benefits of his name and his military prowess. To betray him now would sully the spiritual purity of democratic republican governance itself. Recall for a moment how the officers who assassinated High Council chairman Lebello were greeted by the kaiser. Above all else, I refuse to have any part in such a disgraceful idea."

Romsky's decision was, if anything, apolitical—nothing more than an expression of shame at the personal level. But that was precisely why he had not inherited the lamentably poor reputation of João Lebello, former High Council chairman of the Free Planets Alliance. He clearly lacked a genius for processing reality, but perhaps he subconsciously accepted that there were moments in history when reality had to come second to ideals.

In any case, Romsky's decision ensured that Yang escaped being sold out to the empire by a civilian government a second time.

II

Yang was neither omniscient nor omnipotent, so there was no way he could have sensed the full extent of the animosity and maneuvering directed at him. Above all else, Reinhard von Lohengramm's star shone so brilliantly before him that the meandering of asteroids simply did not register.

With the decisive battle approaching, Yang was reconsidering his position. Why was he fighting? Why was it necessary to wrest from Kaiser Reinhard a promise to permit the establishment of a self-governing territory?

The answer: to ensure that knowledge of democracy's fundamental principles, systems, and methods was transmitted to future generations. That required a base of operations, however slight.

Autocracy might have secured a temporary victory, but with the passage of time and the change of generations, the self-control of the ruling class would inevitably crumble. Exempt from criticism, above the law, deprived of any intellectual grounds for self-examination, their egos would swell grotesquely until they finally ran amok. An autocrat could not be punished—indeed, it was precisely immunity from punishment that defined an autocrat. Kaiser Rudolf, Sigismund the Foolish, August the Bloodletter—individuals like this used absolute authority as a steamroller to crush the people, staining the paths of history red.

Doubts about the virtues of such a social system were bound to emerge eventually. And when they did, could not the period of struggle, of trial and error, be shortened if a model of a different system existed?

This was the merest seed of hope and nothing more, far from the full-throated slogans of the Free Planets Alliance—"Death to despotism! Democracy forever!" But then Yang did not believe that any political system could last forever.

The duality within the human heart condemned democracy to coexist with dictatorship along every possible axis of space and time. Even in an age when democracy seemed to reign triumphant, there were always those who longed for its opposite. These longings came not only from the desire to rule others but also the desire to *be ruled by* others—to obey without question. After all, things were easier that way. Learn what was permissible and what was forbidden, follow orders and adhere to instructions, and security and happiness were within your reach. A satisfying life was surely possible on those terms. But whatever freedom and safety cattle might be allowed in their pen, the day always came when they were slaughtered for the table.

Power could be turned to more brutal ends in an autocracy than in a democracy, because the right of criticism and the authority to rectify abuses were established neither by law nor in custom. Yang Wen-li's criticisms of head of state Job Trünicht and his party were caustic and frequent, but he had never been legally sanctioned for them. He had faced harassment more than once, but on each of those occasions, the powers that be had been forced to find some other pretext. That was entirely thanks to the stated principle of democratic republican governance: freedom of speech. Political principles in general deserved respect. They were the greatest weapon for preventing those in power from running wild, and the greatest armor for the weak. To convey the existence of those principles to future generations, Yang would be forced to discard any personal feelings of love and respect and fight against autocracy itself.

Yang's work of reconsideration moved on to practicalities. Kaiser Reinhard was a military genius. How could Yang defeat him?

If he led the fleet outside the corridor, the Imperial Navy clearly had the numbers to surround them. Even if the plan was to emerge just long enough to draw the empire back into the corridor with them, Mittermeier was known for his preternaturally fast maneuvers. If he cut off the corridor's entrance, the Yang Fleet would be surrounded and annihilated by overwhelming force before their strategy could even be put into action.

"I'll just have to draw them into the corridor first."

Of course, there was no guarantee of victory in that case either.

There were two opposing ways Kaiser Reinhard might be lured into the corridor: stoke his pride by intentionally handing him a minor success, or fight at full strength, win, and enrage him with embarrassment over his defeat.

But no—neither of those ideas would work. If Reinhard were the sort to preen over small victories or rage over temporary setbacks, he would not be the formidable foe he was. Even back when he had been one admiral among many serving the Goldenbaum Dynasty, hadn't he met all the criteria perfectly at the strategic level before displaying dazzling creativity at the tactical one? Reinhard's stunning victory over all comers at the Battle of Astarte had been little more than an amusing diversion for him, and in his subsequent campaigning he had demonstrated the vast range of his talents: his facility with massed forces, his mastery of supply, his direction of subordinates, his ability to secure topographical advantage, and the timing with which he commenced his operations. In the last days of the Free Planets Alliance, Reinhard had determined the strategic conditions for every one of their battles, and the victor of each had been all but decided before the first shot was even fired.

Iserlohn Fortress was of no strategic importance. With both ends of the corridor under the control of imperial forces, it was isolated inside a blockaded cul-de-sac...or so Yang had thought. But perhaps he had been too hasty. The reason the Imperial Navy's operational and supply lines were stretched to their current extent was that Iserlohn was not in their possession. This was not a fact to be viewed lightly.

The tactical strengths of Iserlohn Fortress were even greater. It was impregnable to pure military force, and its main cannons, known collectively as Thor's Hammer, offered unparalleled destructive power.

It also had political import. Yang the Undefeated, continuing his resistance against the new dynasty from within Iserlohn the Impregnable: that alone was a manifesto, addressed to the entire galaxy, for the continuance of democratic republican governance, as well as a comfort to those who supported their cause. Yang had to concede his own value as an idol in that respect, too, however reluctantly.

But whatever importance Iserlohn Fortress might have, he would surrender it to the empire in a second if doing so would bring peace. He had many fond memories of the base, but if he had to use it as a political bargaining chip, so be it.

Either way, the sheer difference in military strength between the two sides made it clear how ridiculous the idea of competing at the tactical level was. That had always been the case, but in the vast wall of the empire's military might, cracks might yet appear.

The golden-haired conqueror, avatar of some god of war, wanted to fight Yang. Yang knew this. To snatch victory from this situation, he would have to exploit whatever chinks existed in Reinhard's psyche.

Yang's plan was an ambitious one. Achieve a tactical victory to drag Reinhard into peace talks, and then force him to accept the existence of a single planet with the right to self-governance as a democratic republic. It did not matter if that planet was El Facil or some undeveloped world farther out on the periphery. When the winter of despotism came to every other part of the galaxy, they would need that tiny greenhouse to nurture the weak shoots of democracy until they matured enough to withstand the trials ahead.

The first step was defeating Reinhard, Yang thought—then wondered if it might not be better to lose against him. If Yang were defeated, the troops who had followed him would surely be treated with magnanimity.

The kaiser would send them on their way with the highest honors, and to the greatest extent possible leave them to determine their own fate.

Perhaps that really would be better. There were limits to what Yang could achieve. Could he guarantee a richer future for those who followed him by withdrawing altogether?

Yang's feet were still up on his office desk when Julian arrived with his tea.

"Looks like Kaiser Reinhard's itching for a fight with me," Yang said. "I doubt he'll ever forgive me if I cheat him out of one."

He spoke lightly and humorously, but the observation was quite accurate—all the more reason why the coming clash was inevitable.

Julian's tea was perfect as always. Yang let out a sigh of satisfaction. "To be honest, I wish the idea was just my own delusions of grandeur. But the kaiser really does rate me higher than my record deserves. It should be an honor, but…"

Reinhard had reached out to Yang once, after the Vermillion War. In exchange for Yang's allegiance, he had offered to make heavy use of him. Yang had been the one to refuse. Like the late Alexandor Bucock, he could not take the hand of an autocrat, no matter how fair, how warm that hand might be. As Reinhard had his own nature, so Yang had his, and it had proved inescapable.

"So this is your fate, then?" said Julian casually.

Yang frowned, and Julian reddened. He realized that his choice of words had not reflected his own life or thoughts. Yang always responded with sincerity and warmth when Julian spoke in his own words, however naive the thoughts behind them might be.

"'Fortune' I could live with, but 'fate'—now there's an awful word. It disrespects humanity in two ways: by shutting down any analytical consideration of our situation, and by selling short our free will. There's no such thing as a 'fateful showdown,' Julian. Whatever our circumstances might be, our choices are ultimately our own."

Yang was largely arguing with himself.

He had no interest in justifying his own choices with a convenient word like "fate." He had never once thought of himself as absolutely correct, but was always searching for a better way, a more correct path. This had been true in his days at the Officer's Academy, and had remained true after he had taken command of a great military force. There were many who trusted Yang, and many others who criticized him, but there were none who did his thinking for him. He simply had to agonize over his decisions as best as his limitations allowed.

It would certainly be easier if everything could be ascribed to the work- ings of fate, Yang mused. But even if he should err, he wanted to err on the side of his own sense of responsibility.

Julian looked closely at his beloved commander. Since their first meeting six years before, Julian had grown thirty-five centimeters. If he grew out his hair five millimeters longer, he would be 180 centimeters tall. He was already taller than Yang. Of course, Julian did not consider this a source of pride. He might have grown taller, but he did not feel that his psyche and intellect had kept pace.

The historians of the future were largely united in their view of Julian Mintz. "If not a great man, certainly a capable and loyal leader who made no small mark on history. Accepting the role he was to play, avoiding the two pitfalls of overconfidence and self-righteousness, he made the best of his talents in building on the achievements of those who came before."

There were harsher assessments, too, of course. "Julian Mintz was like a well-polished mirror reflecting only Yang. His ideas on democratic republican governance were all inherited from the older man. Yang was a philosopher of both military matters and politics, however dogmatic, but Mintz amounted to no more than a technician in either."

This assessment, however, ignored one fact: Julian had adopted the role of technician intentionally, knowingly, to better and more faithfully implement Yang's ideas. Some might dismiss this as a foolish way to live, but if Julian had aimed to surpass Yang and had fallen short of the mark, what would they have said about him then? He would surely have been mocked as a man who did not know his own limitations. But Julian knew his limitations well. No doubt there were some who found this displeasing. But as Yang himself had once told him, "If half the people are on your side, that's quite an achievement."

III

In the high-ranking officers' club, the two "problem adults" of the Yang Fleet were deep in conversation.

"I wasn't trying to keep her existence a secret," said Walter von Schönkopf, whiskey glass in hand. "I didn't know she existed at all! I've done nothing dishonorable, and I resent anyone who points the finger at me."

"Karin would point more than a finger at you if she heard that," said von Schönkopf's drinking partner, Olivier Poplin, acid wit in his green eyes. The two were enjoying drinks over cheese and crackers as they discussed von Schönkopf's daughter, Katerose "Karin" von Kreutzer. Both suffered from the same affliction: no matter how serious they were inside, they would rather die than show it.

A few tables away, Dusty Attenborough was tipping back his own glass. He had declined an invitation to sit with the other two, professing concern that their impurity might be contagious.

Julian suspected that Attenborough was still sulking over the "No over-thirties" incident the other day. He had worn his isolation ostentatiously at first, but it must have been boring him now, because he had dragged Julian to the club to keep him company after they'd run into each other in the halls. Attenborough had put away three drinks by the time Julian had finished his first. Not even slightly flushed, Attenborough began expounding a theory of the relationship between Yang's own nature and the complete absence of any visible fear among the leadership of the Yang Fleet even as the decisive battle approached.

"The character of an army's commander is influential—contagious, really—to a degree that's frankly terrifying. I mean, look at our leadership. Before the birth of the Yang Fleet, they were probably hardworking, upright military men. Merkatzes to a one."

"Surely there are some exceptions, sir."

"You mean Admiral von Schönkopf?"

"Well, not *only* him…"

"Poplin, then? Yes, that unfortunate personality of his does seem to be inborn."

Attenborough's invidious grin drew a rueful smile from Julian too. Attenborough had known Yang since officer school almost fifteen years ago. If Yang's personality was infectious, Attenborough's exposure was off the charts compared to von Schönkopf and the others.

"Listen up, Julian. I'm going to tell you something useful."

"What's that, sir?"

"The most powerful expression known to man. No logic or rhetoric can withstand it."

"'So long as it's free?'"

"That's not a bad one either. But this is even better: 'So what?'"

Julian was at a loss for words, although he would have blamed the alcohol in his system for that.

After a private chuckle, Attenborough made another announcement: he was going to reply, in his own name, to Wittenfeld's communiqué.

"If you make too much fun of him, sir, you might regret it," said Julian.

"Julian, if we fought the Imperial Navy head-on, what would our chances of victory be?"

"Zero."

"Admirably succinct. But do you know what that means? Nothing we do can make the odds any worse. And *that* means we can do whatever we like."

"I don't think that syllogism is quite valid, sir."

"So what?"

Grinning more like a mischievous child than a fearless warrior, the self-proclaimed boy revolutionary poured himself another drink.

"I'm fighting this war on foppery and whim," he said. "There's no point in getting all po-faced about it now. We'll never match the Imperial Navy for seriousness. Dogs bite, cats scratch: everyone has to fight in their own way."

Julian nodded, rotating his empty glass with his finger. He had actually had a reason of his own for accepting Attenborough's invitation: not long before, he had had something like a fight with Katerose.

He hadn't brought it up, because he suspected he would be teased about it—"So you're close enough to fight! Sounds like things are going well!"—but it was no joke to him.

Julian had seen Karin reading a pilot training manual for the spartanian fighter as she strolled along, repair tools in hand. He was just admiring her ability to multitask when she walked right into the wall and dropped everything she was holding. As he helped her retrieve her possessions, they had exchanged a few words, and this had somehow escalated into something rather beyond the bounds of everyday conversation.

Karin had fired the first shot. "Of course, the sublieutenant would never make a mistake like this," she said. "I understand you can do anything you turn your hand to, unlike clumsy little me."

Even for someone far less perceptive and sensitive than Julian, misunderstanding her true meaning would have been difficult. Deciding how to respond to her barbed compliment was even more of a challenge. Holding his tongue was not an option, and so Julian flipped through the language files in the back of his mind. "I've just picked up a few things from being surrounded by people who really can do anything," he said.

"Yes, I hear you've been blessed with excellent teachers."

Julian wondered uneasily if Karin was jealous of him. Perhaps she viewed his upbringing surrounded by men like Poplin and her own father, von Schönkopf, as an outrageous monopolization of privilege. After all, in the sixteen years of her life, Karin had spoken to her father only once herself—and the atmosphere of that conversation had hardly been suffused with parental love. Julian wished he could help repair the rift between the two, but if even Poplin couldn't smooth things over, there was no way that Julian could. After a brief hesitation, Julian carefully selected what seemed like the least exciting page from his mental files.

"Admiral von Schönkopf is a good man," he said.

Tentacles of regret were curling around the words before the last were even spoken. The glance Karin favored him with was a mixture of scorn and contempt painted over with indignation.

"Is that so?" she said. "I suppose his position must seem rather enviable to other men. Does as he pleases, shares his bed with any woman willing."

Julian grew angry. The tentacles snapped, and this time it was irritation that wrapped itself around the words he spoke. "That's a one-sided way to put it. Was your mother just 'any woman'?"

The girl's indigo eyes flashed with a rage that was almost pure.

"I am under no obligation to listen to such things—*sublieutenant*." The last word was added not out of politeness but rather its opposite.

"You started it," Julian said, bitterly aware even as he did that the rejoinder was neither generous nor wise. These were the times he envied von Schönkopf and Poplin their confidence and maturity. Any wit or adroitness he displayed himself was always thanks to an interlocutor who possessed those qualities in sufficient abundance to keep things at a level where even Julian could keep up. Yang, Caselnes, von Schönkopf, Poplin, Attenborough—how immature and narrow-minded he was by comparison, squabbling with a girl several years his junior.

In the end, with a final glare that stung more than a double forehand-backhand slap would have, Karin spun around and departed, hair the color of lightly brewed tea streaming behind her as she moved at a pace between a walk and a run. Julian watched her go for as long as it would take an angel to pass by, trip, and then get back on its feet, and had still not managed to put his emotional or rational mind in order again when Attenborough dragooned him into a visit to the officers' club.

Later, Julian, being absent, became the topic of conversation over afternoon tea at the Caselnes household. Alex Caselnes, having slipped home for some rest during a break in his punishing work schedule, was speaking to his wife, as his daughters clambered over him, about a rather heated-looking exchange between Julian and Karin he had happened to witness. He did not, of course, mention that this would improve the position of their own daughter, Charlotte Phyllis.

"Looks like Julian's more awkward than I realized. A more thoughtful lad would know how to deal with girls by his age."

"Oh my, but Julian's always been awkward," his wife said, cutting him a slice of homemade cheesecake. "An excellent student and a quick study, but no interest whatsoever in making things easier for himself with a little compromise on principles. That's a recipe for awkwardness if ever I heard one. I suppose Yang's influence has rubbed off on him."

"So his guardian's to blame," said Caselnes.

"Not the man who introduced them?"

"You had no objection at the time!"

"Of course not. I thought it was for the best. I still do. You don't regret doing that good deed, do you, dear?—even if it was out of character."

The storied admiral finished his cheesecake in two bites, then quickly returned to the mountain of paperwork that awaited him.

IV

The tension seemed to be rising among even the undisciplined officers of the Yang Fleet, and a faint tinge of excitement could be heard in their whispered conversations.

"If charging the Black Lancers head-on is the plan, best to delete your personal records first. Wish I'd known earlier—I'd've gotten married *and* divorced. Once each."

"All on your own? Now that's talent."

"You looking to breathe through a hole in your back?!"

"Whoa, whoa…Anyway, seems to me we're waving a hatchet made of wax here. But maybe we can knock the elephant off his stride if we hit the right spot. Can't hurt to try."

Those serving under Yang didn't feel the same need to defend their position as their commander, and Dusty Attenborough, was, as always, the perfect example. He had sat down to write a reply to Wittenfeld, but discarded his first draft as too crass and his second as too radical. His third, entirely rewritten draft he presented to Yang at a staff meeting aboard *Ulysses*, requesting approval to send it.

"In other words, this is the classy, moderate version?"

Yang shook his head, looking somehow like a teacher marking an essay, then read the work aloud.

"'My dearest Admiral Wittenfeld. My congratulations on your miraculous rise through the ranks, notwithstanding your uninterrupted record of failure. The imbalance between your bravery and your intellect is your weak point. Should you wish to remedy this flaw, by all means, attack our forces. It will give you one last opportunity to learn from your mistakes…'"

With a shrug, Yang handed the document to the committee member sitting beside him. He pulled off his black beret and ran his fingers through his hair.

"Admiral Wittenfeld's not going to like this," he said.

"That's exactly the point," said Attenborough. "With luck, that hot blood of his will boil over into his brain and make him do something foolish."

Wittenfeld did have a bad reputation for losing his battles, but this could hardly be called a fair assessment. His inflexible tactics had brought him to defeat only once, at the Battle of Amritsar. In countless other engagements against the Free Planets Alliance and the League of Just Lords, he had been victorious. Even colleagues like von Reuentahl and Mittermeier acknowledged his iron will and destructive power. However, Attenborough explained, exaggeration would be more useful here than impartial analysis.

"I understand the intention, but this writing can hardly be called refined," said Admiral von Schönkopf. "Maybe you shouldn't have used yourself as the yardstick for class."

Attenborough frowned at this criticism. "A more refined missive runs the risk of being misinterpreted. All we're doing is buying what Wittenfeld's selling, then sending it right back with added value. I think it'll be effective."

"You expect Wittenfeld to just charge us like an angry boar? The kaiser's surely ordered him to control himself. I doubt even he would be that rash."

Or perhaps, von Schönkopf went on, the provocation would have the opposite effect, inciting the Imperial Navy to attack from all sides and start the real fighting before the Yang Fleet was fully prepared. Fahrenheit and Wittenfeld had led fleets into battle a hundred times; a crafty scheme or two would not be enough to hold them off.

Von Schönkopf's views were sensible, but as a ground war commander he had no role in fleet battle, which some felt predisposed him to harsh assessments of other leaders' strategic proposals. Of course, as Poplin had once pointed out, this implied that there were times when he was *not* harsh, an assertion unsupported by evidence.

Just then, a raised hand seeking permission to speak in favor of Attenborough's proposal came from unexpected quarters: Admiral Wiliabard Joachim Merkatz, who had been a senior admiral in the Imperial Navy until not long ago. When Yang had told Merkatz that Wittenfeld's Black

Lancers and the Fahrenheit Fleet were acting as the spearhead of the Imperial Navy, Merkatz had shown little emotion. "Fahrenheit, you say? We share an odd bond, him and I. Today we square off from opposite sides of the galaxy, but just three or four years ago we held our formations together side by side as we went into battle against the same enemy..."

Bernhard von Schneider, Merkatz's aide, cast a slightly anxious glance at the superior officer he loved and respected. Merkatz had not so much defected to the alliance as been washed into it by circumstance. He had made the choice himself, just before the conclusion of the Lippstadt War, but von Schneider had been the one to show him that he had that choice in the first place, and the younger man still appeared to worry about whether he had done the right thing or not.

Taking the long view, perhaps, Merkatz had never spoken of the wife and children he had left behind in imperial territory. He went about his duties without comment, holding a position somewhere between chief of staff and inspector of the fleet. He still wore his imperial uniform, but not even the fastidious Murai had ever complained about that.

"I don't think that the imperial uniform would have suited the late Marshal Bucock," had been Yang's comment on the matter. "And, in the same way..." His unspoken meaning had been clear to all.

Given the floor, Merkatz spoke with his usual quiet composure.

"If we can turn Fahrenheit and Wittenfeld's fleets alone into independent targets, we may be able to close some of the distance in terms of military strength. I think it's worth trying."

Von Schönkopf's suspicious look may have indicated concern that the grave and dignified Merkatz was finally succumbing to the irresponsible ways of the Yang Fleet. Of course, von Schönkopf was one of the most prominent upholders of those bad habits, even if he felt himself above them.

Merkatz, perhaps the only innocent among the fleet's admiralty, continued to speak.

"If we charge at them just as we send that message, they won't simply take evasive action and retreat. Neither of them can help striking back when attacked. It's in their nature, much deeper than mere personality.

If we eliminate them first and then wait for Reinhard to arrive with his main force later, we may score a preemptive psychological victory against the proud kaiser."

"Hear, hear," Attenborough muttered fervently.

Yang remained silent, turning his beret over in his hands.

"We're talking about the Black Lancers here," said Murai, with characteristic caution. "When we toss out the chum, we might get our arm bitten off." Warning his comrades of what the reaction might be if they failed was one of his roles in the Yang Fleet. It seemed to Julian that von Schönkopf and Attenborough did not recognize how valuable this was, even if Yang did.

"It still seems like a dirty trick to me," murmured Yang, but Frederica and Julian saw the sparks of ingenuity flying from the flint behind his dark eyes. Yang turned to face the veteran overseer, fully present again.

"Admiral Merkatz, would you mind if I borrowed your name for a while?"

A plan had risen at the back of his mind—a plan that, if publicized, would give him a worse reputation for charlatanism than ever.

∪

The groans weren't particularly loud or unsettling. If Yang hadn't noticed the slight lack of color in Julian's demeanor that afternoon, leaving an afterimage that still flickered somewhere in his memory circuits, his hearing might not have picked it up at all. It helped, of course, that aboard a battleship even high-ranking officers were assigned tiny cabins with thin walls.

Yang had been Julian's guardian since SE 794. Alex Caselnes, a man so devilish it seemed he must be hiding a tail, had conspired to put them together. On their first meeting, Julian had barely reached Yang's shoulder. He had been just a boy, with flaxen hair and wise eyes, but his diminutive frame belied a number of virtues Yang lacked—not least diligence and a passion for order.

Yang got out of bed and pulled a dressing gown on over his pajamas. Frederica was either sleeping or, in pretending to, silently signaling her assent to her husband's nocturnal excursion.

Scratching his head with one hand, Yang pushed open the door with the other and stepped out of the bedroom. "Evening," he said.

Julian looked up and realized that he had been overheard. "Sorry to disturb you," he said. "I've had a long day. It was a reminder of how green I still am. I was just blowing off some steam." *Which is another sign of immaturity*, he thought with embarrassment.

Yang rubbed his chin. His mild eyes regarded the boy with interest. "I wouldn't call you green," he said. "Yellow, maybe."

The man praised as a master tactician, a wizard even, apparently meant this attempt at humor to be comforting.

Seeing that Julian was struggling to reply, Yang pulled a bottle of brandy and two glasses from the sideboard built into the wall and held them up for inspection. "How about a drink?" he said.

"Thank you," said Julian. "But are you sure you won't get in trouble sneaking out of bed like that?"

Rather than answering directly, Yang poured two glasses of the amber liquor with what was, for him, an unusual degree of care.

"Admiral Caselnes once grumbled to me that he'd never know the pleasure of drinking with a son, you know," he said. "Serves him right for being so hard on his men all those years, mind you."

With these far-from-virtuous remarks, Yang touched his glass to Julian's. Julian tipped his glass back, feeling the brandy's strong scent extend its sharp tendrils into him, and then went into a coughing fit.

"Becoming an adult is about learning how much you can drink," said Yang. Julian was coughing too much to argue.

The conversation they had that night, sitting together on the bed and speaking until dawn, was one Julian never forgot. Yang had little to impart about matters of the heart. These could only be learned by experience, although some people spent their whole lives escaping enlightenment in that regard. In any case, as Caselnes might have said, taking advice from Yang about the female mind was about as wise as taking on the entire Imperial Navy single-handedly.

Of course, what Yang was actually planning to do—was already doing—was very nearly as outrageous.

If Kaiser Reinhard had been a brutal, inhuman conqueror who reveled in pointless bloodshed and pillage, it would have been easy to resist him. So far, however, Reinhard had proved to be one of the finest dictators in history, magnanimous and wise even as he brought the galaxy to heel. He showed his enemies no mercy, but did not harm civilians, and a certain level of social order was even now being established in the territories occupied by his forces.

Yang and his allies were facing the ultimate contradiction. If autocracy was affirmed and accepted by a majority of the people, fighting for popular sovereignty would actually make them the enemies of that majority. Yang's campaign would amount to a rejection of the people's happiness and the popular will.

"We do not want sovereignty or even the franchise," the argument would be. "The kaiser is ruling justly, so why not give him free rein? A political system is just a means of realizing the happiness of the people. With that achieved, why not shrug it off the same way you would a heavy, stifling suit?"

Could Yang argue against that? The question worried him. Too many people in the past had justified bloody acts in the present with fear of what the future might bring.

"To guard against the possibility that a wicked dictator might one day take control, we must take arms against our enlightened ruler today, for only by defeating him can we ensure the survival of democratic republican governance based on the separation of powers."

The paradox was laughable. If the institution of democracy could only be protected by toppling virtuous rulers, that made democracy itself an enemy of good governance.

Yang hoped to establish a seedbed of democracy where they could lie low during periods of enlightened rule but spring into action when despotism loomed. It was looking increasingly likely, however, that the people themselves would reject this plan as unnecessary. He thought back on the many solivision programs cranked out in the days of the former alliance. "If there was such a thing as absolute good and evil in this world, Julian," he said, "life would be a lot easier."

VI

In mid-April of that year, on the alliance's former capital Planet Heinessen, a minor incident took place, amounting to less than a grain of sand in the vast, slow-turning gears of history.

Whitcher Hill, about two hundred kilometers south of Heinessenpolis, was home to a large psychiatric hospital. One night, a fire broke out there, killing approximately ten patients. The reason that the number could not be calculated precisely was a certain mismatch between the patients confirmed alive and those found dead. The patient in room 809 of the special wing—one Andrew Fork—could not be found by any of the hospital staff, alive or dead.

The name "Andrew Fork" was already old and stagnant water in the well of popular memory. Four years prior, in SE 796, the alliance army had been defeated so thoroughly at Amritsar that they were almost destroyed entirely. Fork had been the strategist responsible. After an episode of hysterical conversion disorder, he had been reassigned to the reserves. The following year, in 797, he had attempted to assassinate the man who was at the time director of Joint Operational Headquarters, Admiral Cubresly, and the possibilities for his life were closed up within thick hospital walls.

No one man could be entirely blamed for the Free Planets Alliance's military crumbling like a wall made of baking powder. But nor could it be denied that Fork was part of the ill-fated combination of factors leading to that catastrophe. He had made commodore at just twenty-six years old, rising even faster than the famed Yang Wen-li, and his fall, when it came, had been just as dramatic in both speed and scale.

The hospital fire itself could not be concealed, but Fork's disappearance was buried in the official statistic "Dead or missing: 11." The planet was occupied territory now, and holes had opened in its governance. The lower-ranking bureaucrats in the alliance feared being reprimanded and punished for their incompetence by the Imperial Navy. They swept the matter under the rug, and everything was fine—or should have been. They were more than used to this approach from the days of the former High Commissioner Lennenkamp.

A lone ship traversed the void of space. In one of its cabins, a group sat in a circle around a thin, pinched man just past thirty. If Julian Mintz or Olivier Poplin had been granted a clairvoyant vision of the room, they would no doubt have had to reorganize their visual memories. The man was Archbishop de Villiers, secretary-general of the Church of Terra.

By rights, de Villiers should have been buried under billions of tons of earth and stone, with nothing to do but wait for discovery as a fossil in the distant future. But despite the destruction of the main Terraist temple by Admiral Wahlen of the Imperial Navy, the church's innermost circles had survived, along with, unsurprisingly, their loathing of their enemies.

One of the subordinates around de Villiers spoke, eyes filled with oil and fire.

"Our recent history is one of repeated error, but this time, by the grace of God, it seems that all went well."

Another subordinate nodded. "We must not allow peace between the kaiser and Yang Wen-li. Their armies must battle each other to the last man. The success of this mission is imperative."

Archbishop de Villiers raised his hand. The gesture seemed partly intended to restrain the fervor of his minions and partly to do the reverse and fan the flames higher. Although not omniscient, he was able to foresee, more or less accurately, the end point of Yang Wen-li's political leanings. The mutual destruction of both sides, the Church of Terra's preferred result, seemed unlikely. If the church were to avoid being routed utterly, they would have to push the combatants over the edge themselves. Fortunately, they had just the tool for the job. It had been three years since they had last used it, but a few sweet whispers should be enough to remove the rust and grime.

"It is you, Commodore Fork, who will be the true savior of democratic republican governance. Yang Wen-li seeks compromise with the dicta-tor Reinhard von Lohengramm. He would make peace with a tyrant in exchange for a secure position and special privileges within imperial hegemony. Yang Wen-li must die. He is the vilest turncoat, eager to betray the principles of democracy itself. Commodore Fork, by rights you should have been a full admiral by now, the entire alliance fleet under your command, preparing for a decisive battle that could split the galaxy in two. We will prepare everything you need. Kill Yang Wen-li, save democracy, and regain your rightful position."

A fanatic needs not the truth as it is, but a fantasy painted to suit his tastes. Simply allow him to believe what he wanted to in the first place, and bending him to your will is a simple matter. Within the fragile realm of Fork's psychology burned a feverish longing to be the hero who saved democracy. His vivid hatred for Yang Wen-li, the man who had usurped his place as that hero, was essentially no different from the hatred of the anti-Terran forces nursed by the Church of Terra's leaders since before the Space Era. This the conspiracy's architect knew well.

De Villiers laughed at a volume just barely audible, sending out waves of malice directed both at those who were present and those who were not.

"Let me add one thing, although I expect none of you to remember it. Since antiquity, the victims of assassination have always been those who left their mark on history for other reasons. Assassins, however, are remembered for that act alone."

If not for his vainglorious tone, de Villiers' words would have been deeply moving. What he said was correct both as a matter of fact and on a deeper level.

"Andrew Fork will go down in history as the monster who killed Yang Wen-li. But even this is better than being forgotten. Call it an act of charity bestowed upon a fool who seeks glory but lacks the ability to achieve it."

De Villiers waved his black-robed subordinates away and, in a dark mood, mentally reviewed what he had told them. He did not feel as if he had prophesied his own future, exactly, but some intangible hook had caught in the folds of the sensitivity he armored with ambition.

Shaking his head, he focused his thoughts—corroded by worldly desire rather than fanaticism—on another man. A man who could either pave the way for de Villiers or bore deep holes in that road to hinder him. A man with a hairless head, watchful eyes, and a muscular body: Adrian Rubinsky, former ruler of Phezzan.

The apostate must not be granted a single molecule of oxygen. The loathing and sense of impending crisis de Villiers felt at the thought of the man, psychologically kin to himself, continued to fester.

CHAPTER 3:
THE INVINCIBLE AND THE UNDEFEATED

I

THE BATTLE BETWEEN Reinhard von Lohengramm and Yang Wen-li was in a sense epic, and made the easily remembered year of SE 800 one of the most tragic in human history. Humanity had endured countless battles since adopting the Space Era calendar, just as they had beforehand. Battles between law and the lawless. Between tyrants and liberators. Between privileged classes and unprivileged classes. Even between the forces of autocracy and of republicanism. But in no previous year had such an imbalance of external conditions coexisted with such evenly matched internal factors...

First, let us consider those external conditions. On one side was an empire of unprecedented scale, ruling most of the galaxy; on the other, a band of fugitive mercenaries. It was a clash between a dinosaur and a sparrow. Even to argue over the outcome was pointless.

But in terms of internal factors, it was a battle between two men who were spiritual twins. The only strategist whose field of vision was as broad and far-reaching as Reinhard von Lohengramm's, whose imagination was as rich, whose grasp of military and civilian organization was as sure, was Yang Wen-li himself. The only tactician whose powers of observation were as sharp as Yang Wen-li's, who had the same ability to see situations as they were and respond as they shifted, and who inspired the same loyalty in his men was Reinhard von Lohengramm. The invincible and the undefeated were closing for the final battle...

They also shared a common antipathy toward the Goldenbaum Dynasty, which had ruled humanity for five centuries after its founding by Rudolf the Great. Both Reinhard and Yang despised its system of aristocracy, rejecting the nobility's monopolization of wealth and unjust legal advantages. Both men dreamed of a revolution to overturn the noxious "Goldenbaumian social system" which held humanity in chains and affronted its dignity. Both men were in perfect agreement with the view that government's purpose was to abolish injustice and increase the degree of freedom around individual choice. Was there another pair alive at that moment who shared such deep mutual respect and appreciation? And yet, the two men were forced to make their respective cases with bloodshed...

What compelled them to wage war on each other was a single difference in values. Was a just society best realized by concentrating authority or dispersing it? To argue that question, the greatest military minds of contemporary human society clashed, leaving a trail of blood spilled by millions of soldiers both within and without Iserlohn Corridor. Was there truly no way this tragedy could have been avoided?

—J. J. Pisadore, *The Heroic History*

On the first of May in SE 800—year 2 of the New Imperial Calendar—the Imperial Navy welcomed Kaiser Reinhard to the vanguard. Their invasion of Iserlohn Corridor could now begin. It would be the first time in history that an imperial fleet had sought to capture Iserlohn Fortress from the former alliance side of the corridor.

At this time, the leadership of the Revolutionary Government of El Facil was fleeing into the depths of the corridor. The planet of El Facil itself surrendered. This was proof that Yang Wen-li and his allies hoped to drag the Imperial Navy deeper into the corridor. As Countess Hildegard von Mariendorf put it, Yang was prioritizing the establishment of his strategic position.

"So Yang Wen-li, too, has his mind set on battle," murmured the young kaiser to himself. Hilda watched the blood rush to his porcelain cheeks, feeling both admiration and unease.

There were those within the imperial government who quietly but publicly criticized Reinhard's expedition as a misuse of military resources. Minister of Domestic Affairs Franz von Mariendorf had, not without some circumspection, communicated his opinion to the kaiser as well.

"Using the entire Galactic Imperial Navy to crush Yang Wen-li—under Your Majesty's personal command, no less—is like exterminating a rat with cannonry. I confess my ignorance of military affairs, but surely if we simply blockaded Iserlohn Corridor from both ends, those inside would be forced to surrender eventually. To force a resolution by hastening into battle seems quite unnecessary. I beseech Your Majesty to consider the wisdom of returning to the capital."

Reinhard had already heard the same arguments from Hilda, Mittermeier, and von Reuentahl. He did not dispute them, but led his forces regardless. As he himself had subtly revealed with the phrase "Yang Wen-li, *too*," Reinhard also looked forward to their battle, even if he had established superiority at the strategic level. He accepted that Yang would have the topographical advantage. That was the sole factor in Yang's favor.

Vice Admiral Fusseneger, chief of staff to Senior Admiral Karl Gustav Kempf, was chief information officer at imperial headquarters, and had gathered the meager intelligence available in response to the kaiser's inquiries. "The Yang Fleet is currently lurking within Iserlohn Corridor, with the exception of part of its frontline forces. Communication at the entrances to the corridors is already impossible."

Technically, there was no force called the Yang Fleet. Its formal name was the El Facil Revolutionary Reserve Force, but as this was neither inspiring nor easy to say, it had been all but forgotten the day after its announcement. According to Dusty Attenborough's account, everyone on the former alliance side, apart from Yang Wen-li himself, called it the Yang Fleet through force of habit. Public records on the imperial side were unified in their references to "the so-called Yang Fleet." However uncomfortable it made Yang himself, such was his esteem in the eyes of others. As Mittermeier put it, the Revolutionary Government of El Facil itself was "a mere crest on the head of the rooster that was Yang."

Accordingly, Reinhard spared not a glance for the leadership of that government as they escaped into the corridor leaving El Facil undefended, only flashing a cold smile at their timidity. His interest was entirely directed toward Yang, the black-haired magician, and the tricks he would deploy in the battle to come.

"Is there no way to force Yang to bend the knee without combat?" Hilda asked him, not for the first or even second time. Reinhard ignored her, not only at the urging of the part of him that loved war, but also because he knew her question was largely intended to distract him.

If treated as a thought experiment, he could imagine any number of nonmilitary courses of action. Even Mittermeier, whose psychic topography was a hostile environment for alternatives to combat, had surely entertained some thoughts along these lines. For if one thing unified everyone, it was the certainty that, but for the presence of Yang, the kaiser and his admirals would have faced a much simpler task.

What about luring Yang to putative peace talks and assassinating him when he arrived? Perhaps his own men could be persuaded to capture him with the promise of pardons for everyone else in their "rebellious battalion." Conversely, they could be deceived into thinking that Yang was plotting to sell them out in exchange for his own salvation. The possibilities were endless.

But none would be adopted. Wittenfeld's disgusted rejection of such a proposal by his own staff officer was in accordance with the principles of the new Lohengramm Dynasty's military, which made direct fleet-to-fleet battle its domain. They had a ten-to-one numerical advantage at Iserlohn; they were led by the brilliant warrior Kaiser Reinhard, and the fighting would be directed by the "Twin Ramparts" of the Imperial Navy, von Reuentahl and Mittermeier, as well as a host of other legendary commanders. What did they have to fear?

Even so, the Imperial Navy was not entirely without points on which it felt uncertain or vulnerable. Its route and supply lines were now the longest in human history, and more than half of that length was in occupied territory. They were susceptible to interference of many kinds—guerrilla attacks, terrorism, and sabotage only being the most obvious. Hadn't one of the empire's highest officials, minister of works Bruno von Silberberg, been killed in a terrorist bombing? Minister of domestic affairs Count Franz von Mariendorf's concern was not unwarranted. The empire's core leadership was now divided between their capital planet Odin, Phezzan, and the frontline imperial headquarters, which in terms of efficiency in governance was very far from ideal. Would it not be better to correct this imbalance before swatting the last few irritating flies?

Accordingly, some historians of later ages assessed the situation with a certain pompous condescension. *A brief excursion into enemy territory to achieve a flawless victory in a decisive battle: since antiquity, how many tacticians and conquerors have been led to graves in foreign soil by this dream? Not even a man of Reinhard von Lohengramm's genius proved able to overcome the sweetness of this temptation.*

But this was no mere temptation, Reinhard reassured himself as he sat in his private chambers aboard *Brünhild*. It was the reason for his existence.

His bodyguard Emil von Selle approached quietly to clear away the porcelain coffee cup that sat empty by Reinhard's hand. Emil had been striving of late to emulate the silent way of walking favored by Günter Kissling, head of the imperial guard. His goal was to avoid disturbing the solitude of the kaiser he worshiped, but when he was successful in this he was faced with a new dilemma: when to speak.

Reinhard sat in his armchair, legs crossed, deep in thought, excluding the boy's movements from his attention with natural grace.

Had it really been ten years?

The slightest movement showed in Reinhard's ice-blue eyes.

The sands of time ran backward. Ten years ago, in SE 790—year 481 under the old Imperial Calendar—Reinhard had been a boy of fourteen attending the Children's Academy. Younger brother to Kaiser Friedrich IV's beloved wife, he had relinquished his position at the head of the class to nobody. Even so—or perhaps because of this—he had been lonely, watched always by staring eyes. He had had only one ally, but this priceless friend had been unimpeachably reliable and loyal, and Reinhard recalled the day he had revealed his heart's deepest ambition to that red-haired companion, though couched in the form of a question.

Do you think that what was possible for Rudolf is impossible for me?

As he opened the windows of remembrance, rich imagery of sentiment that had long been forgotten, that should never have been forgotten, came borne on wind and light to fill the fields of his mind once more. Why, he wondered, had the colors been so vivid back then, even in the dead of winter? Why had his rough and overwashed old shirts felt to him like the finest silk? Why had the ambition in his breast bewitched his ears with its melody? Why had he accepted without hesitation that the word "future" contained a thousand possibilities, and that the fulfillment of ambition was synonymous with happiness? Had be simply been foolish? Had the innocent arrogance that enfolded him been powerful enough for him to believe in his own rectitude? Reinhard could not answer these questions, but he was sure of one thing: at the time, there had been no need to concern himself with such matters.

The kaiser's brief silence was ended when his chief aide Vice Admiral Arthur von Streit presented a clearly nervous Fusseneger with urgent news.

"My apologies for the disturbance, Your Majesty," said the chief information officer in a voice as pale as his complexion. "I have just received word that our vanguard, led by Admirals Wittenfeld and Fahrenheit, has already engaged the enemy. The battle has begun."

II

The news that the battle was underway naturally came as an unpleasant shock to Reinhard. To arrange the full forces under his command in perfect alignment and to compete with the enemy on the field of tactical prowess had been the young emperor's intention. Unlike the Vermillion War of the previous year, the topography of this confrontation left Reinhard unable to dictate where the battle would take place, and he had concluded that the only way to force a short, decisive battle on Yang Wen-li would be a direct advance into Iserlohn Corridor.

"Why did they open hostilities before my arrival?" Reinhard demanded, cheeks flushed with rage. "Do they mean to undo all my preparations to satisfy their own reckless bravado?"

Brünhild's bridge trembled with Reinhard's fury. His staff officers remained silent, but Reinhard swept back the golden locks that had fallen onto his brow and forced calm upon himself. *Yang must have lured Fahrenheit and Wittenfeld into battle through trickery*, he surmised, *in order to divide the imperial forces.*

That surmise was quite correct. The facts, soon discovered, were as follows:

The story began with the Imperial Navy's presence at the empire-facing entrance to Iserlohn Corridor. There were 15,900 ships stationed there under the command of the navy's rear supreme commander, Senior Admiral Ernest Mecklinger.

On orders from the kaiser via distant Phezzan, Mecklinger had entered the corridor in advance of Wittenfeld and Fahrenheit, who were approaching from the opposite end. His chief expected role would be to harass Yang Wen-li's fleet from the rear when they made their move, but if circumstances allowed him to enter battle and secure the rear line before the arrival of the other imperial admirals, they would be able to trap Yang in one swift pincer movement. However, advance reconnaissance had revealed Mecklinger's entry into the corridor to Yang, who responded by deploying a force of over twenty thousand ships.

"Over twenty thousand?!"

Mecklinger was speechless. He was a man of superior strategic wisdom who had achieved a steady string of victories by deploying and investing the necessary forces for each situation, never incorporating into his tactics elements of chance or personal bravery. Based on this way of thinking, he calculated that Yang must have at least fifty thousand ships in total if he were prepared to send twenty thousand to meet Mecklinger's forces. After all, to deploy one's full forces away from the main battlefield and leave nothing in reserve would be an affront to military learning itself.

Yang had taken great care to manipulate the figures as former alliance ships had flowed toward Iserlohn Fortress to prevent the Imperial Navy from grasping the true numbers. Forcing errors of judgment like Mecklinger's had been his aim.

"We must not engage!" said Mecklinger. "All ships, about-face! Leave the corridor!"

He gave the order not out of cowardice but logic. The forces under his command numbered 15,900 ships in total—somewhat less than the twenty thousand Yang had sent. What was worse, if the Mecklinger Fleet were defeated there would be no significant concentration of mobile forces standing between the Yang Fleet and imperial territory. Perhaps a hundred thousand ships or so could be diverted from among those guarding the periphery and other key points, but with no one to command them as a unified force, they would simply be eliminated one by one as they engaged Yang in order of proximity. And then, beyond the sea of stars, the imperial capital Odin would stand defenseless and alone...

That, in other words, was the thin foundation on which the Imperial Navy's military advantage rested. Faced with this stimulus to his long-trusted sense for danger, Mecklinger's character, strategic understanding, and sense of responsibility left him no choice but to avoid immediate engagement and retreat to the entrance of Iserlohn Corridor to regroup.

Having achieved this goal, Yang's ships changed course immediately, heading straight for Wittenfeld's Black Lancers.

Wittenfeld had no way of knowing about Mecklinger's retreat. As far as he was concerned, Mecklinger was still right behind Yang. In later years the fierce admiral would say, through gritted teeth, "If Mecklinger hadn't run from that first battle—if he'd just supported our attack on Yang Wen-li for a couple of days—things would have been completely different. We could have surrounded Yang, penned him in tightly around Iserlohn Fortress. The Black Lancers could have attacked the fortress, and when Yang hurried to return, Mecklinger would have been free to fire on him from the rear—and brought himself great personal glory, I might add!"

Wittenfeld was entirely correct in this assessment, but Mecklinger's position was valid too, even if the Artist-Admiral had no wish to make that argument too loudly.

"No other military commander in all of history understood the importance of intelligence and communications as well as Yang Wen-li," was Mecklinger's conclusion. "Fearing that Iserlohn Fortress would intercept or sabotage its communications, our forces sent messages to each other solely via Phezzan. This inevitably created delays, and Yang exploited that to escape the danger of encirclement, partly through strategy and partly through force. His true greatness lay not in the accuracy of his predictions but rather in his knack for restricting his enemy's actions and decisions to within the bounds of those predictions. Even the greatest generals of the Galactic Empire were but dancing on the stage he had prepared for them."

By the time of this reminiscence, however, Yang's stage-building days were over.

Wittenfeld was still fuming over the highly uncivil message he had received from Dusty Attenborough when another communication arrived on April 27. That he chose to convene a meeting with Fahrenheit to discuss the matter rather than deciding on a course of action himself was, for him, a kind of personal courtesy.

According to the new message, Merkatz, the admiral who had defected to the alliance, was regretting his decision and wished to tender his surrender to Kaiser Reinhard, along with an offer to act as a double agent within the enemy forces.

"It isn't worth discussing," said Fahrenheit at once. "It's a trap. Admiral Merkatz is an enemy to the Imperial Navy, but not the type to bend his principles at a juncture like this."

"Of course it's a trap. I don't need you to tell me that. What interests me is what the trap is meant to achieve."

Wittenfeld insisted that the enemy must be hoping to lull the Imperial Navy into a false sense of security so they could launch a surprise attack. Fahrenheit had to admit that this made sense. In fact, it was the *only* thing that made sense. Fahrenheit did find it suspicious that Yang and Merkatz should attempt such a shallow trick, but Wittenfeld had an answer for that too.

"What if it's a suicide mission?"

In other words, Merkatz really would flee to Imperial Navy headquarters, but when the Imperial Navy had let down its guard, Yang would launch his attack. Naturally, Merkatz would be killed for having allowed himself to be used as a decoy, but the attack might still succeed. This was also known as a "dead agent" strategy—an infiltrator sent behind enemy lines with the understanding that he would not survive. It was cold-blooded, but it was plausible that Merkatz would propose such a thing himself.

"I imagine Merkatz is looking for a place to bury his bones. I'm sure he would volunteer to sacrifice himself for the cause. After the next transmission is when things will get dangerous for us."

It seemed to Fahrenheit that Wittenfeld was relishing the prospect rather than simply predicting it, but there was no reason to oppose strengthening their defenses and heightening their responsive capabilities. He put his fleet on alert level two and waited for Yang to make his move.

Before long, a second transmission was received. With Fahrenheit's agreement, Wittenfeld sent a reply agreeing to welcome Merkatz as their guest. At this point, Wittenfeld should have reported the situation to the kaiser. He had intended to, but they received the response they had expected earlier than predicted, and they were forced to respond to the attack by force before they had time to make the report. If Mecklinger had in fact been closing in on Iserlohn Fortress from behind, the opportunity to encircle their enemy would have been too good to pass up.

Thus did Fahrenheit and Wittenfeld stride boldly onto the stage Yang had prepared for them.

On April 29, SE 800, the curtain rose on the Battle of the Corridor. The millions of troops fated to take part felt their hearts beat faster in sympathy with the soundless bell that rang out, announcing to the whole galaxy that the show was about to begin.

III

The disarray that Yang's ships fell into when Wittenfeld detected their surreptitious approach and rained gunfire upon them was painful for Wittenfeld to watch. He did not know, of course, that Yang's staff officer Vice Admiral Murai had once glumly observed that the only thing the Yang Fleet ever got better at was pretending to be routed.

Attenborough faced what was quite literally the performance of his life. The challenge was real. If they failed to evade the jaws of the ferocious Black

Lancers, they would without question be torn to shreds. Attenborough maintained the brazen, unflustered expression he needed to control his subordinates, but rivulets of cold sweat ran down his back.

He maintained the life-or-death charade regardless, putting on a show of fleeing in defeat and remaining just out of range of the pursuing Imperial Navy's main cannonry. Whenever the imperial ships flagged in the chase, Attenborough's would turn around and insolently return fire. As a seasoned tactician whose taste for combat was now aroused, Wittenfeld responded by intentionally slowing his fleet and then lunging forward to attack the moment Attenborough's turned back.

These fleet maneuvers were sublimely accomplished, and even though Attenborough was being more than careful, he very nearly found himself half-surrounded. No longer acting, Attenborough and his fleet fled for dear life into the corridor. Fahrenheit tutted as he watched this on-screen from the bridge of his flagship *Ahsgrimm*.

"Wittenfeld, you slippery dog. You had this planned from the start, didn't you? Why can't you just obey the kaiser's orders?"

This was in fact a misapprehension on Fahrenheit's part, but Wittenfeld's command was so precise as the Black Lancers charged into Iserlohn Corridor that anyone might have mistaken it for a planned maneuver.

When Yang saw on his screen the mass of points of light representing the Black Lancers pour into the corridor, a raging flood of metal and nonmetal, he knew the battle was his. Everything so far had gone according to plan.

Yang Wen-li looked around the staff on the bridge: his wife and aide Frederica, vice admirals von Schönkopf and Murai, his staff officer Patrichev, and Lieutenant Commander Soon "Soul" Soulzzcuaritter. Caselnes had been left behind to guard Iserlohn Fortress, and Merkatz and Fischer were off pursuing their own assigned missions. And then there was Julian Mintz, who had been a staff officer without portfolio at headquarters since the beginning of the year. This was the so-called Yang Family of that period in its unassuming battle formation.

"The Imperial Navy is led by the greatest emperor in history and commanded by too many great generals to count. They can't all fit inside Iserlohn Corridor at once, and that fact is going to be the key to our survival. Let's lean on it as hard as we can."

Yang spoke as if calmly explaining facts rather than brimming with confidence, but it was exactly this that planted in the hearts of his subordinates the seed of the idea that victory was assured. One of the reasons that Yang was known as "the Magician" was surely his almost supernatural ability to inspire faith in others, right up until his own death. His subordinates had a joke that they had borrowed from the ancients to express that faith:

"What's the best plan Yang Wen-li ever came up with?"

"Whatever plan he comes up with next!"

1045: Reports arrived of a sudden approach by the Imperial Navy. The entire Yang Fleet was put on alert level one. 1130: Attenborough's advance guard arrived and joined Yang's main forces on its left wing to stare down the advancing enemy.

"Good work," said Yang through the viewscreen.

"Just remember this when you're divvying up the spoils," said Attenborough. There was no time for further banter.

The posture Yang adopted when commanding a fleet had not changed since the first time he had captured Iserlohn Fortress. He always sat on the command desk, one leg crossed over the other with his knee in the air, and today was no exception. Every so often his staff would glance over at Yang sitting in this way to calm their breathing.

An operator's voice betraying an understandably nervous quaver rang out across the bridge.

"Enemy has passed through the yellow zone and entered the red zone. Distance to main cannon firing range 0.4 four light-seconds."

"Ready cannons," said Yang. He raised one hand, but not to give the signal to open fire. Instead, he removed his black beret and ruffled his ungovernable black hair. Oliver Poplin, currently in the cockpit of a spartanian fighter craft far from the bridge, had once compared this habit to the way cats raise their fur when threatened.

"Enemy has entered firing range!"

Yang put his black beret back on and raised his right hand. Julian took a deep breath, and at the moment he filled his lungs completely and began to exhale, Yang's hand fell again.

"Fire!"

"Fire!"

Vast gouts of light and energy raised silent winds that roiled their corner of the galaxy.

The screen bloomed with explosions. Concentrating their firepower was the Yang Fleet's specialty. They might even have been better at it than feigning retreat.

The wall of light and heat brought the charging Black Lancers to a sudden stop. Wittenfeld was enraged, and the barrels of the fleet's cannons began erupting in vengeful flame.

It would be pointless to view the battle waged in and around Iserlohn Corridor in SE 800—year 2 of the New Imperial Calendar—after the complete collapse of the Free Planets Alliance as a struggle between good and evil. Rather, it was a clash between peace and freedom, or between will to power and faith in institutions. The imperfect scales of justice might come down on either side depending on whether the one who held them supported—or simply preferred—Reinhard von Lohengramm or Yang Wen-li.

To those fighting the battle, of course, no such neutral standpoint was possible. Death, and the meaning of death, rested on the outcome of this battle.

Fahrenheit had rushed forward to fight alongside the Black Lancers after sending word to the kaiser that the battle had begun, and now the two imperial fleets adopted spindle formations as they faced the C-shaped fleet under Yang's command.

The Yang Fleet's formation had the advantage in a frontal firefight, being able to deploy a far greater number of cannons. Both imperial commanders itched to regroup, but with the risk of getting in each other's way and the immediate danger from the enemy guns ahead, that would be almost impossible.

"We should let the boars of the Black Lancers use their tusks to dig their own graves," hissed Commander Sanders. Fahrenheit reprimanded his adjutant curtly for the rage- and persecution complex–inspired outburst, but he was unable to put aside his own discomfort with the situation either. As it happened, Wittenfeld was dissatisfied also. Fahrenheit, he felt, should have hung back as a secondary force; his insistence on advancing alongside Wittenfeld would only restrict both from maneuvering freely in the narrow corridor.

Wittenfeld's vice chief of staff Rear Admiral Eugen's brow was almost undetectably furrowed. Eugen was said to be the most cautious man in the Black Lancers, and it took a few more seconds of hesitation before he decided to offer his opinion to their commander. Wittenfeld was standing before the main screen, arms folded and orange hair tousled.

"Your Excellency, it appears that this was a trap to lure our forces into the corridor. If we are to avoid arousing the kaiser's anger any further, I believe we must retreat—even if this does entail certain sacrifices."

It was the phrase "the kaiser's anger" that seemed to make an impact on Wittenfeld. In truth, he had already reached the same conclusion as Eugen himself. But if they retreated in this formation, they were in danger of being pursued and half-surrounded by the Yang Fleet. Would it not be better to push forward and break through the enemy at their center? Wittenfeld made a decision that would have surprised no one who knew him.

The Black Lancers began to stir. In a direct, frontal attack, they were said to be the most destructive battalion in the galaxy. It seemed to Wittenfeld that the only way to overcome their current situation was to use this destructive power to the fullest and create their own path through the center of the Yang Fleet.

At Wittenfeld's command, the main guns of each ship in his fleet showered the other side in a triple volley of fire. Then the Black Lancers surged forward in a furious charge.

The Yang Fleet fell back to absorb the attack gently. Or, at least, the center of the fleet did. The left and right wing, on the contrary, moved forward. In moments, the fleet had adopted a deep formation like an elongated V. The timing, flexibility, and perfect coordination they displayed was the fruit of much hard work on the part of Vice Admiral Fischer, master of fleet operations.

The Yang Fleet's deep defensive line erupted into a wall of fire, shattering the Black Lancers as they approached. Imperial ships black as lacquer became tumbling fireballs that melted into the black lacquer of space.

The Imperial Navy returned fire. Exposed to the Yang Fleet's cannons though they were, they continued to advance in perfect formation. They hoped to force a close-range battle, even a mixed one, and to use their overwhelming offensive capabilities to obliterate the Yang Fleet entirely. If Yang lost control of the situation for the merest moment, his fleet would dissolve into nothing more than a band of washouts.

IV

"Remember the Vermillion War last year, imperials? Remember what a crippling, devastating, inexcusable loss that was for you? You would have been ground into space dust if we hadn't taken pity on you. We saved your lives, and you repay us with yet another invasion? Your kaiser may have a pretty face, but he's nothing but a good-for-nothing punk."

Attenborough's taunts enraged the Imperial Navy as he pulled off the impressive feat of pivoting directly from successfully completing his mission to drag the Black Lancers into Iserlohn Corridor to joining the Yang Fleet on its left wing for a new attack on the enemy.

The communication channels on both sides filled with belligerent cries.

"Sieg Kaiser!"

"Damn the kaiser!"

The Black Lancers attacked in harrowing waves. Each time they charged, the front lines absorbed the disciplined fire of the Yang Fleet that produced fireballs in great quantity before the front receded. But before long they regrouped and charged again, and each time they did they battered the Yang Fleet severely and unavoidably. On the bridge of Yang's flagship

Ulysses, explosions bloomed into a flower bed of light, and the unleashed energy created such turbulence that it disturbed the once-even density of their formation.

A Yang Fleet patrol ship exploded with white-hot light, and a lacquer-black warship burst through the afterimage toward them. Yang's staff officers felt their hearts leap in their chests. Energy beams emerged like blades from *Ulysses*'s starboard and port sides, and in the concentrated cannon fire the enemy ship was annihilated, leaving only a mass of heat.

"Does that idiot Wittenfeld think he can win just by charging?" muttered lieutenant commander Soon Soul. But Yang wasn't so quick to dismiss Wittenfeld's acumen.

From a purely military perspective, the Imperial Navy's capacity to recover was effectively infinite, while the Yang Fleet's was close to zero. Accordingly, in the worst case, the imperial side could simply force a war of attrition. As long as the Yang Fleet's losses matched their own, before long the enemy would be wiped out and they would be the victorious survivors. It was hardly worth dignifying with the word "tactic," but ultimately this was where the purpose of fielding a massive army lay.

"Our two fleets together add up to thirty thousand ships," Wittenfeld had said to Fahrenheit. "We could bury them all, ship for ship, and still have ten thousand to spare!"

As irresponsible as this sounded, it did evince an understanding of the strategic high road. However, even the veteran orange-haired commander had to admit that the true situation was far from "ship for ship." In fact, their losses were staggering compared to the enemy. Sometime after the tenth wave was shattered, Wittenfeld's chief of staff Admiral Gräbner and vice chief of staff Rear Admiral Eugen decided that the Black Lancers would have to temporarily retreat and let the Fahrenheit Fleet take over as the main offensive force.

"A massive army doesn't need tactical finesse," Fahrenheit told his officers. "Stay on the attack. Keep pressing forward and hit them hard."

His judgment and decision were correct. If their momentum faltered, they would only give Yang room to bring them down through his artistic and magical tactics. The Fahrenheit Fleet had to keep up its offensive, not giving the enemy time to respond.

Their initial charge was so ferocious that even the Black Lancers went pale with shock. The guns of the Yang Fleet pounded the uninvited guests with fire and flame. But, at this point, Yang's side was at a disadvantage in terms of fatigue in the ranks. After exchanging fire a few times, Fahrenheit detected this and concentrated his forces on the left wing of the Yang Fleet, where Attenborough had command. His plan was to break through the left wing and then come around clockwise to strike at the flank of Yang's main fleet.

The maneuver was successful. With the two parts of the Yang Fleet temporarily severed, Fahrenheit's attack on the main body's flank was brutal, but met with a ferocious response.

Fahrenheit's fleet bored into the mass of enemy ships, taking high-density fire from left and right and becoming a mass of fireballs exploding in chain reaction. They formed a brilliant necklace of death and destruction.

Wittenfeld watched his comrades' bitter struggle from afar. His own fleet had already finished regrouping, and he had no doubt that the Yang Fleet was nearing exhaustion, so he ordered a new attack. This time the charging Black Lancers were met with only scattered and sporadic fire, allowing them to throw part of the Yang Fleet into disarray.

It appeared that Wittenfeld and Fahrenheit had successfully merged and recombined their forces. They were unaware, however, that this was the key to the devious trap that had been laid for them. The two imperial marshals had concentrated their ships at the center of what moments later became a ring of fire and closed in on them.

Even had they foreseen this outcome, no other way had been open to them. Neither could have left the other to stand alone. In less than half an hour, every screen in the Imperial Navy blazed with gunfire and the tide of the battle had turned completely. Despite Yang Wen-li's numerical disadvantage relative to the imperial fleets, he had managed to corner the enemy by making good use of the hazardous area at the end of the corridor. This time it was the right wing of the Yang Fleet that forced Fahrenheit's ships back against the danger zone, and the man directing that wing was none other than imperial defector Admiral Wiliabard Joachim Merkatz.

"Merkatz?!"

When Fahrenheit heard the name of his old acquaintance, an electric flash ran through his blue eyes and he turned his gaze to the points of light that filled his screen. An expression far from animosity crossed the angular face of the famed general who had been revered under two dynasties yet was still only thirty-five years old.

"Fine. This suits me better anyway," muttered Fahrenheit. Now hemmed in between enemy fire on one side and the danger zone on the other, he put his remarkable tactical prowess to work reorganizing the fleet under his command and focusing their firepower on a single point in the net that surrounded them in order to open a hole. Meanwhile, Wittenfeld knocked another corner of the Yang Fleet into disarray and fled for the corridor's exit, abandoning any further resistance. But these actions, too, were exactly what Yang had anticipated. He responded by opening the net that surrounded the two enemy fleets and then reforming around them, engulfing their ships in a deep battle situation.

Yang had used the nature of the corridor itself to put Fahrenheit and Wittenfeld in a brutal position. Their only route of retreat was now a long, narrow sector where the Yang Fleet's firepower was concentrated. To leave the corridor, they would have to pass through a storm of fire and heat. If they tried to adopt an offensive stance en route, they would only succeed in marching in orderly ranks right into the wall of enemy fire; if they decided not to commit the error of turning their head to face the enemy, they would have to flee as fast as they could while the Yang Fleet shredded their exposed flanks.

"A terrifying thing, Yang Wen-li's ingenuity. And yet, even with that knowledge, I have ended up just where he wants me…Looks like my military service has been mined out."

A self-mocking shadow flowed soundlessly down Fahrenheit's cheeks.

At the open gates of Yang's flagship *Ulysses*, spartanians were about to emerge.

"Dry Gin, Liqueur, Sherry, Absinthe. All companies, are you ready to scramble?"

Commander Olivier Poplin's voice was so free of tension that it might have been about to lead them on nothing more than a long hike. He had once revealed his secret for cheating death to a curious interlocutor: "Underestimate everything." Certainly he was a master of that particular art.

His subordinates shared the same devil-may-care attitude—or perhaps arrogance. They were veterans who had survived countless battles, large and small, since the days of the Free Planets.

At least, most of them were.

Poplin glanced at Corporal Katerose "Karin" von Kreutzer's face on one corner of the screen in his ship, watching her prepare for her first sortie. He grinned, and light danced in his green eyes like sunbeams.

"Feeling scared, Karin?"

"No, Commander, I am not feeling scared!"

"That's right, never let it show. Even clothes that are too big at first fill out as you grow. The same goes for courage."

"Yes, sir."

"This has been Poplin's Irresponsible Life Advice Line, where we say what we like because it's not our problem."

Seeing Karin struggle for a formal reply to this, the young ace laughed.

"All right, Karin, off you go. If you can do 62.4 percent of what I've taught you, you'll be fine."

Karin felt as if she'd used up that 62.4 percent within moments of takeoff. The absence of "up" and "down," the protestations of her inner ears, the anxiety of not knowing quite where you were—in less than a minute, she had experienced them all.

Katerose von Kreutzer, pull yourself together! Do you want him *to laugh at you?!*

Him? Who was *him?* For a moment, Karin had the unpleasant feeling that the path of her heart was not a straight line.

The spartanians soared through the battlefield of space. The speed felt pleasant in body and soul, but her course was not as stable as it might have been. The vast hull of a warship filled her vision and she hurried to pull up the nose of her craft. Executing a roll, she realized that she did not even know if the warship had been friend or foe. Your first sortie was also where you first realized how unprepared you were. She felt the truth of this in her every nerve. She struck her helmet with a closed fist, then checked her instruments, checked her position, spoke the figures aloud. Seeing a ship coming from the other direction, she put her hand to the neutron cannons in terror, then realized that it was a Yang Fleet craft and was terrified again by what she had almost done.

U-238 slugs left fire trails behind them, weaving a deadly embroidery in the void. Red, yellow, white—dazzling knives sliced eternal night into a thousand slivers, each one greedily consuming countless human lives.

"Underestimate everything!"

The moralizers of the world would surely narrow their eyes in disapproval of these words, but Karin recited them as if they were the holiest of incantations. And it was true that if an enemy of education such as Walter von Schönkopf could roam the universe unpunished by the heavens, the framework of society deserved all the underestimation it got.

A ball of energy burst out of a half-destroyed cruiser in a raging torrent. Karin pulled up the nose of her craft again. Her vision and heart whirled. Just as she finally managed to reconfirm her position, a single imperial walküre flew into her field of vision. It followed its own line of fire toward her, scraping far too closely over her head.

"Under—estimate—*everything*!"

Karin forced the syllables out in bursts as she strained to bring her beloved fighter about. The walküre completed its 180-degree turn first and fired on her again, but hit only empty space. Karin captured it in the sights of her neutron cannons and tossed her hair, so like the color of weakly brewed tea, inside her helmet.

"*Damn the kaiser—!*"

"I have been informed that Corporal Katerose von Kreutzer returned safely with one confirmed kill."

Vice Admiral Walter von Schönkopf, Karin's biological father, was given this information on *Ulysses*'s bridge as he opened his flask of whiskey. He raised the drink high and smiled cryptically. "Three cheers for the tomboy!"

Was he sincere, or only using his daughter as a pretext? The defiance in his expression was so resolute that it was impossible to tell.

At 2315 on April 30, Fahrenheit's flagship *Ahsgrimm* was finally caught in the Yang Fleet's net of firepower. Fahrenheit was using the ship as a last line of defense, supporting his fleet's retreat to prevent it from becoming a total rout, but as the other ships slipped away the density of the enemy gunfire directed at his own increased in inexorable proportion.

Right at the moment the limits of *Ahsgrimm's* energy-neutralization system were exceeded, a sizzling spear of light pierced its hull. This set off further explosions, and a serpent of flame writhed through the ship. Fahrenheit was thrown from his commander's chair and against the wall, then dashed against the floor for good measure. Agony spiraled up through him, and he retched breath and blood from the bottom of his wounded lungs.

Sitting upright with some difficulty, Fahrenheit heard the rapidly approaching tread of death in the depths of his ear canals. A smile found his bloody face. His blue eyes caught the lighting and glinted with metallic reflected light.

The home I was born to was as poor as His Majesty the Kaiser's was. I joined the navy because I needed to eat. I met my share of useless commanders and senior officers, but my reward in the end was service under the greatest man of all—Kaiser Reinhard himself. I call that a fortunate enough life. If things had been the other way around, I should never have been able to meet his eyes…

Blood spilled from the corner of Fahrenheit's mouth, a new agony made solid. In his darkening field of vision he saw that the student from the elementary school who served as his orderly was still by his side. Fahrenheit looked the boy directly in his grimy, tearstained face. "What are you doing?" he shouted. "Hurry up and abandon ship!"

"Your Excellency…"

"Go! Now! Do you know how they'll look at me in Valhalla if I bring a child with me?"

The boy coughed amid the fire and smoke and stench of death. He was determined to uphold the principles of the school.

"In that case, please give me a token. I will see that it gets to His Majesty the Kaiser even at the cost of my own life."

The fearless admiral glanced back from death's door with something like exasperation. He attempted a rueful smile, but was already too weak.

"A token? Very well."

His control over his vocal cords was failing rapidly.

"Here is your token: *your life*. Bear it all the way to the kaiser. You are *not* to die. Do you hear me?"

It seems doubtful that Fahrenheit himself heard the last words he spoke.

At 2325, the flagship followed its commander into death, leaving only a handful of survivors who threw themselves into the shuttles to escape the bloodshed.

On May 2, the defeated troops rejoined the main fleet under Kaiser Reinhard. Wittenfeld's Black Lancers had lost 6,220 of their original 15,900 ships and 695,700 of their original 1,908,000 men. Fahrenheit's fleet had lost 8,490 of its 15,200 ships and 1,095,400 of its 1,857,600 men. And, above all, a senior admiral of the Lohengramm Dynasty had fallen on the battlefield for the first time.

"Fahrenheit is dead, then…"

Reinhard's ice-blue eyes sank into grief. In this opening skirmish to the decisive battle, they had lost a member of their top military leadership. Despite fighting on the side of the kaiser's enemies in the Lippstadt War, his genius in combat had seen him forgiven and welcomed by the blond conqueror. Reinhard surely regretted the loss deeply, but said nothing more. His gaze fell like a crystal sword on the other senior admiral, who had returned alive. This was Wittenfeld's first taste of loss since the Battle of Amritsar, and the fearless admiral, face haggard but back as straight as he could manage, waited for the kaiser to unleash his wrath.

"Wittenfeld!"

"Yes, sir."

"This error was very like you. Aware that it was a trap, you nevertheless stepped directly into it and attempted to tear your way through. Thousands died, and not one hero to be remembered."

"I caused the needless death of a brother-in-arms and squandered thousands of Your Majesty's troops," said Wittenfeld, using all his strength to keep his voice steady. "I will resent no punishment you may deem appropriate for my idiocy."

Reinhard shook his head, luxurious golden hair rippling like solid sunlight. "I do not mean to criticize you," he said. "Better an error like you than unlike you. The task before you now is to take further action in keeping with your character to regain this lost ground. This is, I feel sure, what Admiral Fahrenheit would have wanted too. I, too, am more determined than ever to defeat Yang Wen-li. Lend me your strength."

It was known that Fahrenheit had been named the fourth marshal of the Lohengramm Dynasty. Wittenfeld bowed his head deeply and was unable to raise it for some time. He was frankly touched by the magnanimity of his liege.

Von Reuentahl, however, standing beside the young conqueror, observed something rather different. He knew both consciously and unconsciously that the kaiser's conquering spirit was currently focused entirely on one man: Yang Wen-li.

"Is it to be victory or death, then, mein Kaiser?" asked von Reuentahl.

Hilda, chief secretary to Kaiser Reinhard, stirred slightly and divided her gaze equally between the kaiser and von Reuentahl, who was also secretary-general of Supreme Command Headquarters.

"No," said Reinhard. "The options are not victory or death. They are victory…or more perfect victory." He laughed in a translucent voice. Sometimes he wondered if even he went over the top in his speech. For now, however, he had wanted to reaffirm his raison d'être. He felt at that moment throughout his entire body the bliss of pursuing victory on the battlefield.

It was the kaiser's first smile in some time. This above all else made his bodyguard Emil von Selle happy.

CHAPTER 4:

KALEIDOSCOPE

I

IN KAISER REINHARD'S NAME, Imperial Military Command Headquarters announced publicly that Senior Admiral Adalbert Fahrenheit had fallen in battle and would be promoted posthumously to the rank of marshal.

This news also reached the Yang Fleet back in Iserlohn Fortress. Admiral Merkatz took a day to mourn his former brother-in-arms, a friend since their days in the Goldenbaum Dynasty, and was absent from the May 1 strategy meeting. His aide von Schneider took his place, but even he wore a mourning ribbon on his breast. This drew some barbed looks from Vice Admiral Murai, possibly the fleet's sole stickler for protocol, but even he did not say anything. Walter von Schönkopf made certain highly unmilitary observations, including "Nothing like mourning dress for bringing out a woman's beauty" that also drew Murai's ire, including some looks that were not so much barbed as bristling with needles.

Yang was exhausted. He appeared to want nothing so much as a glass full of sherry and a bath full of hot water, but this was not unusual for him. Before battle, when he was dreaming up ways to achieve the impossible, he came off like a creative artist, full of intelligence and vitality, but afterward, when the plan was carried out and the objectives achieved, he lolled around like an old hunting dog.

"Once the fighting's over, he remembers that he hates it and gets put in a bad mood," was Julian Mintz's assessment. This was not meant cynically; if anything, it was intended as a defense of Yang's sloth. Frederica Greenhill Yang, on the other hand, saw no need to defend her husband at all—in her opinion, his idleness was better counted as one of his virtues. Neither of the two were capable of a strict and objective assessment of his character.

"Our fleet has won the first battle, but will this affect the Imperial Navy's basic strategy?" asked Murai. It was the custom in the Yang Fleet for him to open the strategy meetings with a suitably meeting-like question.

The youthful staff officers, assured, arrogant, and anarchical, quite obviously kept Murai at arm's length. Captain Kasper Rinz, head of the Rosen Ritter brigade, had wanted to be a painter in his youth, and often sketched the other staff officers at meetings. When Rinz drew Murai, though, instead of capturing his face he simply filled the space between beret and collar with the word ORDER. Of course, without Murai's eyes and mouth, it was highly doubtful whether this "band of fugitive mercenaries" could have maintained cohesion as a military unit.

"I don't think it'll change things much," said Yang. "This wasn't another Amritsar or Vermillion. We were just hiding meanly in our hole so that even the kaiser couldn't choose his own field of battle."

That "meanly" wasn't Yang being humble—it was the truth. In tactical terms, Yang was neither generous nor an idealist. Until victory was achieved, he fought with extreme bitterness, giving no quarter whatsoever.

At this time, Dusty Attenborough had already begun giving orders for five million chain mines to be deployed at the entrance to the corridor, demonstrating that Olivier Poplin had been correct when he said that preparing for a fight was the only thing Attenborough wasn't lazy about.

The consensus was that the mines would at least buy some time, and Yang did not argue against it. The ceaseless fighting had taken its toll on the Yang Fleet. Their tank beds, which left their users fully refreshed in no time at all, were running at full capacity, but with excitement, agitation, and anxiety tap-dancing through their minds, some of the troops visited the beds several types a day. As might be expected, there did not seem to be many in the "merry Yang Family" who were on the same psychological level as von Schönkopf, Attenborough, and Poplin. As for Julian, he was not suffering from fatigue, but he did feel as if his heart and lungs might suddenly destabilize at any moment.

How were things with the Imperial Navy?

Fahrenheit's death and the defeat of the Black Lancers in the early fighting had come as a shock, of course, but had not critically wounded their psychology. Fahrenheit had been a talented general. The Black Lancers were strong and fearless. But neither were Kaiser Reinhard. And was not that justly praised leader proudly unfurling his perfect, uninjured golden wings even now?

Morale among the fighting men was high, but the navy's leaders could not formulate strategy relying on morale alone. The Twin Ramparts of the navy met for discussion daily.

It was a commonplace notion in military studies that while a large force and significant strength were essential elements in establishing superiority at the strategic level, this was not necessarily true at the tactical level. Depending on the geography of the battlefield, superior size could even factor into defeat.

Mittermeier and von Reuentahl knew this to be true from their own experience. If force size had been the only thing that determined victory, the Goldenbaum Dynasty should have utterly eliminated the Free Planets Alliance at the Battle of Dagon; meanwhile, the alliance should have won at the Battle of Amritsar. A large military force could not function as intended unless it was supplied perfectly, provided with accurate information, and was free of idle soldiers—in that order. Faced with Iserlohn Corridor's unique topography, von Reuentahl and Mittermeier were forced to keep that third item particularly in mind.

Not all accepted the view that the Battle of the Corridor was the final, glorious act in Kaiser Reinhard's "Great Campaign" and therefore the most important battle of all for the kaiser. Some of the military historians of later ages argued that the "splendid refinement" that characterized the kaiser's previous military actions was nowhere to be seen at Iserlohn, which instead played host to nothing but "an ostentatious display of military superiority"—but were these criticisms or regrets? In any case, Reinhard's "military superiority" had never wavered, but that was because it had been employed in environments where military force was effective.

News that the Yang Fleet had mined the entrance to Iserlohn Corridor caused some furrowed brows among the Imperial Navy leadership. They could not grasp, immediately, what Yang Wen-li was planning. Was not dragging the enemy *into* the corridor his only tactical route to victory? Was he simply buying time before he would be forced to meet their invasion?"

"Why even carry directional Seffl particles, if not for cases like this?" said one attendee at the meeting. "Why not use them to open a path through the minefield, just as we did at Amritsar? What Yang is planning is irrelevant."

Marshal von Reuentahl, secretary-general of Supreme Command Headquarters, dismissed this opinion at once. Their circumstances at Amritsar had been entirely different. Even if that had not been the case, their battlefield here was Iserlohn Corridor. It was cramped and narrow, and if it were "plugged" with a minefield their freedom of movement would be severely restricted.

"Suppose we use the Seffl particles to bore a hole in that plug," von Reuentahl said. "The Yang Fleet will be waiting for us on the other side, ready to concentrate fire on that freshly bored hole. They will snipe our ships as they emerge from the hole, leaving us no opportunity to even return fire. The entire fleet could be lost."

The fact remained, however, that to crush the Yang Fleet they would have to enter the corridor somehow.

"But perhaps we do not have to discard your idea entirely," muttered von Reuentahl.

After half a day of thought, he presented his own proposal to Reinhard.

The kaiser nodded his assent, golden hair swaying. "Very good," he said. "Our forces are seven or eight times the size of theirs. Surely enough to eliminate Yang Wen-li if we can only get inside the corridor."

"Thank you, Your Majesty. With your assent, I shall move forward with execution. If you see any areas requiring additional work, of course, I shall amend them…"

"I see none at this time. If even your stratagem does not bring us victory, I will think of another method to counteract Yang's scheming. You have done well."

Oskar von Reuentahl, just like both his prince and his enemies, contained contradictions. A range of circumstantial evidence raises doubts about whether he truly hoped to see Kaiser Reinhard victorious in the end, but the strategy he had proposed on this occasion was probably the best, given the circumstances and conditions at the time.

Wolfgang Mittermeier, out of consideration for their kaiser as well as for his friend, also examined the proposal in detail, but he, too, found nothing that required amendment.

"A passing grade from the Gale Wolf! What an honor," said von Reuentahl. "Perhaps there's room on the staff at the space armada for me, too, eh?"

Mittermeier's gray eyes, rich in vitality, flashed with recognition of his friend's hidden meaning.

"No, I think not," he said. "At least not among my staff officers. Our kaiser might not be the type to feel jealous of talented subordinates, but I am."

Von Reuentahl smiled faintly at this feeble response to his own feeble joke. The smile came through differently in his black right eye, his blue left eye, and his even lips.

"The Gale Wolf is too modest! The only men in the galaxy who can outthink me as strategists are mein Kaiser, Yang Wen-li, Merkatz, and you. That I only need to fight two of those is my great good fortune."

Von Reuentahl's voice put one in mind of the sound of an ocean current with multiple layers at different temperatures. After half a second of silence, Mittermeier seized his own earlobe.

"By your logic, more than half of today's five greatest commanders are in our camp. If we work together for a common purpose, victory will be within our reach."

Irritation showed suddenly on Mittermeier's face.

"Enough, von Reuentahl. I do not understand why you and I always speak so archly. It was never necessary until very recently."

Von Reuentahl nodded, smiling frankly at his old friend. "Just as you say," he said. "Evening is here, and we have not yet even started drinking. I have a white from 446. No match for a 410, perhaps, but what do you say?"

II

At 0630 on May 3, SE 800, year 2 of the New Imperial Calendar, the Galactic Imperial Navy began its entry into Iserlohn Corridor under the direct command of Kaiser Reinhard. Even after losing more than a million souls in the first skirmishes of the battle, the imperial forces still numbered 146,600 ships and 16.2 million officers and men, with more in reserve at the rear—specifically, 15,200 ships under the command of Senior Admiral August Samuel Wahlen, currently stationed between the corridor and the former alliance capital Planet Heinessen. Yang Wen-li's fleet, on the other hand, was already down to fewer than 20,000 ships. In terms of sheer numbers, the two sides simply bore no comparison.

Kaiser Reinhard was on the bridge of the fleet flagship *Brünhild*, where the viewscreen showed the Imperial Navy vanguard clearing mines as they advanced.

The "Silent Commander," Senior Admiral Ernst von Eisenach, had been chosen by the kaiser to lead the strike force that would follow.

"These orders are the greatest honor a warrior could possibly receive. I shall spare no effort to carry out Your Majesty's wishes, and if those efforts should be insufficient I shall apologize with my life. Sieg Kaiser!"

…is what Eisenach did *not* say, instead making only a deferential, silent bow before leaving the kaiser's presence.

One by one, the other admirals received their orders and set off to their posts. Wittenfeld, who had tasted the bitter chalice of defeat in the first engagement, was given temporary command of the former Fahrenheit

Fleet in addition to his own, giving him almost twenty thousand ships in total. The implication was as clear to Wittenfeld as it was to everyone else: the kaiser had high expectations of the ferocious commander's burning desire for revenge.

Neidhart Müller, youngest of the senior admirals, was assigned to guard the rear. He had played this role at almost every stage of the kaiser's Great Campaign since its commencement the previous year. The truth was that the Imperial Navy simply could not eliminate the uncertainty that lay in its wake as it advanced across the galaxy. Behind them stretched a vast territory that had once belonged to their now-defeated enemy. If organized rebellion should arise, it might be beyond the ability of even the seasoned Wahlen to put down. In such a case, Müller would turn back from the battlefield and cooperate with Wahlen to secure the widest possible route back to the empire's home territory for the rest of the fleet. He was also responsible for defending against enemy attack from the rear, although that seemed impossible in their present situation.

The man who had been entrusted with the vanguard and tasked with cleaning the minefield as he plunged into the depths of the corridor was Vice Admiral Rolf Otto Brauhitsch. It was a grueling operation of more than half a day, but he completed this assignment eventually.

Brauhitsch had formerly served under Siegfried Kircheis. After Kircheis's death, he had come under the direct command of Reinhard. Whether on the front lines or at the rear, his ability to deal with situations as they arose was first-rate, and his meticulous advance preparations and decisive leadership in battle belied his youth. Sometimes, however, he was accused of forgetting the preparations he himself had made and rushing in blindly. Perhaps it was simply that while his bravery was inborn, his attention to detail was the fruit of conscious effort.

At 2100 on May 3, Brauhitsch fired his first volley at the Yang Fleet. Return fire tore through the dark void toward him precisely fifteen seconds later. Points and beams of light multiplied by the half second until his screen had become a vast, rippling curtain of light.

From this moment on, Iserlohn Corridor was a dizzying kaleidoscope of devastation and slaughter.

In short order, the Brauhitsch Fleet was taking concentrated fire. Worse yet, the minefield behind them made retreat all but impossible.

This was all as expected—indeed, part of their strategy. Brauhitsch carried out the instructions he had received from the kaiser and divided his 6,400 ships into squadrons of one hundred to avoid the concentration of enemy fire, but the fleet took no little damage while executing this maneuver. With walls of fire and light penning them in both fore and aft, the vanguard of the Imperial Navy had been forced into a perilous position.

At 0220 on May 4, secretary-general of Supreme Command Headquarters Marshal von Reuentahl ordered the commencement of the operation's second phase.

The release of directional Seffl particles began. The minefield was run through by five invisible pillars of cloud, which when ignited became five vast dragons of flame dancing in the void. It was both a magnificent sight and a ferocious manifestation of the terror within that very magnificence. Eventually the dragons burned themselves out, leaving five tunnels through the minefield like the fingers of some colossal god that had seized the dragons and crushed them.

High-speed cruisers poured into the five tunnels.

When they emerged into the corridor, the former alliance forces quickly showered them in fire, and many exploded into balls of flame. However, it was impossible to maintain suppressive fire on five entrances at once—and, above all, the cruisers were a diversion. While the Yang Fleet's attention was focused on the five tunnels, the Imperial Navy's main forces were making their entry through the path that Brauhitsch had so painstakingly cleared into the corridor proper.

After two hours of pitched battle, the imperial military finally established what might be called a bridgehead within Iserlohn Corridor.

The pure-white form of Kaiser Reinhard's flagship *Brünhild* emerged into the corridor at 1200 on May 5, and the Yang Fleet's communications channel filled at once with vocalized tension and anxiety.

"The kaiser's made his appearance. Are we ready to present our bouquet?" asked Attenborough, in a rather subdued style for him. He steadied his breathing and heartbeat, then slapped his commander's desk and shouted, "Fire!"

Attenborough was the most accomplished student of the Yang Wen-li school of one-point concentrated fire. Tens of thousands of beams of light fell on hundreds of individual points in space like torrential rain. It was a perfect combination of calculation and practice.

The densely packed Imperial Navy was unable to avoid the frontal cannon fire. An inaudible roar of destruction pounded ships and humans alike, and waterfalls of heat and light poured in every direction.

The corridor filled with tiny, newly created stars. Spirals of energy sparked a chain reaction and flooded the narrow corridor with dark, torrential flows. Both sides were thrown into disarray, and the energy beams were also knocked off course, reducing their hit rate. For a moment, the front lines were pure chaos. The first to regain some grip on order was the Yang Fleet, which was accustomed to fighting in the corridor. Just as Mittermeier was struggling against harassing fire and Iserlohn's cramped dimensions to scrape together a proper formation, the Yang Fleet closed in and showered his ships in cannon fire.

"Left wing, fall back! Right wing and center, advance!"

Mittermeier hoped to draw in the vanguard of the Yang Fleet with the retreat of his left wing, while simultaneously rotating in a half circle counterclockwise to attack the enemy from their port flank. None but the Gale Wolf could have even hoped to execute such a dynamic maneuver.

Had Mittermeier succeeded, Yang would doubtless have been put in a difficult position. The movement of the imperial fleet, however, did not match the speed of his orders at that moment. His communication systems were also functioning imperfectly, and he lacked sufficient room to maneuver his enormous forces freely. Yang did not miss the moment when the Imperial Navy fell into slight confusion, and gave orders to fire.

Brünhild's screen filled with billowing explosions. Hundreds of the ships guarding the unspoiled white goddess erupted into pulsing flame and were torn to pieces. But the fleet flagship remained hidden behind the rest of the Imperial Navy's dense formation.

Mittermeier made a noise of frustration and turned to his aide, Lieutenant Commander Amsdorf.

"While I was letting them flatter me with titles like 'marshal' and 'commander in chief of the Imperial Space Armada,' it seems that my feel for command in battle was dulled," he said. "Can you imagine? Formulating a plan without ensuring that the entire fleet could keep up!"

Mittermeier sought and received permission from the kaiser to transfer from *Brünhild* to his own flagship *Beowulf* and enter the fray at the front. It was 2015 hours on May 4.

III

"The Gale Wolf has arrived at the front lines!"

The Imperial Navy's communications channel filled with cheers. The only man in the imperial military whose popularity among the enlisted men compared to Mittermeier's was the kaiser himself. Even von Reuentahl would come in third.

Calmly exposing himself to enemy fire, Mittermeier reformulated the fleet's tactics and then gave orders to his subordinates for execution.

"Bayerlein, go!"

The young officer felt his heart race faster at the order from his beloved and respected commander. Bayerlein had around six thousand ships under him at that time. It was not a large force in the context of the Imperial Navy, but it was superbly agile and responsive. Mittermeier, restricted by the shape of the corridor from much more than advancing in a single column, had Bayerlein form a wing for potential half encirclement.

They were met by Dusty Attenborough's battalion. Yang had recognized Mittermeier's strategic intentions and deemed it imperative that Bayerlein be stopped.

As commanders in battle, Bayerlein and Attenborough were more or less equals. The imbalance was one of resources. Attenborough could muster only 80 percent of the forces that his enemy could develop as a vanguard. If the situation slipped from frontal clash to mixed battle, he would be overwhelmed before long.

As a result, he decided to lure Bayerlein into a position between Attenborough's battalion and the main body of the Yang Fleet in order to launch a pincer attack. And so, just five minutes after their first engagement, Attenborough began his retreat and invited the enemy to charge.

Bayerlein recognized the trap, but nothing would be achieved by turning back now. Trusting in Mittermeier to think of something, he accepted Attenborough's invitation and surged ahead, accelerating as he went and wildly firing energy beams and missiles, almost as if to intentionally waste energy.

Yang's tactical activities at this point were unusually refined. While checking Mittermeier's movements with cannon fire, he directed his vanguard to move forward with full speed at a ten o'clock angle.

By the time Bayerlein realized what was happening, Yang almost had him half-encircled. A hurried retreat allowed Bayerlein to keep his losses to a minimum.

Mittermeier couldn't suppress a short but rather serious rueful chuckle. "The Magician's toying with Bayerlein now? He's in a class of his own."

Without Yang Wen-li's leadership and strategy, the El Facil Revolutionary Reserve Force would have been a disorderly rabble at best. On the other hand, so long as Yang was guiding them, the units under his command were the crème de la crème, the strongest in the galaxy, striking on the left and parrying on the right, first advancing and then falling back, so vigorous and active that their twenty thousand ships could stand against five times that many. Of course, this came at the cost of attrition by fatigue. Even if their spirits remained high, their bodies would gradually falter when trying to obey orders.

That, Mittermeier mused, was when his chance of victory would arrive—but there was no guarantee that the Imperial Navy would hold together that long. If that were not enough, the topography would force them to deploy their resources piecemeal—almost one by one.

Reinhard, von Reuentahl, and Mittermeier were all thoroughly aware of how unwise this was, but having been drawn into the corridor, they had no other choice. The only option they could see was to continue piling force upon force and grinding the Yang Fleet down as best they could.

Nevertheless, Mittermeier's tactical direction, too, was near supernatural in its accuracy and alacrity. Just like his close friend von Reuentahl, Mittermeier nursed some private criticisms on the strategic level regarding the kaiser's campaign of conquest. Having received his orders, however, he confined his thinking to the tactical level and concentrated all his knowledge and ability as a commander on establishing an advantage in the battlefield before him. He used the forces he had available to create thousand-ship battle units of two types, one focused on mobility and the other on firepower, and used these units to reinforce the battle lines wherever they seemed in danger of collapsing. He also kept the supply and medical ships running at full capacity to keep fleet logistics knitted organically together.

As a result, although the Imperial Navy recognized the advantage the Yang Fleet enjoyed, it did not flee, and indeed stubbornly maintained order to a degree that even Yang had to admire.

"That's the Gale Wolf for you," he said. "Nothing ostentatious about his tactics, but not just any admiral could pull them off."

In truth, Mittermeier would have dismissed this praise as foolishness. The Imperial Navy was vastly more powerful than its enemy, and yet they had entered a battlefield so cramped that it robbed them of their very freedom of movement. Those at the rear of their forces were unable to join the fray at all, and could only watch the situation unfold from afar through a wall of their allies.

"I've left men idle," Mittermeier muttered to himself. "What kind of commander am I?" He felt deeply embarrassed at this failure to master and apply even the fundamentals of military learning.

On May 6, Yang attacked the Imperial Navy using a strategy suggested by Merkatz. Yang, Merkatz, and Attenborough hammered the enemy's left wing—narrow, but still there—in succession. When the Imperial Navy began pouring its main force into that wing to reinforce it, Commodore Marino led a strike team into the core of their main force. This was not an unorthodox plan; if anything, it was the height of orthodoxy, but that was exactly why it was likely to succeed—and, indeed, it very nearly did.

"All right, go!" Marino shouted, stamping his foot. "Let's give that lovely kaiser of theirs the loveliest funeral they've ever seen!"

Excited by his own voice, breathing fast, Marino dove toward *Brünhild* like lightning to a lightning rod.

Senior Admiral Steinmetz realized the danger to his prince. His fleet was in a long, narrow formation, not necessarily the most advantageous for battle, but they did have the edge in numbers. They lunged toward Marino from the front and left to stop his approach.

Unnerved by the size and momentum of the enemy fleet, Marino's strike force broke right. After a thirty-minute skirmish, Marino had lost 40 percent of his ships. Their formation was collapsing and they were on the verge of a rout. What saved them was the main body of the Yang Fleet.

"Main enemy force approaching in tight formation!" bellowed Steinmetz's operator. Steinmetz ordered his men to welcome the intruders with cannon fire, but their aim was far less precise than the gunners of the Yang Fleet. Soon the Steinmetz Fleet was a mass of fireballs and light stretching over tens of thousands of kilometers.

By this point the main Yang Fleet and Merkatz's fleet had wordlessly united. Side by side, they alternated attacks on the Steinmetz Fleet until, surprisingly quickly, it was taken apart.

Steinmetz's flagship *Vonkel* took three simultaneous rail gun slugs at 1150 on May 6. Fire followed explosion, and the ship's interior was engulfed in panic. The god of flames swung his sword on the bridge, laying the officers low and sending equipment and instruments flying with a wave of intense heat. As shrieks of agony gave way to dying groans, Steinmetz's adjutant Commander Serbel looked around for the admiral through the blood and fire and smoke. Steinmetz had fallen facedown beside him. Serbel coughed up a bloody mass and then opened his redly stained mouth to speak.

"Your Excellency's left leg is utterly crushed," he said.

"Your reports always were accurate," Steinmetz replied, unsmiling. "I don't know how many times they've saved me." He looked at the left side of his lower body in an almost businesslike manner. He had almost no feeling in his leg. "I think this is it for me, though. Are you wounded?"

He got no reply. Serbel had already collapsed facedown in a pool of his own blood, now rapidly evaporating from the heat coming through the floor from the level below. He was completely still.

Steinmetz called for his chief of staff, Bohlen. As expected, there was no reply. The numbness spread to his right leg and hip as his hemorrhaging worsened. Night fell on his field of vision, and invisible barriers went up in his ear canals.

"Gretchen!" he murmured, and breathed his last.

Even von Reuentahl had to pause for a moment as his heterochromiac eyes reflected the rainbow of light engulfing the *Vonkel*. Reinhard glanced back over his shoulder at his secretary-general. The young emperor's face was half lit up by the beams of light from the screen like a sculpture of porcelain and obsidian.

"Did Steinmetz abandon ship?" Reinhard asked.

"I will check right away, mein Kaiser."

Von Reuentahl did not even notice the four half moments of stunned silence he had required before replying.

The only member of Steinmetz's command center to survive was Rear Admiral Markgraf. It took three minutes before he was able to report the death of his commander. Kaiser Reinhard put one hand to his fair brow at the news of a second admiral lost. His long-lashed lids were closed for only a moment before they opened again and his ice-blue eyes sought out a single person.

"Fräulein von Mariendorf."

"Yes, Your Majesty."

"I hereby appoint you the new chief advisor of imperial headquarters. You are to take Steinmetz's place as my lieutenant."

Hilda was taken aback, notwithstanding her usual insight.

"But, Your Majesty, I—"

Reinhard raised his hand, as white as if it had been carved from halite, and silenced the countess's objection.

"I know. You have never led so much as a single soldier. But leading the troops is the job of the frontline commanders, and leading the commanders is the job of the kaiser. All I ask is that you advise me. Who will object to me selecting my staff as I see fit?"

Hilda bowed respectfully, tactfully refraining from naming the one person who would indeed object, with very high probability.

IV

At this point in the battle, the Imperial Navy's formation was collapsing, and even Mittermeier's preternatural direction could not entirely reverse the trend. The fleet Steinmetz had commanded was not by any means underpowered, but with its command center gone it could not coordinate its movements, and even its valiant defense against the Yang Fleet's offensive was almost entirely ineffective. In fact, because it was spreading in a disorderly fashion to both left and right, it was actually making things worse by confusing the chain of command among its allies.

Kaiser Reinhard stood on the fleet flagship's bridge, calmly watching the enemy fire that now reached almost as far as *Brünhild* itself. Von Reuentahl beside him watched the kaiser closely, but saw only the slightest of furrows on his elegant brow.

Is this where I end my life, then, alongside this golden-haired conquering king?

Well, there were worse fates. Von Reuentahl smiled in secret at the mirror he kept in the dimly lit recesses of his heart. He had, of course, taken precautions to protect imperial headquarters itself from risk.

Rear Admiral Alexander Barthauser was known as one of the bravest leaders under von Reuentahl's command. He possessed neither startling talent nor much capacity for handling large forces, but on the battlefield he did whatever was necessary to faithfully carry out his orders, and on this point he had earned von Reuentahl's trust.

Barthauser's 2,400 ships positioned themselves parallel to the Yang Fleet along its starboard side and showered it with relentless cannon fire, successfully slowing its advance. They did not buy much time, but it was enough for *Brünhild* to escape. Reinhard's pride made the retreat a reluctant one, but von Reuentahl was able to persuade him that falling back would allow them to lure Yang's main fleet into a trap and half encircle them. However, the coordination between the many fleets of the Imperial Navy was not rapid enough to realize this aim. Before they could position themselves within the space opened up by the withdrawal of *Brünhild*, the Yang Fleet had already charged forward to occupy it instead.

When his operator shouted that Yang was pressing mercilessly forward, von Reuentahl thought it odd, but spread out his gunships to meet them with arms.

Just then, the Yang Fleet changed course, swooping *under* the Imperial Navy's defensive formations to hit Reinhard's main force with energy beams and missiles from below and charge into their ranks from close range.

The admirals of the Imperial Navy shared a horrified shudder. At that moment, Yang seemed to them less inspired commander than brutal warlord. The cannon fire was intense, shattering the Imperial Navy's resistance and reaching almost to *Brünhild*, eternal flagship of the kaiser.

Reinhard shuddered too, but his was less out of fear than having reached the pinnacle of excitement.

"Yes, yes! This is exactly what I hoped for!"

His porcelain skin flushed with life. His breathing became faster, richer.

Immense waves of light and energy billowed across that corner of the galaxy, and at the center of it all Reinhard seemed to shine as if personifying his own vitality.

"Von Reuentahl! Concentrate fire lines at two o'clock, elevation minus thirty degrees. If you open a gap in the enemy formation, keep applying pressure there until you break through."

Reinhard said nothing more, but his meaning was clear to the heterochromiac von Reuentahl. Even as the enemy's cannon fire and high-speed maneuvering had drawn closer, Reinhard had not slipped into panic. Instead, he had identified the point where the enemy formation was maintained so that the counterattack could be focused there. If they could pierce the Yang Fleet's ranks, the enemy's battle lines would be thrown off-balance. In the best case, this might be the first blow of the chisel that cut the diamond, and the entire Yang Fleet might collapse. Even in the worst case, Yang would have to halt his attack while he reconstructed the fleet's formation. The battlefield was vast, and such crucial points were rare, but Reinhard had identified one immediately. *Praise be to our kaiser's genius*, thought von Reuentahl.

Reinhard laughed, sweeping back his fine golden hair. His beaming face was as dazzling as an overturned box of jewels.

"I knew that Yang Wen-li would attack aggressively. Only by challenging me personally can he defeat me, after all—recall the Vermillion War. I…"

Suddenly Reinhard fell silent, and unthinkingly raised his left hand to his mouth. Teeth like virgin snow bit gently into his ring finger. Hilda was surprised to see that anger had entered his expression. The look remained on his face even after word was received that Yang Wen-li's offensive had been halted and the Yang Fleet forced to withdraw.

For several days now, Yang Wen-li's flagship *Ulysses* had also been adrift on a sea of life-or-death struggle.

"Looks like you'll be using up your whole life's stock of seriousness before this is through, Commander," said von Schönkopf. He was a skilled and valiant commander in ground battle and close combat, but had no role in a fleet battle and was simply observing, whiskey flask in hand.

To the others, this looked like an enviable position. Attenborough, for example, would spread out a blanket on the floor of his flagship *Massasoit's* bridge as soon as the battle was over and sleep all the way back to Iserlohn Fortress. Such was the ferocity of the combat and the extent to which he was draining his own physical reserves to fight it.

The same was true of Olivier Poplin, who would sortie fourteen times before the fight was over. After his final mission was complete, Poplin would sleep for six hours in the cockpit of his beloved ship, then fourteen more in the bed of his private chambers—"On his own, if you can believe that," as Attenborough would later note.

To maintain its tactical advantage, the Yang Fleet was standing one-legged on thin ice. It simply did not have the numbers. On the imperial side, Steinmetz had been eliminated and his fleet effectively neutralized, but Müller, Wittenfeld, and von Eisenach still waited unharmed in the wings—to name just three. That latent power was terrifying. They had not been able to enter the fray yet due to the cramped conditions in the corridor, but if Kaiser Reinhard decided to adopt the tactics that Yang most feared right now, what response would be possible?

Yang saw no choice but to stay on the offensive and hope to overwhelm the Imperial Navy before that worst-case scenario came to pass.

And so, at 2300 hours on May 7, the Yang Fleet launched another frontal assault.

What protected the kaiser this time was Müller, who successfully positioned his ships to absorb the enemy cannon fire.

Hearing that a squadron of enemy ships whose commander was yet unclear had formed a defensive wall in front of Kaiser Reinhard, Yang Wen-li let out a small sigh. "That'll be Iron Wall Müller, living up to his name," he said. "Just having Müller under his command would be enough to keep Reinhard's name alive in song for centuries."

It was as if the memory of Müller's fortuitous arrival that had saved Reinhard's life the previous year during the Vermillion War had come back to life again.

This time, Müller waited until his fleet was arranged more or less perfectly, then slipped between Reinhard and the Yang Fleet. Yang only managed to get one blow in before the wall went up and he was forced to retreat and reform.

Even at this late stage of his battle with the Galactic Empire, Yang couldn't help admiring the sheer amount of talent Reinhard commanded. It was not just Müller. Fahrenheit and Steinmetz had not given their lives for the idea of autocratic government. Instead, they had willingly thrown away the rest of their allotted span out of personal loyalty to Reinhard von Lohengramm. This was how the kaiser's favor was repaid.

"In other words, people are loyal to people, not ideals or systems of governance," Yang mused, dedicating a portion of his neurons to what could not be called urgent matters even amid the intense whirlwind of battle.

Why fight at all? Even Yang, an artist whose medium was combat, brooded on this question constantly. The more he pursued it logically, however, the more convinced he became that fighting was meaningless.

To blur this "why," the most important core of that logic, and appeal to emotion instead was to engage in demagoguery. Since antiquity, wars rooted in religious hatred had always seen the fiercest combat and the least mercy, because the will to fight was rooted in emotion rather than principle. Loathing of enemies, loyalty to commanders—all were ruled by emotion. Nor did Yang exclude himself from this analysis: he knew that his own allegiance to the principles of democratic governance was also, in part, simple enmity toward autocracy.

Yang's greatest worry regarding his ward, Julian Mintz, was that, after six years under Yang's influence, he might be fighting *for* Yang. That would not do at all, Yang though. He did not want Julian to hate the enemy and love to wage war on them out of personal loyalty to Yang. He wanted the object of that loyalty to be democratic thought and practice.

But did he want Julian to continue the fight against imperial governance even after Yang himself was dead? Here Yang hesitated. After all, he had been opposed to Julian's joining the military in the first place. In the end, he had acceded to Julian's wishes and granted his permission, and now he recognized Julian's talent—but regret came to him often.

Yang Wen-li contained multitudes, but the largest contradiction within him was surely the fact that despite his tendency to devote half his mind to abstract musings such as these even in pitched battle, he was yet undefeated. The enemy before him now was the military genius Reinhard von Lohengramm, a man who combined within him the spirit of Mars and the mind of Minerva—and yet, even this indomitable conqueror had so far proved incapable of defeating this "band of fugitive mercenaries."

On May 8, the Yang Fleet and the Imperial Navy were still locked in combat. Müller's intervention had forced Yang into a temporary retreat, but there had been no dramatic change in the fortunes of either side. Unlike in the Vermillion War, Yang had not been surprised by Müller joining the fray, and was ready with countermeasures.

"Allies fore and aft, port and starboard, above and below, so dense that we can't see past them—so why does the other side have the upper hand?" muttered Mittermeier's staff officer Admiral Büro in frustration and disappointment. It was just as Büro said: despite enjoying its customary numerical superiority, the Imperial Navy could not seize the initiative from the Yang Fleet.

In comparison with the war in the Vermillion Stellar Region a year ago, the Battle of the Corridor was a series of temporally and spatially small but intense skirmishes and maneuvers. Yang's severe numeric disadvantage left him only one route to victory: divide the enemy with minefields and concentrated fire, and then destroy the pieces one by one, carefully spacing the battles out in time. Even Müller could not move his forces freely, and was forced to endure an endless series of localized clashes.

Such were the brutal conditions under which the report of Mittermeier's death arrived at the bridge of the Imperial Navy's fleet flagship *Brünhild*, enveloping it in gray horror. For a moment, Reinhard's bodyguard Emil thought he saw the kaiser's golden hair turn silver. Von Reuentahl's face went pallid, as if the pale blue of his eye was being diluted, and had to steady his gaunt form with one arm on Reinhard's command console. The trembling of that arm was transmitted in minute vibrations through the console to the kaiser himself.

"Apparently I have the luck of Loki, for I remain in this world yet. The enemy's cannons have yet to force open the gates of Valhalla here..."

This transmission from Mittermeier himself denying the false report restored vitality to headquarters. Mittermeier's flagship *Beowulf* remained at the head of the Imperial Navy, wounded but intact.

At this moment, Reinhard made the decision to execute the final horrible stratagem remaining to him.

On May 10, the curtain rose on the second act of the Battle of the Corridor, although it had begun the day before, at the Imperial Conference. The members of Imperial Navy high command who gathered in the kaiser's presence now included only marshals von Reuentahl and Mittermeier, senior admirals Müller, Wittenfeld, and von Eisenach, and a few high-ranking officers directly attached to headquarters. Mittermeier could not suppress a pang of sadness at how lonely the scene was compared to conferences past. Even since beginning this very battle, they had already lost Fahrenheit and Steinmetz. Had even Kaiser Reinhard imagined that, after the Free Planets Alliance was destroyed, Yang Wen-li and his allies—politically nothing more than the alliance's last gasp—would force such bitter fighting on the empire? What was more, in light of the differences in military capacity and goals, it had to be conceded that so far the Imperial Navy was on the losing side of the struggle.

Reinhard opened the conference by announcing Steinmetz's posthumous promotion to marshal, along with the appointment of his new chief advisor, Countess Hildegard "Hilda" von Mariendorf, who would herself be made a vice admiral. As he had predicted, no one objected to his decision on this matter, although some were, of course, more welcoming than others. Hilda noted that von Reuentahl's heterochromiac eyes in particular showed little enthusiasm—but perhaps she was just being oversensitive.

"I have never, in all my battles, been rewarded for adopting a passive attitude," Reinhard said. "When I have forgotten this, Mars has never failed to punish me. This, I am sure, is why victory eludes us now."

His cheeks blazed as if they contained the sun within them. The vividness of his coloring made Hilda uneasy. It seemed to her more than the result of mental agitation alone.

Ignoring Hilda's concerned gaze, Reinhard continued his passionate declamation.

"Yang Wen-li has used the narrow topography of the corridor against us, forcing a column formation upon us and attacking our massed forces. I sought an elegant response to his designs, but in this I was in error. We must smash his resistance head-on to ensure that he never rises again. That, I am sure, is the road that I—and my navy—must now take."

At 0645 hours on May 11, the Imperial Navy began a new attack based on a wave pattern. Yang Wen-li felt his blood run cold. This was precisely what he had feared most.

Strategically, it was the height of simplicity. Send a column forward in a charge, laying down concentrated fire. Have the column turn just before reaching the enemy and then retreat, continuing to bombard the enemy. Once the first column had fallen back, send a second column, and then a third. Keep the chain going and wait for the enemy to succumb to fatigue, attrition, or simply a lack of supplies.

The Yang Fleet was at a severe disadvantage in these terms. Facing this strategy, its military capabilities would slowly be ground down, worn away, and consumed until the remnants finally melted into the cosmic void.

The best course of action would probably have been to fall back to Iserlohn Fortress and use its main battery, Thor's Hammer, to push back against the empire's wave attacks. This was Merkatz's suggestion, and Attenborough agreed. Yang also wanted to do just that, but Müller, commander of the Imperial Navy's reconstructed first formation, kept up the wave attack without interruption and denied the Yang Fleet any room to rest. If Yang pulled his forces back, he was sure that Müller would surge forward and create a mixed battle through parallel pursuit, cutting them off before they could reach the fortress or its cannons.

Yang could read that much, and having read it he was unable to move. He was already swamped by the need for countermeasures at the tactical level: firing back at the ceaselessly marauding waves, plugging the gaps that appeared in his own side's formations, sending the mobile forces directly attached to the command center to rescue allies from dangerous situations, and so on. Keeping Yang occupied—denying him the opportunity to think up a new strategy while maximizing his physical and mental fatigue—was one of the empire's goals.

After keeping up the attack for thirty hours straight, the Müller Fleet finally withdrew. Müller himself was exhausted, and his fleet had taken damage from enemy fire each time they had turned to withdraw, but he had successfully denied the Yang Fleet the opportunity to launch a serious attack of its own. The second attack group moved into position: the vast force commanded by Admiral Ernst von Eisenach. They were almost as numerous as the entire Yang Fleet, and hardly fatigued at all. Their first wave fired so ferociously that they might have been trying to empty their energy tanks, forcing the Yang Fleet into a temporary retreat. They then seized that opportunity to leap forward, riding the edge of the corridor to attack the Yang Fleet from its flank.

Von Eisenach's powerful broadside attack seemed likely to split Attenborough's division from the main Yang Fleet, providing ample proof of
his skill as a tactician.

"If this keeps up, we'll be isolated and surrounded by the enemy! What's
Marshal Yang going to do?" said Commander Lao, one of Attenborough's
staff officers, voice cracking.

"Never fear," Attenborough said with a smile. "They don't realize it,
but they've stumbled into their own grave. Close off their escape route
and hit them hard."

Commander Lao looked dubious. He was not pessimistic by nature, but
the tendency seemed to have been cultivated within him through service
as a staff officer to men like Yang and Attenborough.

However, in this case his fears did seem ungrounded. As soon as the
Eisenach Fleet succeeded in splitting Yang's forces, they were exposed to
attack from both sides.

Commodore Marino, former captain of Yang's flagship *Hyperion*, sank
fangs of beam and missile into von Eisenach's port side, opening a wound
that temporarily reached deep into the fleet.

Von Eisenach's flagship *Vidar* was surrounded by fireballs and flashes
of light on three sides as its escorts exploded into flames one by one. Von
Eisenach seemed to be in a crisis, but he did not so much as twitch an
eyebrow. Calmly issuing the orders that would close the wound in his
fleet's side even as he fended off Marino's assault, he successfully disengaged from the danger zone, holding the enemy back with heavy fire.

Nevertheless, the damage to the Eisenach Fleet could not be ignored.
As von Eisenach's staff urged him to withdraw, his lip trembled slightly.
Perhaps he was cursing God and the devil inside his mouth, but no sound
waves reached anyone's ears. In any case, well-timed retreat was the foundation of imperial military strategy, so von Eisenach did not impose his
own will—but when the fleet turned and withdrew, he did make sure to
leave visible gaps in its formation.

Yang, of course, resisted this temptation. For one thing, he had too much
to do before the next wave of attacks came. There were ships to resupply
with weapons, ammunition, food, and energy; wounded to evacuate; and
damaged parts of the battle lines that needed reinforcement.

"We're reaching our limit," said Caselnes. Nodding at the warning, Yang finished resupply, evacuation, and reinforcement, and then went on to successfully repulse a third attack, this time from Bayerlein and Büro. In fact, at 2200, on May 14, the Yang Fleet actually went on the offensive, hoping to knock the Imperial Navy into disarray. They did succeed in sowing enough confusion to temporarily delay the fourth attack, a coordinated effort by the Black Lancers and Fahrenheit's former fleet.

But the attack could not be forestalled forever. Wittenfeld's flagship *Königs Tiger* charged in to attack at 0440 on May 15 with all the dignity and ferocity its name implied. It was not alone, of course, but with only a limited number of the finest pilots it attempted to smash the Yang Fleet in a single blow. Wittenfeld's military genius showed not only in the responsiveness of his ships but also in his ability to accurately locate the center of the enemy fleet and focus his efforts there.

Yang halted the charge of his left wing battalion and temporarily shortened the battle lines to organize a counterattack against the imperial forces. This was a rare miscalculation on his part. Wittenfeld had been thoroughly defeated in their earlier encounter, but rather than it dulling his taste for combat, the memory of that loss fueled the roaring morale and powerful charges with which he now sought to regain that lost honor. Yang slowed him with a wall of beams and missiles, and then played for time while executing a delicate change of formation. Intentionally avoiding a frontal attack, Yang brushed Wittenfeld's attack off slightly portward, and then had Merkatz move in from the flank once Wittenfeld had been lured in.

The Black Lancers were thus completely trapped in a pincer formation— except that they were far stronger than the forces that had them half-surrounded. Their numbers had fallen, but that only seemed to strengthen the unity of their command.

The cannon fire they returned and the ship-on-ship charges that followed were staggering in their brutality. Ships disintegrated into the void, crew and all, were carved up by beams, and were wheeled out of the fighting zone, losing energy in uncontrollable streams before finally exploding.

Yang held off the Black Lancers while launching broadsides at Fahrenheit's former fleet and putting pressure on the enemy's command systems, expending firepower so freely that it seemed that his supplies and energy would run out entirely. As a result, Wittenfeld's attack reached its limit and became difficult to sustain.

When the Black Lancers finally withdrew, it was 1920 on May 15.

In terms of human resources, however, the Yang Fleet had already suffered an irreplaceable loss. Vice Admiral Edwin Fischer, master of fleet operations, had been killed. Wittenfeld might have been grinding his teeth over his failure to eliminate Yang Wen-li, but he had knocked one of Yang's legs out from under him. A sustained attack on the Imperial Navy would no longer be possible.

If the Imperial Navy had attempted another attack on all fronts, Yang would have been forced to flee to Iserlohn Fortress. But even the kaiser was not omniscient. The imperial side had no way of knowing that they had inflicted a near-critical wound on their enemy.

What was more, the top leadership of the imperial military had a secret of their own: His Majesty the Kaiser was not well. The fever that had plagued Reinhard repeatedly since his coronation had come again on May 16, and von Reuentahl, as secretary-general of Supreme Command Headquarters, had consulted with Mittermeier and Hilda and decided that the entire fleet would withdraw from the corridor. Knowledge of the kaiser's illness, of course, was not to leave headquarters.

Von Reuentahl's strategic vision was cooler and more realistic than Reinhard's, particularly regarding Yang Wen-li and his allies. As he saw it, the kaiser was throwing away tremendous and carefully accumulated strategic advantage out of an obsession with tactical victory. He would not go so far as to call it pointless, but it did seem to him that Reinhard was actively pursuing bloodshed that could have been avoided.

Although he remained as tight-lipped as ever, von Reuentahl could not help feeling surprised when he realized anew that Reinhard, conqueror of the entire galaxy, had prioritized his desire for battle above his tremendous intellect and the conclusions it had reached. It was not, he thought, that Reinhard loved war by nature; rather, war was like a vital nutrient that the golden-haired emperor needed to survive. And were these repeated fevers of late not a sign that the boundless craving of that spirit within him was too powerful for his body to bear, young and healthy though he was?

In any case, on May 17 in year 2 of the New Imperial Calendar, the Imperial Navy lost two million officers and men and 24,400 ships as it was ignominiously forced back out of Iserlohn Corridor.

"We can conquer an entire galaxy, but not this one man," murmured Mittermeier, gray eyes filled with melancholy and exhaustion from the endless life-or-death battles.

They had sent vast forces into the narrow corridor and waged a fourteen-day war that had ended in failure to defeat a numerically inferior enemy. The two great pillars of the Yang Fleet—Iserlohn Fortress and Yang Wen-li himself—were still standing.

Yang Wen-li did not pursue the imperial fleet when he learned it was retreating. There were no weak links in von Reuentahl and Mittermeier's command of their forces, and Müller was guarding the rear of the entire Imperial Navy, poised to counterattack whenever necessary. Days of fighting without a break had left the Yang Fleet at an extreme of exhaustion and attrition, as well. Above all, Yang was still deeply and heavily shaken by the death of Fischer.

When that awful news had arrived, Attenborough had turned to his staff officer Lao and heaved an uncharacteristically deep sigh. "That's a blow. Our living star chart is now a dead star chart. We won't be able to go for a hike in the forest without him."

Fischer had been reserved and unassuming by nature, but everyone knew his importance to the fate of the Yang Fleet. Yang had never once lost on the tactical level, and this miracle had been made possible by Fischer's ability to seamlessly synchronize the fleet's movements to Yang's unorthodox thinking. His unparalleled artistry in fleet operations and Yang's willingness to let him exercise it had been an ideal combination, allowing both to demonstrate their abilities and maintain a flawless record of victory.

Yang put his sunglasses on, brought his hands to his forehead with fingers interlaced, and sat that way motionless for a time. He seemed to be partly mourning Fischer's death and partly contemplating how difficult it would be to run the fleet—how elusive victory would be, from that point on. Fischer was the first of the Yang Fleet's leadership to die in battle, and the other officers took it as a bad omen, as if the oil fueling the lamp of luck underlying their undefeated record had finally run out.

On May 18, the Yang Fleet disengaged from the battlefield and began its return to Iserlohn Fortress. But then a new shock was hurled at them.

"A message from Kaiser Reinhard!" said the communications officer aboard *Ulysses*. "He-he..." The businesslike calm with which the officer had begun his sentence failed him, so Julian Mintz took the communications plate and turned it toward him. Now he, too, needed a few moments to put his feelings in order and reenthrone his reason. Cheeks flushed, he conveyed the news to Yang standing beside him.

"A message from Kaiser Reinhard. He proposes a cease-fire and a meeting!"

The staff glanced at each other in quick succession before their gazes finally settled on a single shared object. Yang Wen-li was still sitting cross-legged on his command console, fanning his face with his black beret, and when he stopped fanning he ran his other hand through his black hair.

CHAPTER 5:

I
YANG WEN-LI DID NOT IMMEDIATELY RESPOND to

Kaiser Reinhard's proposal that they meet. This was not due to extended rumination on the matter. His physical and mental exhaustion after days of fighting was simply so severe that neither shock nor jubilation could keep sleep at bay.

"My brain cells are porridge," he said. "I'm in no condition to think. Just let me get some rest."

If Yang himself had reached this point, it was unsurprising that his staff officers all felt the same way—with the exception of von Schönkopf, who had spent the battle cheekily watching from the sidelines.

"I want my bed. I don't even care if there's no woman in it," said Olivier Poplin, as if renouncing half of his life.

"Anyone who wakes me will face the firing squad as a counterrevolutionary," said Dusty Attenborough, already half-asleep as he disappeared into his own quarters.

Even the sober Merkatz gave the bare minimum of orders and then retired to his chambers. "Forget an infinite future," he muttered. "Right now I'd settle for a good night's sleep."

Merkatz's aide von Schneider tutted. "What does he intend to do if the enemy attacks again? Still, I suppose death isn't so different from sleep, really." With this rather alarming reasoning, he staggered toward his own quarters, but he must have expended his last strength on the way, because he fell asleep in the elevator, propped up against one wall.

Left in charge was Alex Caselnes, who now shook his head. "We'll need at least a million princesses to wake up all these sleeping beauties," he said.

Von Schönkopf was the only one to disembark from *Ulysses* steady on his feet. "If you need assistance, Admiral Caselnes, I volunteer to summon all of the female soldiers back from the land of Nod myself," he said with a wink. When Caselnes ignored this heartwarming proposal, he strolled off to occupy the empty bar.

Thus did the sandman sprinkle the dust of slumber throughout Iserlohn Fortress. Yang and Frederica, Julian, Karin, the staff officers—all flung themselves down the well of sleep and slipped beneath the waterline of reality. As von Schneider mused uneasily before the last of his reason succumbed to fatigue, had the Imperial Navy attacked at that moment, the impregnable Iserlohn Fortress would have had to remove the "im-" from its epithet.

However, the Imperial Navy was of course extremely fatigued as well, and would remain without sleep themselves until the Müller Fleet, still guarding the rear, had withdrawn completely from the battlefield. Their assessment of the fighting capability of Yang's faction was accurate or better, so they could not relax their guard against the possibility of a sneak attack or ambush. When their safety was finally secured, Müller tumbled straight into bed, but faced no criticism for it.

Once they were rested, the Yang Fleet emerged from their rooms like an army of starving children, filling every mess and cafeteria in the fortress. Officers and enlisted troops alike looked like refugees—except for Olivier Poplin, who went to the trouble of shaving and even putting on cologne before appearing in public. Of course, in the time he spent on this unnecessary grooming, the officer's mess filled to capacity, and he was forced to wolf down his white stew standing in the corridor. "A textbook illustration of wasted effort," was von Schönkopf's assessment.

At 1330 on May 20, the staff officers were finally ready to consider Kaiser Reinhard's proposal.

As scent particles from three cups of tea and five times as much coffee clashed in the conference room, the discussion began, but in fact Yang had already made up his mind. Inducing the kaiser to negotiate had always been the final goal of Yang's war.

"First we drag the kaiser into Iserlohn Corridor, then we drag him out to the negotiating table. I wish we could fit him for some silver skates to make things easier for us."

When Yang explained his fundamental political and military strategy like this, his staff officers were uncertain whether to nod solemnly or treat it as a joke. None of them were willing to defend the spirit of democracy to the last soldier. To survive and extract a political compromise from the house of Lohengramm was why they had to win. This, however exasperating it might look to outsiders, was the reason they fought.

"After all, old Büro already beat us to the hero's death," said Dusty Attenborough, neither entirely joking nor entirely serious. "No one will praise us for a copycat suicide. If we don't live vigorously and well, we're the losers."

The Yang Fleet was prone to this sort of mildly tasteless dark humor, but it was true that none of the fleet's leadership were so "principled" that they would doom themselves to destruction by rejecting compromise with a dictator out of hand with no consideration of the power relationships involved.

Accordingly, the message from Kaiser Reinhard itself was to be welcomed. But they were not in the fortunate position of being able to trust in it innocently. Suspicion that the kaiser was laying a trap inevitably set the basic tone for the discussion. Even if the Imperial Navy had given up hope of resolving the situation through military force, their new course would not necessarily be entirely congenial to the Yang Fleet's aims.

"Perhaps they are just using this talk of a conference and cease-fire and what have you to lure the commander out of Iserlohn Fortress and assassinate him," said Vice Admiral Murai. In starting the discussion this way, he was acting something like an experimental chemist seeking to draw out counterarguments and uncertainties.

Yang removed his black beret and turned it over and over in his hands.

Von Schönkopf returned his coffee cup to its saucer after one sip, perhaps not finding it to his liking. "Unlikely, I think," he said. "That isn't how the kaiser works. Our golden-haired boy has too much pride to resort to assassination, even if he has failed on the battlefield."

Von Schönkopf spoke dismissively of history's greatest conqueror, but, in his indirect way, he did grant that the framework of Reinhard's psyche contained little in the way of mendacity.

"That may be true of the kaiser," said Poplin, who probably would not have bothered arguing had anyone but von Schönkopf made the comment. "But surely he has a few people on staff whose values are a little different. They've seen a lot of bloodshed and no victory to show for it. The kaiser's reputation as a military genius must be suffering as well. An excess of loyalty and a shortage of good judgment could inspire some of them to trickery."

Julian sat in silence, watching Yang as the debate unfolded. He could sense that Yang already intended to accept the kaiser's proposal. What concerned Julian now was one question: When Yang went to meet Reinhard, would Julian go with him?

Still—the kaiser relished battle. Why would he suddenly conceive the desire to settle differences through talking? This was beyond Julian's ability to discern.

"The magnificent Kaiser Reinhard von Lohengramm was well acquainted with victory but knew nothing of peace" was one of the more biting criticisms thrown at the kaiser by the historians of later ages. Though not necessarily fair or objective, it did cut one facet of the brilliant diamond of Reinhard's individuality. At the very least, the falsity of the statement's opposite was undeniable fact.

Reinhard's right-hand woman and lieutenant, Hildegard von Mariendorf, was as surprised as anyone to hear that the feverish kaiser had requested a meeting with Yang Wen-li from his sickbed. Such a meeting was something she had hoped for but never expected to see. On more than one occasion as Reinhard prepared for the Battle of the Corridor she had urged him to take that path instead to avoid pointless bloodshed.

"I doubt that Yang Wen-li wants the whole galaxy," she said. "If a concession to him is necessary, then Your Majesty has the authority and, if I may be so bold, the duty to offer such."

Kaiser had swept back the golden hair that tumbled forward over his brow and turned to look at his beautiful chief secretary.

"Fräulein von Mariendorf," he said. "It sounds as though you are arguing that the responsibility for having made a cornered rat of Yang Wen-li rests with me."

"Yes, Your Majesty. That is what I mean to say."

Reinhard accepted Hilda's rebuke with an expression more wounded than disgruntled. Even his hurt frown was elegant and youthful.

"Fräulein, you are the only one alive who dares speak so frankly to the ruler of the galaxy. Your bravery and forthrightness are to be praised, but do not think that they will always be welcome."

Two things stopped Hilda from pressing her point further: her knowledge of what gave Reinhard spiritual nourishment, and her constant apprehension that losing this might mean losing his very reason for existence. And yet, were he to defeat Yang Wen-li in battle as he so fervently wished, perfecting his dominion over the galaxy, where would those ice-blue eyes turn? For what would those fair hands reach? Insightful as she was, it was impossible for Hilda to foresee.

She had been relieved by the decision to withdraw the fleet without revealing Reinhard's illness. His fever was due to overwork rather than any troubling pathology, but at least the final phase of the war had been postponed.

Perhaps it was not right to think such things. No doubt she should rejoice at the idea of a peaceful resolution of the problem facing the kaiser and his empire, and pray for its success. To avoid prolonging the fight itself had always been her goal.

Nevertheless, some things about the development did not sit right with her. Along with the rest of the staff of imperial headquarters, she had advised Reinhard to take this course of action many times before,

LEGEND OF THE GALACTIC HEROES: DESOLATION

but he had always waved this away with his customary grandeur, fixated on the idea of forcing Yang to kneel to him in direct confrontation. If not for this fever, he would have maintained this course and continued the bloodshed until Yang was buried and Reinhard could move on. To repeatedly strike with greater force than your enemy could recover from in order to wear them down and, ultimately, eliminate them was not in itself a misguided strategy—so why had Reinhard departed from his original "blood and steel" ethos? Surely it was not because the fever had weakened his will...

Propped up in bed, Reinhard answered the question he saw in Hilda's eyes.

"It was Kircheis," he said. "He came to warn me."

The youthful, golden-haired emperor was quite serious. Hilda stared at him until she realized her own rudeness in doing so. The fever had given his porcelain cheeks a pale ruddiness like the lingering trace of a kiss from the goddess of the dawn.

" 'No more,' he told me. 'End your war with Yang Wen-li.' Still giving me advice, even in death..."

Reinhard seemed not to realize that the authority and formality he used when dealing with the living had slipped from his speech. Hilda kept her silence. It was clear that no reply was expected.

This could all be explained scientifically. From the thoughts and feelings that mingled beneath the surface of consciousness, multiple streams had risen in a tangle. Grief for friends forever lost, and the accompanying ever-growing remorse for his own mistakes. Respect for Yang Wen-li as an enemy. Self-recrimination over Fahrenheit, Steinmetz, and the millions of others who had died in the corridor. Irritation over the unprecedentedly slow pace of change in the battle overall. Professional interest as a strategist in whether there was a more effective way than war to resolve the matter.

From this chaos, the clearest parts had been unified and crystallized into the person of Siegfried Kircheis. Reinhard had subconsciously anthropomorphized the most effective way to defeat his own stubbornness in argument and change his attitude...

An analysis of the phenomenon would follow along these lines. But Hilda was well aware that there are times in this world when it is better not to analyze. Siegfried Kircheis had appeared in a dream and urged him to stop the war: though medieval, this interpretation was sufficient and indeed correct. If Kircheis had been alive, he would certainly have made the same recommendation as both a sworn friend to the kaiser and a high-ranking retainer of the empire.

"Fine, then, Kircheis. As usual, you get your way. You were only born two months before me, but you were always playing big brother and breaking up my fights. I'm the one who's older now, because you've stopped aging—but fine. I'll try talking to Yang. That's as far as it goes, though. I can't promise that the talks won't break down."

In the end, what had been impossible for Hilda, Mittermeier, and von Reuentahl, a spirit of the dead had achieved. Realizing this, Hilda felt as though she had been granted a sudden glimpse at the wavering emotions of several of the advisors that surrounded the kaiser.

Seeing that the discussion between His Majesty the Kaiser and Fräulein von Mariendorf had come to an end, the kaiser's bodyguard Emil von Selle brought out hot milk with honey for the invalid. The fragrance did not entirely restore Hilda's cheer.

It was not that Reinhard was disinterested in or irresponsible about governance. He was a conscientious administrator, and this could be seen in his attitude as well as his results. But he was, fundamentally, a military man. Reinhard the bureaucrat was the product of conscious effort, while Reinhard the warrior came naturally. Accordingly, wherever he wielded authority, across his entire empire, military strategy always took precedence over its political counterpart. At this time, on the boundary of his psyche, there was a part of him that rejected the idea of talks with Yang.

"Partly because of my worthlessness in falling ill, our officers and troops are exhausted and running low on supplies," he said. "Talks with Yang do not necessarily mean compromise. We must earn time to finish preparing for the next battle."

Some of his admirals were relieved to hear about the talks, while others thought them regrettable. Wittenfeld, who had achieved the greatest victory on the battlefield without even realizing it, struggled to control his desire for combat.

"The negotiations are bound to break down," Wittenfeld said, publicly if not loudly. "When that happens, we go back on the offensive at once." Those who had served under Fahrenheit and Steinmetz also had difficulty keeping their desire to avenge their fallen commanders in check. Recognizing the genuine danger that things might explode, Mittermeier decided to step in himself and set about reorganizing the two fleets. The gray eyes of the Gale Wolf had the power to silence men two feet taller than he was at a single glance.

Mittermeier would turn thirty-two that year. He had already risen to the rank of imperial marshal and, as commander in chief of the Imperial Space Armada, was in the imperial military's highest echelons of command. To most of the troops, he was dizzyingly highly placed, and yet he looked even younger than his years. He moved with lightness and agility, and was not overformal with the enlisted men and women.

More than just a tactician, Mittermeier also enjoyed strategic insight. When the remnants of the Free Planets Alliance had gathered at Iserlohn Fortress and in the El Facil system, he had known that their disadvantages would only grow. The empire had always known where its enemies were massed, and although attacking them had proved difficult, blockading them would have been easy. Mittermeier saw no reason to insist on victory through military force, especially if it would require so many to sacrifice their lives.

What was more, the forces gathered at Iserlohn were currently unified by a closely linked group of individuals centered on Yang Wen-li. If Yang ceased to exist, this group might also melt away. This was Mittermeier's view of things. Put in the most extreme terms, the empire could simply close Yang up inside the corridor and patiently await his death.

Of course, similar issues could be seen in the Imperial Navy—and the Lohengramm Dynasty itself. If Reinhard were slain in battle, there was no leader in the military or political sphere who could take his place. For this reason, the kaiser's fever and confinement to bed sent a chill wind through even the fearless Mittermeier's nervous system. The admiralty had not even been forced to avoid making public the fact that their retreat from Iserlohn Corridor was due to Reinhard's illness. If that overpaid team of doctors had correctly diagnosed it as overexertion—if the youthful kaiser was already physically overburdened by psychological energies within and obligations without—what did the future hold?

The Lohengramm Dynasty might end with its first generation, and plunge them all back into the chaos of war. Mittermeier could not help wishing that the kaiser would recover his health and marry. It had never occurred to him that a new age of conflict would give him the opportunity to seize power for himself. The very idea would have been alien to this brave general at the height of imperial command.

Meanwhile, Mittermeier's close friend Oskar von Reuentahl had done a flawless job of overseeing the expeditionary force as the bedridden kaiser's representative with barely a murmur of complaint. Apart from a single observation to Mittermeier to the effect that the kaiser was not the sort of man to die of illness, he would have impressed even the taciturn von Eisenach with the dignified silence in which he worked, often taking only white wine and cheese for breakfast and unwittingly giving his close friends something to worry about.

Here a minor event took place. Marshal Paul von Oberstein, minister of military affairs on distant Phezzan, offered an opinion to the kaiser regarding a certain matter. The kaiser rejected von Oberstein's suggestion out of hand. In its details, revealed only to Hilda and the other two marshals, it was almost identical to the proposed plot that Wittenfeld had angrily rejected when a staff officer had made it. In one respect, however, von Oberstein's vision was even more cynical. Since Yang was unlikely to simply come when summoned, a high-ranking advisor should be sent to Yang's camp to serve first as messenger and then as hostage. Mittermeier and von Reuentahl were both too taken aback even to voice their criticisms of this notion.

Upon his arrival at the Imperial Navy, the unsuspecting Yang was to be killed to avoid any further agonizing. Yang's side would be enraged, and would retaliate by killing their hostage. In the name of retaliation for *that* killing, the Imperial Navy would use military force to suppress the now leaderless Yang faction, and the entire galaxy would be unified under the Lohengramm Dynasty. All through one man's sacrifice…But was there a senior advisor who would willingly offer themselves as a hostage, knowing what lay in store?

"If there are no other candidates for the role of messenger, I will accept that responsibility myself," said von Oberstein. This unflinching, almost indifferent offer to serve as the sacrificial pawn in his own stratagem was, perhaps, an example of why he could not be dismissed as simply callous and cruel. Still, Mittermeier and von Reuentahl felt little urge to praise him.

"Imagine being forced into a double suicide with von Oberstein, of all people," said the Gale Wolf with uncharacteristic venom. "Not even Yang would take that in good humor. Anyway, why would Yang trust von Oberstein in the first place, even if he did claim to be a messenger?"

The heterochromiac secretary-general added his own dark strain to the chorus. "No, I say we let him do as he proposes—always keeping in mind that even if Yang's people slaughter him, we're under no obligation to avenge the fellow."

"I like that. Forget Yang Wen-li—if von Oberstein were gone, the galaxy would be at peace, the Lohengramm Dynasty would flourish, and all would be well."

Neither of them actually hoped for the outcome they spoke of, but it was clear that neither would have been greatly chagrined by it either. It was too late to enact von Oberstein's plan in any case, but they rejoiced at the honor the kaiser had shown in rejecting it.

Mittermeier and von Reuentahl earned their place in military history as outstanding leaders of vast armies, but they were not all-seeing. They could not know that an intrigue like the one von Oberstein had proposed—but even baser—was already threatening the galaxy like a rapidly spreading fungus.

The preparations they now began to ensure the comfort of their honored enemy and invited guest were, in the end, all for naught. Neither would ever meet Yang Wen-li face-to-face.

II

At 1200 on May 25, Yang Wen-li departed Iserlohn Fortress for his second meeting with Kaiser Reinhard. His transport was *Leda II*, the same cruiser he had used when summoned to appear before the alliance government two years earlier. Since the ship had brought him home safely from that adventure, his staff officers had urged it on him again for good luck.

The question of transportation was thus decided with ease, but the path to the meeting was not so smooth. Von Schneider had raised a new concern: even if Kaiser Reinhard's honor as a warrior could be trusted, could his staff officers be? The Imperial Navy was not made up solely of people of good faith like Marshal Mittermeier. Some among them might view this as an opportunity to assassinate Yang, whether on the pretext of loyalty to the emperor or revenge for fallen comrades.

Julian Mintz hesitated for a moment, then said, "Then I shall go, as the commander's representative—forgive my presumption. Once I learn the details of the conditions or proposals on the table, the commander can arrive for the discussion proper."

Yang shook his head. "Won't work," he said. "Sorry, Julian."

The kaiser had requested a dialogue of equals, he explained. To send Julian first would be an insult. If the kaiser felt so insulted that he retracted his proposal, the possibility of peace might be lost forever. They had no chance of winning another frontal battle with the Imperial Navy in their current state. They had suffered irreplaceable losses, the surviving troops were still exhausted, and resupply would take time, given Iserlohn's production capacity. They had not even begun maintenance on the fleet yet.

What Yang emphasized most of all was the degradation of the fleet's mobility following the death of Vice Admiral Fischer.

With Fischer gone, Commodore Marino was the front-runner for the task of reorganizing and running the fleet. Marino was a talented commander, but his achievements and trust among the troops could not compare to his predecessor's. Yang strongly doubted that the fleet would be able to maneuver as perfectly as it had under Fischer in its next battle. This loss of confidence was one of the reasons Yang felt unable to refuse Reinhard's request for talks.

"We can't win by tactical planning alone. If the fleet isn't able to execute the plans to the letter, we'll be out of luck. Rejecting the kaiser's offer and heading right back into battle would be suicide."

The staff officers had no reply to this. They, too, keenly felt the tremendous blow of Fischer's death. They also understood that Yang's ultimate objective was peace. When they weighed the merits of meeting the kaiser for talks versus rebuffing him out of hand, ultimately the former was the only choice.

"Very well," said Caselnes. "For the kaiser to call a cease-fire is effectively a victory for us anyway. And, although we have no guarantee the talks will succeed, they will at least give us room to breathe. We might even see guerilla action against the empire break out on Phezzan or in former alliance territory during that time, further fortifying our advantage. Not that we should expect too much."

The staff officers all nodded eventually at Caselnes's determinedly optimistic summary, although some took longer than others.

The discussion turned to the matter of Yang's entourage.

Officers immediately began recommending themselves and others for the task. As much as they denounced Reinhard as a creature of despotism and military dictatorship, they could not deny the splendor of his presence. None among them were free of the desire to gaze upon the galaxy-conquering golden lion with their own eyes.

Yang's wife Frederica would have accompanied him, of course, but she had come down with influenza and a fever and had been prescribed bed rest by Caselnes's wife Hortense, who was both a teacher of the domestic arts and a master of domestic medicine.

Her husband was also excluded from consideration, as all his efforts would be needed to reconstruct the fleet's capabilities in combat. Similarly, von Schönkopf was required to strengthen the fortress's defenses. Attenborough would have to command the fleet in Yang's absence; Merkatz could not be expected to call Reinhard "Your Highness"; the negligible chance of space combat would make Poplin superfluous; and Murai would be needed to oversee all the others: one by one, officers were mercilessly ruled out.

In the end, only three high-ranking officers were chosen to accompany Yang: his assistant staff officer Rear Admiral Patrichev; Commander

Blumhardt, leader of the Rosen Ritter; and Lieutenant Commander "Soul" Soulzzcuaritter, former aide to Marshal Alexandor Bucock.

The small size of Yang's retinue was partly to compensate for the outsized group chosen by Francesk Romsky, chairman of the Revolutionary Government of El Facil. Romsky would also attend the talks, and had chosen more than ten men to go with him. This, of course, was the official understanding; Oliver Poplin, for his part, believed for some time that he had actually been barred as a troublemaker.

"Blumhardt was chosen as a bodyguard, and Soul as old Bucock's representative," Poplin said. "Patrichev? To make Yang look better, of course. What other use would he be?"

Everyone was surprised by the absence of Julian Mintz from the list: Yang was leaving behind the one who might be called his highest lieutenant. Perhaps a convenient sort of sixth sense had been working overtime; perhaps, as the official explanation had it, he wanted Julian to serve as the overworked Caselnes's deputy; perhaps von Schönkopf was correct in his sardonic suggestion that Yang did not want to be mistaken for Julian's attendant; or perhaps it was simply caprice.

"Take care of the place while I'm gone, Julian," Yang said.

Disappointment filled the young man's face as he nodded, not as a calculated message but simply because he had not managed to put his own feelings in order.

"I wish I could just say 'Leave it to me,' but I'm not happy about being left behind. Wouldn't I be of any use to you? Why Admiral Patrichev…"

Why choose Patrichev over me? This was Julian's pride speaking. He was not entirely without self-awareness of this, and felt himself redden under Yang's gaze. Yang smiled broadly and tweaked his cheek.

"You dummy," Yang said. "Don't you realize how long I've been relying on you? Ever since you first came to live with me, in fact, dragging that trunk that was bigger than you were."

"Thank you. But…"

"If I couldn't go, I'd have you go in my place. But I can go—so I will. That's all there is to it."

"Understood. I'll be standing by for good news. Please be careful."

"Sure. By the way, Julian—"

"Yes, sir?"

Yang leaned closer and lowered his voice to a pointed whisper. "Do you prefer Caselnes's daughter, or von Schönkopf's? Be honest. I need to know which way you're headed so I can start to prepare myself."

"Commander!"

Julian's face burned hot enough to surprise even him. Yang noted this well, and whistled cheerfully if not skillfully. Times like this were when he seemed just the man to lead hopeless cases like von Schönkopf and Poplin.

Next, Yang went to visit his wife on her sickbed. Hortense Caselnes and her two daughters were by Frederica's side already. Charlotte Phyllis, the older of the girls, was peeling an apple as Yang walked in. He noted that her facility with a fruit knife rivaled Frederica's own.

"Well, Frederica," said Yang, "I'm off to meet the most beautiful man in the galaxy. See you in about two weeks."

"Take care. Oh, wait—your hair's a mess."

"Who's going to care?"

"You should, for one! After all, you're going to meet the second most beautiful man in the galaxy."

Frederica took a hairbrush from her night table and quickly tamed Yang's hair as Hortense looked tactfully away.

Leaving one of his typically inept kisses on his wife's feverish cheek, Yang nodded to the Caselnes women and left the room. Julian was waiting in the hallway with Yang's suitcase.

When the door closed, Charlotte Phyllis slapped her mother's knee with excitement and no small amount of emotion. "Did you and Papa ever act like that, Mama?" she asked.

Hortense glanced sideways at Frederica. "Of course we did," she said calmly.

"But you don't anymore?"

"Well, Charlotte Phyllis, do *you* go back and practice the things you learned in kindergarten now that you're in fourth grade?"

Such was Julian's parting from Yang. A faint shadow of unease remained in the young man's breast, but it was far surpassed by his faith in the honor of Kaiser Reinhard. Little did he suspect the anguish that lay in wait mere days away. Gazing directly at the sun that was Reinhard, he had forgotten that the firmament held other stars too.

Three days after Yang's departure, the independent Phezzanese merchant Boris Konev came within communications range of Iserlohn Fortress. Konev had been crisscrossing former alliance territory and the area around Phezzan on assignment from Yang, gathering information and funding for the Yang Fleet. His vessel maintained radio silence to avoid the imperial dragnets, and had actually passed quite near *Leda II* some thirty hours earlier. As soon as he established contact with Iserlohn Fortress, the first words out of his mouth were, "I want to see Yang right now. Is he still alive?"

"You've never been much of a comedian, but this material's your worst yet," said Poplin on his screen. "I'm pleased to report that Death is apparently on vacation and the commander is alive and well."

Only the tiniest of hourglasses would be needed to mark the time it took the dripping sarcasm to evaporate from Poplin's voice as his expression changed completely. Konev bore ill tidings that lit warning lamps of deepest crimson in the minds of Iserlohn's leadership and caused even Gjallarhorn itself to ring out in warning: Andrew Fork, architect of the disaster at Amritsar, had escaped from his psychiatric hospital and was bent on a new goal: the assassination of Yang Wen-li.

Attenborough threw his black beret to the floor with rage. "Andrew Fork! Damn that worthless imbecile! Wasn't killing twenty million at Amritsar four years ago enough for him? If he still isn't satisfied, why doesn't he do civilization and the environment a favor and just kill *himself?*"

"I'm sure he thinks of this as his life's work," said von Schönkopf, voice dark and bitter as overbrewed coffee. "Beating Yang Wen-li, that is. He knows his achievements don't measure up, so he's found another solution: murder the competition."

Julian felt a chill run up and down within him like a broken elevator. Was Andrew Fork free by his own power? Or had someone—or some group—freed him? Was this truly a solitary madman on the run, or was it some monstrous game, with Fork nothing but a tightrope walker whose fall had been planned from the beginning?

"Go after Yang and bring him back," said von Schönkopf to Julian. "Everything else can wait. A small squadron would be best—we don't want to make the empire nervous." He then selected the men who would accompany Julian on his mission.

And so, with confusion still not completely contained, a six-ship squadron of battleships led by *Ulysses* set out from Iserlohn in pursuit of Yang. The confusion they left to Caselnes to deal with. What he found most difficult was keeping the news from Yang's wife on her sickbed. Even for one of the greatest officials in the history of the Free Planets Alliance, this was a great deal to ask.

III

Matters which had stagnated to the point of semifluidity suddenly began to flow in earnest once more. Though all ran in the same direction, there was no overarching order governing the many courses they described.

"Everyone hoped for peace—peace under their own authority," wrote one historian of a later age. "This common objective called for individual victories." This was broadly correct, but Yang had no intention of insisting on his side's authority over the other, which should have made a constructive result from the talks with Reinhard possible. Or, rather, if understanding and cooperation could not be established in that way, the only road left open to them would be a barren one, fueled by hatred and leading to destruction.

What was more, if Yang was assassinated, the route to democratic republican governance would be closed off. Was Andrew Fork so driven by the foul leftovers of interpersonal competition that he meant to slay the philosophy and system he had once claimed to support? Julian Mintz cast around desperately for ways to prevent Fork's profitless scheme from reaching fruition.

The remnants of a radical alliance faction had set their sights on Yang Wen-li's life. What if he reported this fact to the Imperial Navy and had them protect Yang? This idea came to Julian after leaving Iserlohn, as he was stewing in frustration over the limits of his power while traveling.

But at the moment of moving from contemplation to decision, he hesitated. To entrust Yang's life to the Imperial Navy was not in itself shameful. The request for a cease-fire and talks had been theirs, so the responsibility of guaranteeing Yang's safety until his meeting with the kaiser—indeed, until that meeting was over—lay with them. In that light, it would have been acceptable to request from the beginning that they dispatch a battalion to escort Yang to the meeting place.

But Julian could not suppress one terrifying thought.

If elements of the Imperial Navy were to seize on this and harm Yang under the pretext of protecting him...

There were surely those on the imperial side who viewed Yang Wen-li as an impediment to the imperial project of galactic unification who must be eliminated, whether that be through war or treachery. What if they approached him with talk of protection, then murdered him and blamed it on Andrew Fork? How could an escaped madman hope to assassinate Yang, after all? Powerful forces were surely pulling strings in the background. For example, Marshal von Oberstein, minister of military affairs for the empire and font of the Imperial Navy's intrigues...

This was prejudice, or perhaps overestimation of von Oberstein himself. It was true that he was constantly formulating and proposing schemes for crushing the kaiser's enemies and other irritants to the Lohengramm Dynasty. But regarding the danger facing Yang on June 1, SE 800, his hands were in fact clean.

At that time, von Oberstein was still on Phezzan, finding time between the endless tasks required of a minister of military affairs to engross himself in a certain project of his own design. He had not, of course, declared this publicly, but so long as he maintained his silence, it was not unnatural to suppose that he might be plotting against Yang Wen-li, enemy of the empire. Even if he had denied it, it is doubtful he would have been believed. His long personal history had fixed a certain impression and opinion of him in the public mind.

Julian had no actual reason to fear or avoid von Oberstein, but this was a result of other factors. For him to fear an imagined von Oberstein was quite understandable. The outlines of the conspiracy against Yang were much as Julian imagined, even if the conspirators themselves were not.

In short, Julian could not bring himself to seek assistance from the Imperial Navy, and von Schönkopf felt the same way. That left covert action as their only option.

And so, from May 28 through 31, the former alliance end of Iserlohn Corridor and the surrounding sectors fell quietly into chaos.

Somewhere unknown and unknowable, those who had conceived and directed this conspiracy squirmed in secret. However unhealthy and unconstructive their work had been, it had not been completed without the requisite painstaking effort. They had sheltered Andrew Fork, impressing a course to bloodshed on his disordered psyche by carefully pouring into his ear and then his heart the countless rhetorical justifications they had prepared. This done, they had put him in an armed merchant vessel and sent him off toward Iserlohn. As an organization, they had only barely survived the destruction of their religious headquarters, and this project consumed all their resources. They took the utmost care to keep their efforts secret from the Imperial Navy in particular, lest it all come to nothing. In this respect, the judgment of Julian and the others was not correct, but only those who claimed omniscience for themselves could have criticized them for it.

"Your Grace…"

"What is it?"

"If I may be permitted to ask, is it truly safe to leave the assassination of Yang Wen-li to a nonbeliever like Fork?"

Archbishop de Villiers looked at the pinched, dogmatic face of the aged bishop who had asked the question. Concealing a lazy smile within, he said, "Worry not. I am aware that Fork is not a man worthy of such an important task. This time, the goals of our faith *must* be achieved."

His solemn, confident tone alone was enough to satisfy the bishop, but de Villiers continued.

"Andrew Fork is but a mannequin of straw, made only to be burned. The merit for this deed will accrue to good and loyal followers of our faith. Why should we bestow the honor of eliminating the wisest military leader in the galaxy to some heathen fool?"

That honor rightly belongs to me. The young archbishop did not speak these words, but the light that gleamed in the corner of his eyes was eloquent enough. The light was more worldly than holy, but his questioner had already lowered his graying head in reverence and did not see; he departed deeply moved.

To de Villiers, the faith of the Terraists was a means to an end, and the Church of Terra itself nothing more than a concrete manifestation of that means. In his irreligious and calculating attitudes and behavior, the person of de Villiers was if anything a universal type found far beyond the church's narrow confines. Had he been born only slightly nearer to the Galactic Empire's capital planet of Odin, he would surely have devoted himself to advancement in government or military service. Had he been born into the Free Planets Alliance, he could have chosen a path that suited his talents and abilities and ambitions, whether politics, industry, or academia—although whether he would have succeeded is another question.

Instead, he had drawn his first breath on a distant planet on the periphery of the empire, which combined vast territory with an unforgiving philosophy of governance. What was more, that planet was not in the domain of the present or the future but the past, forcing him to choose more obscure means to rise from the miserable position forced upon him. And what, de Villiers thought, could be wrong about entrusting his future to such means?

"Fork!" he muttered. "If he'd had the sense to die after graduating from officers' school, he wouldn't have had to live the shameful life he did."

Contempt on the part of those planning an assassination for those who would carry out the deed was far from uncommon. In this case, de Villiers likely despised Fork for having failed to take advantage of any of the rich possibilities open to him in life. De Villiers himself now sought nearly the only possibility he himself had in the Church of Terra. He would have to strengthen his position internally while expanding its reach overall.

A theocracy with dominion over all of humanity. An autocratic, unimpeachable pope with absolute authority over both the holy and the profane.

If this magnificent fresco could be painted only in blood, de Villiers saw no reason to balk at shedding it.

IV

What did Yang Wen-li himself think the chances were that he might be assassinated?

Less than a year earlier, he had almost been terminated by the very government he served. If he had been able to detect this danger in advance, it was not by peering into a crystal ball. He had sensed watchful eyes that should not have been there on his honeymoon with Frederica, and when matters escalated to improper detention he had been able to analyze the reasons.

Yang was neither omniscient nor omnipotent, so the limits of his prophetic powers were defined by the information he was able to gather and his own powers of analysis. He did not dislike intellectual games, so he had explored the possibility of his own assassination from a variety of angles, but there were limits to this process as well. Had he been able to accurately discern the truth—that the Church of Terra was planning to eliminate him, using Andrew Fork as their tool—he would have been something other than human. In any case, he was faced with a different problem that demanded his primary attention.

"Those who look directly at the sun have no hope of seeing its feebler cousins—and Yang's concentration was fixed on Kaiser Reinhard."

Thus was the judgment of later ages, and although it emphasized the greatness of Reinhard more than was necessary, its thrust was correct. Yang had to think above all on Reinhard's character, his inclinations; the Church of Terra simply did not command his attention.

Additionally, there were certain patterns of thought that only made sense within the church itself—specifically, the fear that Reinhard and Yang would collude, with the former directing the latter to bring the Terraists to heel. Nor did Yang have any way of knowing that de Villiers was plotting his assassination as a show of power to strengthen the archbishop's own position. Yang had taken note of the church even before the discovery of its relationship with Phezzan, but he could never have deduced the murderous intent it harbored toward him from what he knew.

It was also commonly accepted at that juncture that, if any terrorists were planning attacks, Kaiser Reinhard would be their target. As he had neither wife nor issue, the Lohengramm Dynasty was essentially Reinhard and his inner circle; if he died, the dynasty would fall and galactic unity would be lost. Any assassination of Reinhard would be carried out by one who stood against him as an enemy; it would be an act with reason, with meaning. Surely there were some who remained loyal to the Goldenbaum Dynasty that he had deposed.

What, on the other hand, had anyone to gain from assassinating Yang? It would only strengthen Reinhard's grip on power by eliminating his greatest enemy.

In any case, even if there was some danger, Yang was in no position to refuse a meeting with Kaiser Reinhard on those grounds.

Speaking to his secretary Hilda—the Countess von Mariendorf, who would in the very near future become chief advisor of imperial headquarters—Reinhard had said clearly, "I shall reach out to Yang Wen-li, but there will be no second chance for him if he refuses my hand."

Given Reinhard's personality and his dignity as kaiser, this was not unexpected. Yang's insight in this area was precisely why he could not allow his sole opportunity to pass. Warring against an overwhelmingly larger force and destroying more of their ships than his own side had lost—not to mention killing two of the Imperial Navy's greatest generals—was proof, if any was needed, of Yang's tactical abilities and the fighting spirit of his side. But the dust had now settled, and the superiority of the empire's position was unchanged.

And this strategic superiority was not something Reinhard welcomed. Strange as it is to say, the correctness of the "attack from the front and wear the enemy down" strategy was distinctly unpleasant to him as a tactician and a military adventurer.

Larger forces defeating smaller ones is the basis of a strategist's thinking, but tacticians often thrill to victory by a small force over a large one. They locate the height of beauty in dramatically overturning the enemy's strategic advantage by implementing startling ideas on the battlefield.

"Victory beyond belief, snatched against all expectations from the jaws of defeat—how many tacticians have been lured to their doom by the devil whispering of such things?" This warning had been current since human society marked its years with "AD," and its truth was unchanged in Reinhard's time.

Reinhard had so far proved immune to that sweet and deadly temptation. He assembled vast armies, chose the right times and places for their movements, delegated authority to superior commanders, and did not overlook supply lines and communications. He had never once let those on his front lines, including himself, go hungry. That was proof that he was not one of the countless irresponsible military adventurers.

However, after the first Battle of the Corridor in 800 SE—year 2 of the New Imperial Calendar—Reinhard seemed strongly dissatisfied with the performance of his navy as well as his own performance as their leader. For his representatives like Marshals von Reuentahl and Mittermeier, the battle had indeed been unbearable. Despite the rationality shown by the kaiser in establishing strategic security, he had barely made use of it in command on the actual battlefield. In the second half of the battle, Reinhard had forced staggering losses on the Yang Fleet by bombarding them with overwhelming numbers, but whatever the rate of attrition, in absolute terms the Imperial Navy had lost more. And then, just when this war of resources had begun to seem winnable, he had withdrawn.

"Does the kaiser love war, or only bloodshed?"

No small number among the frontline commanders were indignantly asking this question, frustrated by the sense of futility they felt. Of course, they had no way of knowing at that time that the kaiser was confined to his bed with fever.

When Mittermeier heard a commander voice this criticism in person, he slapped the man so hard that he fell to the floor. This treatment seemed harsh, but he had no choice. If he overlooked the discontent, not only would the kaiser's authority be damaged, the officer who had voiced he opinions could be executed for lèse-majesté. Mittermeier's slap had been necessary to end the incident on the spot, and his decisive measure was worthy of praise.

However, Mittermeier himself felt a sense of peril far deeper than the dissatisfaction among his subordinates. The perceptive marshal had seen a crack like a thread of diamond appear in the kaiser's nature. It was an estrangement between his reason as a strategist and his sensitivity as a tactician. Up until now, these had been held together by strong psychological unity, but the bond seemed to be growing weaker.

Mittermeier wondered if illness was weakening the kaiser in mind as well as in body. At the same time, he could not banish the uneasy idea that faltering mental energy might be the cause rather than the result of the kaiser's fever. The doctors had declared it a case of overwork, but was this merely the reason they had come up with to avoid counterarguments, after proving unable to discover any other reason?

But if so, why was the kaiser ill? Mittermeier had only vague theories. Or, rather, he intentionally stopped his thinking in that area before getting too far. Even for the bravest admiral in the Imperial Navy, the prospect of pursuing the true cause of the kaiser's illness was horrifying. Compared to this terror, the concrete manifestation that was the illness itself was almost beneath notice.

Under the circumstances, even the perceptive Mittermeier never considered the possibility that Yang Wen-li might be assassinated by a third party. The same was surely true of von Reuentahl. Thus stood things on the imperial side.

2350, May 31. Bridge of the cruiser *Leda II*.

Following dinner with Romsky and the other government representatives, the military contingent was relaxing in *Leda II*'s officers' club, the Gun Room, before turning in.

Yang was in a good mood. He was a terrible 3-D chess player, despite his fondness for the game, and had not won a game against anyone in two years, but tonight he had beaten Blumhardt twice—once barely, once handily.

"I didn't think I was that bad at the game," said Blumhardt.

Yang glanced sideways at his grumbling opponent as he sipped his tea. He had brewed it himself, and its "better than coffee, at least" flavor reminded him of the priceless treasure he had in Julian. He had been out of contact with his ward for several days now and was finding himself rather bored and not a little uneasy.

Julian and the rest of Yang's staff were still desperately trying to reach Yang, of course. But magnetic storms at several points along the corridor and even stronger artificial barriers had made that impossible.

"Well, I'd better hit the sack before this mood wears off," Yang said. He rose to his feet, acknowledged a round of salutes, and retired to his cabin. The officers reported this to Romsky's secretary and then settled in for a game of poker.

By the time Yang had showered and gone to bed, it was 0025 on June 1. With his slight tendency toward low blood pressure, Yang was not quite an insomniac but did have trouble sleeping, so he always kept a horror novel and pen and paper at his bedside. For the past couple of days his sleep had been particularly shallow for some reason, so he also had sleeping pills on hand. Perhaps corpuscles of nervousness were seeping into the corridors of his psyche after all.

Yang had no strategy whatsoever prepared for his meeting with Kaiser Reinhard. His companion Romsky was far from skilled at diplomacy, so Yang would bear no small responsibility for the outcome of the talks, but the only place he had any interest in matching tactics against the kaiser was the battlefield.

He took a sleeping pill and listlessly read a few pages of his novel.

At 0045 hours, he yawned once and was just reaching for his bedside lamp to turn it off when his hand stopped short. His intercom was ringing. He answered, and Blumhardt's audibly tense voice filled his ears.

The curtain had risen on the first act of the mysterious drama about to engulf *Leda II.*

The ship had received two messages. The first reported that Andrew Fork, formerly a commodore in the alliance, had escaped his psychiatric hospital and, driven by a loathing so obsessive it had crossed over into the realm of madness, was planning to assassinate Yang Wen-li. What was more, the armed merchant vessel stolen by Fork had been spotted in a nearby sector. This message had been followed by a report that the Imperial Navy had dispatched two destroyers to meet Yang partway.

Lieutenant Commander Rysikof, *Leda II*'s captain, had put the ship on alert. At 0120, a merchant vessel appeared on-screen. At 0122, it opened fire on them. Before *Leda II* could return fire, however, two imperial destroyers appeared behind the intruder and utterly eliminated it, along with its crew, with a burst of concentrated fire.

The destroyers signaled a request to open communications, so Rysikof had a channel opened for them. The video was fuzzy, but *Leda II*'s crew saw a man in what looked like an imperial officer's uniform report that the imperial side had learned of the plot against Yang.

"We have taken care of the terrorist," he said. "You are safe now. Since we will be escorting Your Excellency directly to His Majesty the Kaiser, we request permission to board and speak face-to-face."

"The leader of our delegation is Chairman Romsky," said Yang. "I will abide by his decision."

Romsky's judgment was in accord with what might be expected of a gentleman. He gladly granted their rescuers permission to lay aboard.

. .   .
     ●
  .   .
          .

"Yes, Andrew Fork…"

Patrichev half emptied his enormous lungs in a prolonged sigh.

"He always was a sour, arrogant, unpleasant fellow," said Blumhardt dismissively.

Patrichev's voice had more sympathy. "A brilliant man, but reality refused to accommodate him," he said. "Any problem susceptible to formulas or equations he could solve in short order, but he was ill-suited for life in the real world, where there is no instruction manual."

Yang remained silent. He had no interest in commenting. He bore no responsibility for Fork's self-destruction, but it left a bitter aftertaste all the same. He also suspected there was more to the story—how had someone banished from society as a madman gotten hold of a ship and a crew of sympathizers to attempt his act of terror? But the sleeping pill Yang had taken before being dragged out of bed again was starting to take effect. His concentration was faltering; he could not maintain close analysis.

One of the imperial destroyers set about docking with *Leda II*. Hatches extended from both ships and then connected, creating a pressurized passageway between the two ships. Yang's officers watched this procedure on-screen from the Gun Room.

"Is this really necessary?" asked Soul. Yang shrugged. Romsky had made his decision. It was already awkward enough that Yang's invitation had come before Romsky's as a government representative. He felt that he had forgotten, if only temporarily, the procedures of democracy, and he had decided as a result to prioritize Romsky's authority and prestige. Yang viewed the doctor as a fundamentally good man, untouched by intrigue or jealousy. The following somewhat cynical testament was recorded for later generations:

"Yang Wen-li was certainly not satisfied with Romsky, but he supported him out of unwillingness to allow anyone with a worse personality to grasp the reins of power. He considered Romsky's weakness to be the extent of the things he could smilingly permit."

At 0150 hours, docking procedures were complete and imperial officers appeared in the passageway between the two ships. The look of disappointment on their faces as they surveyed those assembled to welcome them aboard *Leda II* was due to Yang's absence. Romsky's aides, emphasizing the priority of diplomacy and foreign relations, had asked Yang and the other military representatives to wait in their chambers until called. Yang, for his part, had no interest in arguing about such a minor issue. What was more, that damned sleeping pill was really starting to take effect. If Romsky would take care of the tiresome glad-handing, so much the better.

But this was not how the men in imperial uniforms interpreted the scene. They assumed that Yang must have sensed danger and gone into hiding. As Romsky smiled warmly, ready to offer gratitude for their "rescue," the barrel of a blaster was pointed in his face. The second act of the drama had begun.

"Where is Yang Wen-li?"

The menacing question seemed to exasperate Romsky more than it surprised him. "I don't know what you think you're doing, but surely you understand that it isn't polite to wave guns around. Put that away."

This response did not escape criticism in the years to come. "There is no point in politely explaining etiquette to a dog," one commentator argued. "Instead of words, Romsky should have thrown a chair at their faces."

The soldier suddenly lowered the blaster to Romsky's chest and fired, but his aim was poor. The shot grazed the doctor's lower jaw to bore through his upper throat. His cervical vertebrae and spinal column were destroyed, and he collapsed wordlessly to the floor. His face still bore an expression of the mildest surprise.

Romsky's aides screamed and fled. Blaster fire followed them, but not a single shot made contact. The assassins may have calculated that the fleeing aides would lead them to Yang.

At 0155 the panicked aides reached Soul and Blumhardt, who recognized the gravity of the situation in the aides' faces before a word was spoken. Blasters in hand, the officers began barricading the door of the Gun Room with furniture. There was a storm of footsteps outside and a dozen or more blaster bolts flew into the room.

The shoot-out had begun.

Romsky's killer was shot right under the nose by Soul, dying instantly. Whether his participation in this dishonorable act of terror was driven by religious beliefs or materialistic desires remained forever mysterious as a result.

The enemy was less disciplined in their fire than Blumhardt and the other officers, but they compensated for this with sheer volume. The officers who had been urging Yang to stay down realized that they would have to change course.

"Run, Commander!"

Blumhardt and Soul both shouted the words at the same time, their voices mingling with the enraged screams of the assassins, the din of blaster fire, and the chaos of chairs and bodies falling to the floor. Blumhardt dropped three of the enemy with expertly placed shots, then shouted at Yang again.

"Run, Commander!"

But where?

Yang shook his head. The fact that he was fully clad, from black beret to half boots, was impressive enough for a man who saw no virtue in personal promptness.

Patrichev reached with an arm at least twice as thick as Yang's own and seized him by the shoulder. He dragged his stunned superior officer to the rear exit, all but heaving him over his shoulder like firewood, then threw him out into the corridor beyond, slammed the door, and turned to stand with his back defiantly against it.

Patrichev's enormous frame was skewered by half a dozen beams of charged particles. The gentle giant, who had supported Yang as his staff officer since the founding of the alliance's Thirteenth Fleet, looked down with supreme calm at the holes in his uniform, already splattered with blood. Then he turned his gaze to the men who had shot him and said, "Cut it out. Don't you know that hurts?"

The unhurried composure of his voice, as if he had left his sense of pain behind in bed that morning, terrified his assailants. Their reaction came two seconds later. Patrichev was battered with screams and blaster fire. Now with too many holes in the broad surface of his chest to count, he sank slowly to the floor.

Patrichev's bulk now blocked the door, which had presumably been his intention. The assassins set about the difficult task of moving him, and Blumhardt and Soul took the opportunity to bombard them with blaster fire. By then they were the only two still fighting against the intruders, but they were startlingly effective.

The assassins concentrated their loathsome fire first on Soul, piercing him through below his left clavicle. The blaster bolt missed his heart and lungs, but when he staggered back he hit his head against the wall and fell over, unconscious.

The possibility of revenge against the young officer who had already shot five of their comrades dead surely tempted the assassins, but loyalty to their original goal was their priority. A handful of assassins trampled over Soul and the spreading pool of his blood as they ran from the room.

VI

At 0204, a fifth ship took the stage. Most of the original passengers on *Leda II* were dead or wounded, and the ship itself was all but under the control of the intruders. As a result, one of them was first to notice the warship now filling the screen.

"Unidentified ship closing fast!"

The ship may have been "unidentified" to the intruders, but its origin was far less obscure than their own. It was *Ulysses*, arriving at top speed with Julian Mintz and his rescue party aboard. Julian's intuition that Yang would be in a sector where communications were scrambled or cut off had proved correct.

One of the destroyers hurriedly began to come around, but *Ulysses*'s cannons had already locked on to their target. A slight difference in angle and output divided victor from defeated and quick from dead. The destroyer was pierced by three spears of light and erupted into a ball of dull-white flame, returning everyone aboard it to their component atoms.

This took care of one of the enemy ships, but Julian and his crew could hardly fire on the other while it was docked with *Leda II*. The two ships hung together like twins united by hate. *Ulysses* approached and made contact with *Leda II*, then used a concentrated spray of acid to open a passage.

Their initial reward was blaster fire. Shots flew wildly, leaving afterimages like blue thread on their retinas.

The assassins still had the numerical advantage. Their leader had devoted most of the organization's people to this plot. But the men who now surged from *Ulysses* into *Leda II* were veterans under the command of Walter von Schönkopf himself, and their rage and fighting prowess dwarfed the faith that sustained the assassins. The hand-to-hand combat that followed the shoot-out was like a pack of wolves warring against carnivorous rabbits. The assassins were more brutal, but before long even the fanatics who had held off the empire on Terra fell one by one to the gore-smeared floor.

Von Schönkopf looked down at one of the defeated assassins soaking in blood and hate at his feet. "Where is Marshal Yang?" he demanded sharply.

The man did not reply.

"Tell me!" von Schönkopf shouted.

"Gone," spat the fallen intruder. "Gone from this world forever."

Von Schönkopf kicked in the man's teeth. He could not don the guise of a gentleman: his fury was too extreme in both quality and quantity.

"Julian, go and save the commander! I'll be right behind you after I mop up here."

Julian did not need to be told. With startling nimbleness given the armor he was wearing, he broke into a run. Machungo and four or five other armored men followed him.

Even as his anxiety reached near-critical levels, Julian held on desperately to the single thread that might lead them to a miracle. They had found Yang's ship before communications had been reestablished. They had come this far. There was hope. Their efforts would surely be rewarded! Wasn't *Ulysses* a lucky ship? And hadn't he arrived here on *Ulysses*?

The man Julian was searching for was wandering, confused, through an unfamiliar sector of the ship. Every so often he would pause with folded arms before starting to walk again. His ability to flee a band of assassins without running around in terror was one of the things that set him apart from other people. He was, of course, trying to determine where he might be safe.

Yang was sincerely glad that he hadn't brought Frederica or Julian. Oddly, it did not even occur to him that his own life might be extended had they been there to sacrifice themselves. Relief that he had not gotten them mixed up in all this took precedence. Even now, he was only wandering around because his subordinates had thrown him off the battlefield, such as it was.

If asked if he wanted to die, his response would have been, "Not especially, no," that added "especially" being an example of what made him unique. The problem with dying was that Frederica would be left alone. She had truly given him her all, first as his aide for three years, and then as his spouse for one. She was happy just to have him around, so he wanted to stay in good health and be there for her as long as he could.

0230 hours. At this moment Yang and Julian were only forty meters apart. But those forty meters included three layers of wall and a looming fortress of machinery. Lacking X-ray vision, their reunion was prevented.

"Marshal Yang!"

Julian fought as he ran, and as he fought he kept up the search for the most important person in his life.

"Marshal Yang! It's Julian! Where are you?"

He was down to three companions: Machungo and two others. Two lives had been lost in the maelstrom of close combat. The enemy never ran; every time they encountered a new one, fighting broke out again. Who knew how much precious time was being wasted this way?

0240. Yang stopped in his tracks. The voice calling him had sounded very close.

"Yang Wen-li?!"

The call was neither question nor request for information. It was simply a reverberation manifesting an intention to fire. When the man who had spoken pulled the trigger, the act was like a convulsion, as if his own voice had galvanized him into action.

A bizarre sensation pierced Yang's left leg like a rod. He staggered back against the wall. The sensation took form as first weight, then heat, and finally a pain that spread to fill his entire body. Blood was pouring out of him as if being sucked out by vacuum pump.

They hit an arterial plexus, Yang concluded with peculiar coolheadedness. If not for the pain corroding his field of consciousness, he could almost have been watching solivision. By contrast, the man who had shot him screamed in terror and exultation, dropped his blaster, and disappeared from Yang's sight like a frenzied shaman.

"I killed him! I killed him!"

Listening to the cracked, off-key voice fade out of hearing, Yang removed his scarf and bandaged his wound. It was already a flowing spring of blood, staining both of his hands bright red. Compared to the blood he had shed in his life, however, it was nothing.

Pain had become the sole, narrow passageway connecting Yang's field of consciousness to reality. *I might really die here*, he thought. Faces came to him: His wife, his ward, his men. These images made him angry at the situation he found himself in. He was disgusted by his own carelessness, getting into trouble like this so far from any of them. Bracing himself against the wall with one hand, he began hobbling down the corridor. Almost as if, by doing so, he could break down the wall of distance that separated him from them.

Strange, Yang thought ruefully with the tiniest sliver of his consciousness. *You'd think losing this much blood would make you lighter. Why do I feel so heavy?* It was as if malevolent, invisible arms had wrapped themselves around his entire body, not just his shins, and were trying to pull him down.

Once ivory white, his slacks were now a crimson that grew darker by the second at the hands of some unseen dyer. The scarf wrapped around his wound had lost all capacity to stanch the hemorrhaging and now served only as a conduit for blood.

Yang had a moment of confusion as his perspective dipped. He had collapsed to his knees. Following an unsuccessful attempt to rise to his feet again, he leaned back lightly against the wall and sat where he was. *Not my finest hour*, he thought, but no longer had the strength even to move. The pool of blood around him grew. *Miracle Yang becomes Yang the Bloody*, he thought. Even thinking was immensely tiring for him now.

His fingers would not move. His vocal cords were failing. So when he spoke—

"Sorry, Frederica. Sorry, Julian. Sorry, everybody…"

—no one heard it but Yang himself. At least, that was what he himself believed.

Yang closed his eyes. It was his last action in this world. In one corner of the consciousness that now fell down a colorless well, twilight turning to lacquer black, he heard a familiar voice calling his name.

At 0255 on June 1, 800 SE, time stopped for Yang Wen-li. He was thirty-three years old.

CHAPTER 6:

AFTER THE FESTIVAL

I
0305, JUNE 1.

A shock unlike any Julian Mintz had experienced before tangled itself around his legs like an unseen rope.

Stopping in his tracks, he touched his blood-smeared tomahawk lightly on the ground and looked around as he forced order upon his agitated breathing and field of vision. The shock had been real. But he could not immediately understand why he had felt it. Foreboding swelled in his throat with nauseous pressure.

The corridor before him was empty. Another dim corridor extended off to the left, and it was—not. Someone was there. Not standing. Not prepared for any sort of fight. Whoever it was seemed to be sitting down, leaning against the wall. On the floor a small object gleamed dully. It was a blaster, abandoned at the corridor's entrance. It looked like an imperial sidearm. The figure in the corridor had one knee raised and the other leg stretched flat. Slumped forward, the figure's face was hidden by a beret and the bangs that fell forward from under it. The black slick on the floor was silent testimony to how much blood the figure had lost.

"Marshal Yang…?"

Even as Julian spoke, praying to be contradicted, part of his brain was already screaming.

"Marshal..."

Julian's knees suddenly began to shake. His body had grasped the situation before his reason and was reacting accordingly. He stepped into the corridor. He did not want to, did not want to face what he knew awaited him there, but he advanced anyway. Forced on by an unwanted sense of duty, he took three steps forward—four—then lost his balance and fell to one knee, bracing himself against the floor with one hand. He was already on the banks of the lake of blood. From his slightly higher vantage point, Julian gazed at the face of the corpse. It could have just been asleep, exhausted.

Hands shaking, Julian removed his helmet. His unruly flaxen hair stuck to his brow, now slick with both cold and hot sweat. His heart, his voice were as disarrayed as his hair, bound by no order.

"Forgive me. Forgive me. I failed. Just when you needed me most of all, I failed you..."

Julian did not notice the warmth that still lingered in the blood that stained his knee. What had he promised Yang four years ago—that he'd always protect him? He had been so confident. This was the reality. Julian had failed. He was a worthless, useless liar! Not only had he failed to protect Yang, he had not even been with his guardian as he drew his final breath.

Disgust coursed through Julian's nervous system, flooding his senses with the stink of reality again. Glancing back over his shoulder, Julian saw them. Five or six men in imperial military uniforms, approaching from behind.

It took less than a hundredth of an instant for the crimson current to electrify through Julian's every nerve and artery.

The men in imperial uniforms were confronted by a being of pure hatred and animosity, baleful energy in the shape of a man. At that moment, Julian was the most dangerous creature in the galaxy.

A charge, a leap, a swung blade, all at once. In a flash of Julian's tomahawk, one of the intruders' skulls was split in two. He collapsed, spattering the corridor with fresh blood and full-throated screaming. A second flash flew in the opposite direction and shattered the clavicle and ribs of another victim. Before this second man hit the floor, blood was gushing from the newly smashed nose of a third.

Hate and confusion filled the shouts echoing off the walls around Julian. The enemy's tomahawks could not even strike his shadow. Had von Schönkopf witnessed the scene, he would no doubt have praised Julian's brutality but criticized his lack of calm. Julian whirled his tomahawk where his boiling passions led, charging forward and painting the floor with a fresh layer of blood.

"Sublieutenant! Sublieutenant Mintz!"

The newly made revenant felt two arms thicker than his own legs wrap themselves around him from behind. Julian was no match for Machungo's brawn, but the larger man still had to strain his every fiber to subdue this active volcano of aggression.

"Please calm down, sir!"

"Let me go!"

Julian whipped his head around. Blood that was not his own flew off his hair and spattered Machungo's dark face.

"Let me go!"

He kicked at the air with both legs, sending arcs of blood through the corridor like broken necklaces of red jasper.

"Let me go! I'll kill them all! It's no more than they deserve!"

"They're all dead already, sir," Machungo said, perspiration in his voice. "More importantly, what about Marshal Yang? You can't just leave his remains on the floor here."

In half an instant, the storm ended. Julian stopped struggling and turned to look at Machungo. Reason—or something like it—had returned to his eyes. He unclenched his fists and his tomahawk dropped to the blood-slick floor, protesting against the rough treatment with a sticky noise.

Machungo opened his arms and let Julian go. Unsteady on his feet as an infant walking for the first time, Julian approached Yang's corpse again and dropped to one knee. Far in the distance, he heard a weak voice addressing the dead man.

"Commander, let's go back to Iserlohn. That's our home—the home we all share. Let's go home…"

Seeing the young man wait for a reply that would never come, the black giant went wordlessly into action. With reverent care, he gathered Yang's lifeless form in his arms. Julian was pulled to his feet too, as if by an unseen rope, and realized that he had begun walking alongside Machungo.

Marshal Yang was gone.

Unparalleled master of the arts of war, unrepentant hater of war itself, he had gone to a place where he need never fight again.

Julian's consciousness retreated through the corridors of memory. Scenes from more than 2,600 days flickered across his mind in a stream of images. He had a memory of Yang for every brain cell, and he had expected to keep accumulating more. To think that that process would be interrupted like this!

For the first time, liquefied fury and despair burst through the gates of his tear ducts. He wept wildly as a child. Machungo looked at him in consternation and muttered something to himself. "I guess at times like this, whoever cries first wins," it sounded like, but Julian was neither watching nor listening. All he was aware of at that moment was the heat of the tears that fell on his hands.

To live is to watch others die. Yang Wen-li had said so himself. The fact that war and terrorism cause the senseless deaths of good people is the main reason they must be opposed—he had said that too. He always spoke truly. But however true the words he left behind, what good were they when the man himself was dead?

Words…Not only had Julian failed to witness Yang's final moments, he had not heard his last words either. Not even a message to pass on to his wife. Regret and self-loathing came forth in a new wave of tears.

At around this time, von Schönkopf discovered his subordinate and apprentice Blumhardt in the Gun Room.

The young man was sprawled on the floor, surrounded by the corpses of seven or eight men in imperial uniforms. The scene was a testament to how bravely Blumhardt had made his final stand. Slipping more than once in the blood on the floor, von Schönkopf approached and knelt beside him. He took off Blumhardt's helmet and shook him by one blood-streaked shoulder. The young officer, now in his final moments, opened his eyes a crack and gathered all his strength to whisper.

"Is Marshal Yang all right?"

Von Schönkopf could not reply right away.

"He's not good at staying on task. I hope he got away."

"Julian went after him. He's fine. He'll be here before you know it."

"Good. If he hadn't survived…this would have been no fun at all."

He trailed off, and von Schönkopf heard two shallow, sharp exhalations. Commander Reiner Blumhardt, leader of the Rosen Ritter, had breathed his last, fifteen minutes after the commander he had fought to protect.

Von Schönkopf cleared his expression and rose to his feet, but particles of sorrow remained lodged in his eyes. He looked up at the ceiling, took a deep breath, and then lowered his gaze again to see someone approaching. Once he determined it was not an enemy but a known friend, the relief in his voice was apparent.

"Julian. Was he all right? I searched these men. They're not Imperial Navy—"

Walter von Schönkopf stopped speaking amid a suddenly rising haze of misfortune. The inside of his mouth became a desert, and the fearless former commander of the Rosen Ritter spoke in a cracked voice as if vomiting up lumps of clay.

"Stop it," he said. "This isn't drama school. I'm not interested in rehearsing a tragedy with you."

He closed his mouth, turned his seething eyes on Julian, and sighed with his shoulders. This was his ritual for accepting reality. Without a word—from him, or from Julian—von Schönkopf saluted Yang where he lay in Machungo's arms. Julian saw von Schönkopf's hand tremble slightly only twice.

This done, von Schönkopf showed Julian a scrap of cloth. It had been found in Baron von Kümmel's residence a year before by Kaiser Reinhard's soldiers. Embroidered letters leapt into Julian's field of vision: "The Holy Land, in Our Hands."

"The Church of Terra!"

Julian reeled with vertigo. The hatred he had been aiming directly at the Imperial Navy could not be redirected instantly. He thought he had used up all his emotions, and was disgusted to find himself surprised once again.

"But why should Terraists assassinate Marshal Yang? Because we infiltrated Earth and searched their base? If so…"

"The inquiry can come later," said von Schönkopf with an eerie, ominous calm. "We know who did this, and that's enough for now. I'm going to deliver them all to the crematorium, along with even the ground they walk on."

Von Schönkopf turned to his subordinates.

"Haul two or three of the survivors onto *Ulysses*. I'll interrogate them at my leisure. There'll be plenty of free time on the way back to Iserlohn."

Soul was unconscious and severely wounded, but alive. This was the only ray of light amid the mass of bad news. Julian was fond of Soul, and expected to learn a lot about the incident from him once he regained consciousness. Although Soul himself would not find this a pleasant experience.

"Are we ready to go?" asked Machungo. Von Schönkopf and Julian nodded together.

Both inside and outside *Leda II*, the killing was still ongoing. Von Schönkopf's men had vast advantages in fighting ability and discipline, but every enemy they encountered fought to the death. Just like the imperial troops who had stormed Terraist headquarters, von Schönkopf's men felt not fear but an uncanny nausea as they forced bloodshed on the enemy and pushed them back skirmish by skirmish.

At 0330, von Schönkopf ordered all troops to withdraw.

"No more wasting time on those ghouls," he said. "We don't want the Imperial Navy to find us and complicate things. All living boarders, evacuate now."

The order was promptly obeyed, with the survivors of the boarding party ending their battles and returning to *Ulysses*. The remains of Yang, Patrichev, and Blumhardt were carried on board as well. Later, the rescue team would be criticized for leaving the bodies of Dr. Romsky and the other revolutionary government officials behind.

II

Many were those who mourned the shocking death of Yang Wen-li. Most of them had fought under his command or even by his side. But among the historians of later generations, some offered severe criticisms of his legacy.

One of the sharpest read:

"What sort of man was Yang Wen-li, in the end? He denounced war, but advanced his personal fortunes by waging it. When his state fell, he declared and led a new war to split the human race in two, then failed at this also, leaving nothing but the seeds of discord and carnage to those who came after. Had Yang never existed, the tumultuous period from the end of the eighth century SE to the early years of the ninth would have deprived far fewer unwilling victims of their lives. We must not give him more credit than he deserves. Yang was not a disappointed idealist or a failed revolutionary; he was nothing but a warmonger paying lip service to the notion of a higher duty. Brush aside the garish adornment of military romanticism, and what remains of his record? We are forced to say: nothing. In neither life nor death did the man bring happiness to humanity."

Some historians offered a more measured assessment:

"If the second meeting of Kaiser Reinhard and Yang Wen-li had taken place, what would its legacy to history have been? Peaceful coexistence between the titanic empire and the tiny republic, or a final, uncompromising war? Whatever we may suspect, the talks did not in fact take place, snuffing out the hopes of both the living and the dead. Yang Wen-li died at the worst possible time. Not of his own choosing, of course; the death was forced on him by a conspiracy, so we can hardly criticize him for it. No, the greatest sin was committed by the reactionary terrorists, whose unconstructive fervor and obsession led them to terminate those historical possibilities. Their act was like a sneer directed at Yang's insistence that terrorism cannot change the course of history: at the very least, it changed the course of his life."

Other chroniclers took a different tack:

"Moral good and political good are not the same. Yang Wen-li's choices and actions from SE 797 to 800 were, perhaps, good in the former sense, but not in the latter. The age, the circumstances demanded a more forceful leader than would be needed in peacetime, and even there none other than Yang had the ability or popular support to perform that role, though he continued to deny this. Whatever personal satisfaction he may have derived from this piety, it ended with the democratic state that was the Free Planets Alliance losing one of its most important pillars of support, and collapsing as a result. Of course, in Yang's historical philosophy, the alliance had already lost both its life and its reason to exist as a state; presumably he saw no reason to ensure the survival of its name alone if the cost was acceptance of military dictatorship. Furthermore, he himself hoped to cede his key place in history to another."

Was that "another" Julian Mintz, Yang's ward?

"If Julian went to work for the kaiser, he could be a marshal one day," was how Yang used to praise the boy's potential, but given what he believed and where he stood this praise seemed doubly thoughtless. Still, two things were clear from Yang's words: he recognized the capacities of both of the individuals he named, and he did not see Julian's talent as superior to the kaiser's. Of course, Yang did not think of himself as more capable than Reinhard either.

"Even I know I'm not equipped for this," he once told Julian with a shrug. He was far from the only one fascinated by Kaiser Reinhard, but he was surely the most deeply conscious of Reinhard's position in history. What was more, he seemed to view his own position opposite the kaiser with a hint of pessimism.

Yang had an instinctive dislike of those who held the reins of power in his own state, as well as those who dwelled in neighboring domains. It was not surprising that his relations with such people were not friendly. He did not welcome their visits, and feigned illness or absence on many occasions to evade meetings with them. This was not out of any particular belief or principle; psychologically speaking, he was on the same level as a child refusing to eat his vegetables.

So overflowing with ideas and strategies on the battlefield that others called him superhuman, Yang knew virtually nothing of interpersonal relations. When he had overused the illness gambit and conversation with an unwanted guest looked unavoidable, Julian had sometimes played the role of invalid instead. After the crisis was averted, Yang would express his gratitude by tucking a ten-dinar note into his ward's pocket, or leaving a box of chocolates on his nightstand. Indeed, he always tried to show care for his subordinates, however clumsily; he was a kind and magnanimous man by nature, but more reserved around his superiors and particularly those who made their homes near the seat of political power.

What Yang liked about life in Iserlohn Fortress was that, as it was only a peripheral military installation, no one outranked him there, so he was far less bothered by entertaining and public responsibilities than he had been on Heinessen. In practical terms he was the dictator of a fortress-city, and could have behaved like some medieval princeling. But there is ample testimony that his lifestyle and behavior fell far short of that extreme. His complete lack of interest in seeking the privileges of a high-ranking military officer was less due to self-control than character, but it was worthy of praise all the same.

Even historians who took a negative view of Yang had to admit that he was by no means an average man. On the other hand, even those who viewed him favorably had to concede a kind of passivity that prevented him from seeking more opportunities with more allies.

At the Rescue of El Facil, where Yang had first made a name for himself, he had been a callow youth of twenty-one. The civilian authorities had stubbornly doubted the viability of his proposal. Unable to reveal to others the brilliant strategy he bore within his breast, Yang had simply repeated "No need for concern"—the least valuable utterance since the birth of civilization—and not even attempted to convince them. Bringing people on different psychological wavelengths, or with different values, around to his way of thinking was an unbearable burden to him, and in that respect he lacked entirely the sort of character necessary for a man of politics.

"If I don't like someone, I don't care if they don't like me either. If I don't want to understand someone, it doesn't matter if they don't understand me"—such, we may conclude, was Yang's true thinking. Of course, we also have evidence that he did not isolate himself to the extent that he needed neither friendship nor understanding: when he discovered that his ward Julian Mintz was able to receive his transmissions, he taught the boy all he knew about tactics and strategy, delighting in his intelligence. It was not Yang's intention to shape his ward into a military man, but he inadvertently cultivated the qualities within Julian that would make him an excellent one all the same. Julian was a kind of mirror reflecting the estrangement between Yang's genius and his hopes.

Having ended what one historian called his "short, variegated life filled with inconsistencies and victories," Yang Wen-li, his remains under the guard of his subordinates, floated through the void back to his castle.

III

Ulysses rendezvoused with the five other craft that had been following closely behind it, and the funeral procession returned to Iserlohn Fortress. They arrived at the base at 1130 on June 3.

Julian and von Schönkopf had had to take care of several problems on the way.

To begin with, the three captured Terraists were interrogated. That the attitude of their interrogators failed, at times, to emphasize empathy and shared humanity, is a fact. When no answers were forthcoming, the men of the Rosen Ritter, who had lost their commander and many brothers-in-arms, grew even more furious.

"Admiral, please turn the Terraists over to us," said Rinz to von Schönkopf. "They'll never talk anyway. Let's give them the vivid martyrdom they crave."

Rinz's subordinates elaborated on this abstract proposal with more specific suggestions.

"Throw them alive into the fusion reactor!"

"No! We slice them up slowly, flushing each slice into the sewer as we go!"

Von Schönkopf looked them over, seeing the thirst for vengeance in them. "No need to rush," he said. "Iserlohn has a fusion reactor too. A big one." In the coldness of his tone was an ominous intensity beyond the experience of even the men of the Rosen Ritter.

The crowd ebbed away, and von Schönkopf and Julian exchanged a look too deep to be called mere melancholy.

"Patrichev and Blumhardt followed the commander into the unknown, then. They'll make good chess partners for him if the imperials are right about Valhalla."

Julian nodded. "Both of them were even worse at the game than him," he said. Wind spiraled through his soul. These meaningless, pointless conversations felt to him like sowing seed on a concrete wasteland. And yet, he feared that unless he kept saying *something*, the concrete would flood into him, reaching his very capillaries, and petrify him from head to toe.

"I didn't defect from the empire to feel like this," said von Schönkopf. "Surely this can't be punishment for betraying my homeland?"

Julian was silent.

"It might have saved me some trouble to destroy the empire instead of just abandoning it. Well, that's in the past now. Our problem is what comes next."

"What comes next?"

"That's right. Yang Wen-li's dead. Don't plug your ears! Marshal Yang is dead. Dead! And it wasn't Kaiser Reinhard who killed him, either. His final surprise for us! Not that I'm happy about it, mind you."

Von Schönkopf pounded the table, which creaked in protest. Julian sensed himself growing as pale as the admiral. An intriguing question: when all the blood ran from your body, where did it go? When you bled from the soul, where did it end up?

"But here we are," von Schönkopf continued. "Alive. That means we have to think about what comes next. How we're going to fight the kaiser from now on."

"From now on?"

Julian heard himself answer in a voice he could barely believe was his own. A string of phonemes devoid of intellect or reason.

"I can't even think about that now. Not with Marshal Yang gone…"

Yang had done all their thinking for them. Why to fight, how to fight, what to do afterward—Yang had supplied all the answers. Julian and the others had just followed him. Now, it seemed, they would have to start thinking for themselves.

"Should we surrender, then?" asked von Schönkopf. "Bend the knee and swear fealty to the kaiser? Fair enough, I suppose. Not unnatural for a band of mercenaries to fall apart when the head mercenary goes."

Julian was at a loss for words. After two and a half seconds, von Schönkopf gave him a short, wordless grin.

"If that doesn't interest you," he said, "we'll have to stick together, since they outnumber us. And if we're going to stick together, we need a leader. We need a successor to Yang."

"I know, but…"

How could we possibly choose a successor to Yang? Just as most of a solar system's mass was in its central star, the constellation that was the Yang Fleet had only shone so brightly because of Yang himself. Could another leader achieve the same feat? On the other hand, von Schönkopf was right—if no successor to Yang could be found, the fleet would be forced to disband.

"One more question," said von Schönkopf.

"There's more?"

"This one might be even more important. Who tells Yang's wife?"

Surely no question could have been as unhappy, as unpleasant, and yet as unavoidable as this one. Nevertheless, wearing the expression of a man with a mouthful of diesel oil, von Schönkopf had done his minor duty as the older of the two and raised it anyway.

Julian felt suffocated by the magnitude of the problem. Von Schönkopf was right—who *would* report the news to Frederica Greenhill Yang? *Your husband died not on the bridge of his flagship facing down the kaiser, but all alone in a corridor of a cruiser.* Cornered and desperate, he suddenly hit on a potential escape route.

"Why don't we ask Mrs. Caselnes?" he said. "She might—"

"Yes, the thought had occurred to me too," said von Schönkopf. "That might be for the best. Shameful as it is, men aren't strong enough for things like this."

The acid-tongued fugitive noble offered no criticism of Julian's attempt to escape. It was the first time Julian had ever seen him like this. His vitality and spirit had seemed limitless, but now it had dried up like a river in a time of drought, exposing the riverbed to the sun.

The same went for the others. The same would go for everyone at Iserlohn, too. Julian shivered. With the loss of their central star, what would become of the planets and moons that had orbited it? He stood rooted to the floor, in the grip of fear so strong it overwhelmed even his grief.

IV

And so, at 1130 on June 3, the funeral procession docked at Iserlohn.

Caselnes, Attenborough, and Merkatz had learned of Yang's death through top secret comm channel, and met *Ulysses* as it arrived. A cluster of alabaster statues under an old fluorescent light—these were invincible men who had led armies of millions back and forth across the galaxy; now they wrapped wounded souls in their uniforms and awaited a single young envoy.

"Julian." Caselnes forced his voice palely from his throat. "Even under the best of circumstances, Yang would have died fifteen years before you. But he was six years younger than me. Hardly seems fair that I should have to be the one to give him the send-off."

These words were the best that one of the highest-ranking officers in the Alliance Armed Forces could come up with. That alone spoke to the depth of his shock.

Julian did not see Olivier Poplin. Later he learned that, upon hearing the news, Poplin had said only "Yang Wen-li's no good to me dead" before locking himself in his quarters with a case of whiskey.

"Has Frederica…?"

"Heard? No. We haven't told her. You'll do that for us, won't you?"

"I don't want to tell her any more than you do. We were hoping your wife might help…"

But when her husband conveyed Julian's request, Hortense Caselnes wanted no part of it. "Julian," she said, calm but firm refusal in her uncharacteristically pallid face, "this is your responsibility and your duty. You're her family. If you can't tell her, who can? And if you don't, you'll come to regret that much more than you would just breaking the news to her."

Julian had to admit that she was right. He even felt ashamed. Frederica, after all, had no one to receive the news of her husband's passing on her behalf. It was something she would have to do herself too. Julian's gaze turned to the officers. Caselnes shook his head hurriedly; von Schönkopf, slowly. Merkatz, his eyes half-closed, said nothing. Attenborough moved his pale lips silently, but Julian read the words they formed: *Are you kidding?* Julian wanted to sigh, but his breathing was already becoming irregular.

Resigned to his fate, he knocked on Frederica's door. His vision and hearing seemed to malfunction the moment she opened it.

"Julian! That was quick. When did you get back?"

Both smile and voice were blurred in outline. Julian managed some kind of reply. An empty conversation began. Three exchanges, four—and then, suddenly, a crystal clear sentence passed through his auditory nerve to pierce his heart.

"He's dead, isn't he?"

Julian trembled. Frederica's hazel eyes seemed to be looking through his physical form into his gallery of memories. Mustering all the vocal-cord function he could, he finally forced out an insubstantial reply: "What makes you think that?"

"Well, what else could you be so obviously unwilling to say? So it's true, then. He's dead."

Julian opened his mouth. Words, not under the control of his will, spooled themselves out. "Yes," he said. "That's right. Marshal Yang has passed on. He was killed by Church of Terra fanatics to prevent his meeting with the kaiser. I tried to save him, but I was too late. I'm so sorry. It took everything I had to bring him back."

"I wish you were a liar, Julian," said Frederica after a brief pause. "Then I wouldn't have to believe this either." She spoke as if deciphering an ancient inscription on a tablet of clay. "I knew something was wrong, somehow. Admiral Caselnes wouldn't show his face, and Mrs. Caselnes was acting strangely, too…"

She trailed off into silence. A gigantic dragon was rising from a trench far beneath her surface of awareness and sensibility. Julian's whole body stiffened as he sensed its presence. Frederica lowered her gaze to the floor. Julian was afraid that he would flee at the moment she began to cry.

Frederica raised her face again. It was dry, but her vitality and reality seemed wiped away by the sponge of grief.

"He wasn't supposed to die this way," she said. "He should have died the way he lived…"

With the tumult of war more than a generation in the past, an old man lives in an age of peace. They say he was once a famous warrior, but few remain who saw this with their own eyes, and he himself never brags of his military service. Treated by his young family members with seven parts affection and three parts neglect, he lives now on his pension. His sunroom has a large rocking chair where he can sit for hours until called for dinner, reading so quietly he almost becomes part of the furniture too. Day after day, as if time has stopped.

One day, the old man's granddaughter is playing outside when she accidentally throws her ball through the sunroom's entrance. It comes to rest by his feet. Normally, he would reach down slowly to pick it up for her, but this time he does not move, as if ignoring her calls. She runs in for her ball, then looks up into her grandfather's face to scold him—but senses something she cannot explain.

—Grandpa?

There is no answer. The setting sun illuminates the man's face, peaceful as if in sleep, from the side. Still clutching her ball, the girl runs into the living room to report what she has seen.

—Mommy! Daddy! Something's wrong with Grandpa!

As the girl's voice recedes into the distance, the old man still sits in his rocking chair. Eternal peace slowly begins to fill his face, as if the tide were coming in...

That, thinks Frederica, is how Yang Wen-li should have died. It is less a certainty than a memory of a real scene witnessed through déjà vu.

Yang had spent his life on the front lines, fighting the greatest enemies, or struggling in the jaws of conspiracies against him. Frederica herself had once saved him from what seemed like certain death. And yet somehow she had always thought of her husband as a man who would not quite go over the edge.

"But perhaps this sort of death was like him after all. If Valhalla exists, he must be busy there apologizing to Marshal Bucock. After all, the marshal left him in charge of things only six months ago..."

The movement of Frederica's tongue and lips ceased. Beneath her skin, now drained of blood, the sea dragon was awakening. She put her last ounce of self-control into her low voice.

"Please, Julian, let me be alone for a while. I'll go and see him once I've pulled myself together a little."

Julian did as he was told.

V

The sun had set on Iserlohn. The boisterous festival was over, ended with the tolling of a type of bell hitherto unimaginable.

At that moment, the entire population of Iserlohn Fortress, down to the lowest-ranking soldier, lay submerged in the well of grief. But, with the passage of time, shock and confusion were sure to give way to a turbulence engulfing every floor of the base. And the luxury of surrendering to that madness would not be permitted to the leadership. They had to reveal the news of Yang's death to the outside world, organize his funeral, and try to fill, however inadequately, the yawning chasm that had opened in their ranks. The responsibilities that came with their position were intense.

As von Schönkopf had foreseen during the voyage back to Iserlohn, that leadership also urged Julian to direct his attention to the matter of Yang's successor. Attenborough spoke to him with particular force, saying, "Humans don't fight for isms or theories! They fight for those who embody them. For the revolutionaries, not the revolution. We'll be fighting in the late marshal Yang's name one way or another, but even then we need someone to represent him in our world."

Giving up the fight entirely was not an option Attenborough seemed to have considered. Of course, Julian felt the same way.

"We need a *leader*," Attenborough insisted.

"We need a political leader too, with Dr. Romsky gone," said Julian.

He thought that Attenborough had simply forgotten this point, but the self-described champion of "foppery and whim" did not seem taken aback in the slightest. Their political leader had already been decided, he explained, as if it were quite obvious.

"Who do you mean?" asked Julian.

"Mrs. Frederica Greenhill Yang, of course."

Astonishment has many colors, but what came to mind for Julian just then were Frederica's hazel eyes.

"We haven't told her yet, of course," said Attenborough. "That'll have to wait a day or two, I suppose, until she calms down a little. But whoever Yang's political successor turns out to be in the long term, right now she's the best we have. No offense to the late Dr. Romsky, but Mrs. Yang has him beat on all fronts—name recognition, chance of sympathy from the republican faction, everything. She might not have the political insight and finesse of the great figures in history, but we only need her to be better than Dr. Romsky. Right?"

Julian couldn't answer right away. What Attenborough said seemed on-target, but would Frederica accept that kind of position? Or would she view it as stepping over her own husband's body to seize power for herself, and refuse?

Julian looked uncertainly at Alex Caselnes, who met his gaze frankly. "Sometimes even Attenborough gets it right," said the great military administrator. "Including the political judgment. If we want to be accepted as legitimate successors in terms of democratic republican governance, we need Mrs. Yang as our political representative. Of course, if she refuses, that'll be the end of that, but…"

"I think she will refuse," said Julian. "She's always been dedicated to her role as an assistant. To accept a post at the top…Especially—"

"Listen, Julian," said Caselnes, leaning forward over the table. "In politics, the second generation is when institutions and legal systems gain their power to bind. The first generation simply doesn't get a say."

If Yang Wen-li had been the political representative of the republican democratic faction in life, for his wife to take on that role now would be a kind of familial succession, essentially taking private control of the position. However, in reality Yang had constantly refused that position, meaning that his wife Frederica could accept it with full political legitimacy. He had left his wife a political bequest of sorts, but not of the kind that mattered to institutions or legal systems.

"With all due respect, sir, that's a stretch," Julian said, somewhat stiffly. He saw the reason in what Caselnes said, but his emotions failed to follow suit. Frederica had just lost her husband. He did not think it right to weigh her down with another heavy burden just to make things easier for themselves.

After Julian left the room, the rest of the leadership exchanged glances.

A visibly tired Caselnes sighed. "I get the feeling Julian won't be eager to accept his own new role either—as the leader of our military," he said.

Von Schönkopf stroked his chin in silence. Both of them had hoped to hand to Julian the chair that Yang's death had left empty.

Granting that position to a teenager would garner some objections, but Reinhard von Lohengramm had been nothing but a "golden brat" himself before conquering the galaxy. Even Yang Wen-li had been just another bookish officer right up until he'd became the hero of El Facil. A hero was something you became, not something you were born into being. Julian might be a callow and inexperienced youth now, but—

"The fact is, he was Yang Wen-li's ward and his apprentice in military tactics. We can't ignore that. It might even be more important than his actual ability."

"His charisma, you mean?"

"I don't care about terminology. What matters is who can best reflect the lingering light of the star that Yang Wen-li was."

Both agreed that Julian was the only reasonable candidate for this. Of course, lieutenants would be both necessary and important. Making Julian bear the weight alone was not the goal. But ultimately, among the responsibilities to be divided, someone had to play the role of "face."

Yang had recognized potential in Julian too, and expected great things of him. With another ten years, that potential might have moved from the domain of hypothesis to reality. At this stage, all they could do was value his possibilities as highly as possible.

"The question is whether the rest of the troops will agree with us. If we put Julian forward as commander, they might respond by feigning allegiance without actually obeying his orders."

"I suppose we need to start with a change in our own thinking."

First, the leadership of Iserlohn itself would have to respect Julian's authority, obey his instructions and orders, and accept that his position and decisions took precedence. They could hardly expect the enlisted men and women to do this if they were not prepared to do it themselves. Eventually a test would come for Julian's abilities and caliber as a military leader. If he could clear that hurdle, he would become a star giving off its own light, however faint.

"There'll be deserters anyway, of course," said Caselnes. "That's unavoidable. More than half of those with us today are here because they wanted to fight under Yang himself."

"The luminaries of the Revolutionary Government of El Facil will no doubt be the first to go," said von Schönkopf. "Opportunists, the lot of them, hoping to use Yang Wen-li's military abilities and fame to achieve their own goals."

Caselnes frowned. "Who cares? Let those who want to leave, leave. Numbers aren't our strength in the first place. What matters is firming up our core."

In fact, that would be better. There would be no pursuing those who left. Forcing them to remain dissatisfied in the ranks would only leave a chain of volcanoes running through the forces. Leaders would have to worry when these would erupt, and if a bloody purge one day proved necessary to eliminate the problem, their wounds would only grow deeper and wider. For now, some contraction was unavoidable.

What could not be dismissed as unavoidable was Julian's own standpoint. When they had asked him earlier to take Yang's place at the head of the Revolutionary Reserves, he had looked at the older men more in exasperation than surprise. It took twenty heartbeats to organize his counteroffensive.

"What about Vice Admiral Attenborough? He made admiral at twenty-seven, even younger than Marshal Yang. He has the record, and he has the support."

"Can't be Attenborough."

"Why not?"

"He said he prefers to stay behind the scenes."

"But…"

"We do, too," said Caselnes. "Julian, enough. It's time to stand up. We'll be there to support your legs, for all the good that'll do."

"And if you fall, we'll all come down together," added von Schönkopf unhelpfully, drawing a frown from Caselnes.

Julian was able to get away with that least creative of replies: "Let me think about it." Commander of the Yang Fleet! The position was sacred to him, inviolable. He had dreamed of being Yang's chief of staff, but the commander's chair was light-years away from any such imagining. After a short period of deep confusion, Julian went to talk with Frederica about it. Mrs. Caselnes had suggested this, hoping to give Frederica an opportunity for distraction.

"Why not?"

Frederica's quiet response took Julian by surprise. "I didn't expect you to agree with them, Frederica," he said. "I mean, come on! Just imagine it! There's no way I could do what Marshal Yang did!"

"Of course not." Frederica's voice remained quiet as she surprised Julian again, this time by agreeing with his objection. "Of course not, Julian. No one could do what Yang Wen-li did."

"Exactly. The gap between our abilities is just too wide."

"No, Julian. It's a difference in personality. You simply have to do what only you can. There's no need to imitate him. In all of history, there's only ever been one Yang Wen-li—but there's also only ever been one Julian Mintz."

Before long, Frederica would be offered an unwanted position of her own. Alex Caselnes visited her, offered some condolences he doubted met muster, and asked her directly to become their political representative.

"If there's no other way, I'll do what I can," she said. "But I'll need support and cooperation from a lot of people. If I'm to be your representative, I need to be able to give instructions, if not orders, and know that they'll be followed. Can I ask for that in advance?"

Caselnes nodded with his whole body.

Julian found it hardest to hide how strange he found it that Frederica had accepted. She explained to him the next time they were alone.

"I spent twelve years with Wen-li. For the first eight, I was just a fan. For the next three, I was his aide, and for the last year, I was his wife. Starting now, my years—decades—as a widow begin. If I have to spend the days and months alone, I want to help something more than dust accumulate on the foundation he laid. Even if I can raise it only a millimeter. And..."

Frederica closed her mouth. She looked to Julian less like someone lost in thought than someone listening to a voice that was counseling and scolding her.

"And if we—the ones Wen-li left behind—fail now, we'll be making a mockery of what he always said about terror not moving history. So, even though I know I'm not right for the job, I intend to fulfill my responsibilities. People called Wen-li lazy, but I can swear to one thing: when something needed doing, and he was the only one who could do it, he always did it."

"Thank you, Frederica. That's inspiring. I won't run from my responsibility either. If they need me as military commander, even just as a figurehead, I'll take the job on."

Frederica shook her head, sending her blond-brown hair moving violently.

"Inspiring? Hardly. To tell you the truth, I don't care if democracy vanishes. The whole galaxy could return to individual atoms, and I wouldn't mind a bit. If only I had him by my side, half-asleep with a book in his lap…"

Julian couldn't decide how to respond. He realized then that decisions were the product not of intellect but of capacity. Cursing his own immaturity from the bottom of his heart, he called Mrs. Caselnes in and prepared to leave.

VI

Schönkopf's observation-cum-prophecy was all too accurate. The news of Yang's death had every corner of the gigantic fortress restless and uneasy. Soldiers and civilians whispered in small, huddled groups. Optimism went into hibernation, and a great flock of pessimism took wing across the cold winter fields of the base's psyche.

"Without Yang, the Yang Fleet is just a band of fugitive mercenaries. Fault lines will open up eventually, and then it'll fall apart. The only questions are, will that happen sooner or later, and will there be bloodshed or not?"

After Yang's death was made public, such talk inevitably arose. The news that Julian would be Yang's successor as military leader only seemed to fuel the unease, although Caselnes had anticipated this before making the announcement. Doubts, objections, even jeering were heard. The turbulence had found the direction it should go.

"Julian Mintz may have been Yang Wen-li's ward, but why should we salute him as commander? Headquarters has plenty of men who can outrank *and* outfight him. I mean, why him of all people?"

"Why give military command to some *flaxen-haired brat*, you mean?" This was Dusty Attenborough, tone withering enough to pierce even the wall of public opinion. "Because what we need isn't a diary of the past but a calendar of the future."

"But he's just too young and inexperienced. You can't compare him to Kaiser Reinhard."

"So what?"

Despite Attenborough's resistance, the Four Horsemen of Dissatisfaction, Uncertainty, Anxiety, and Powerlessness seemed to gallop unseen through the base, poisoning people's reason.

On the morning of June 5, Vice Admiral Murai visited Julian's quarters to make an announcement.

"Julian, starting now, I intend to fulfill my final responsibility to the Yang Fleet. With your permission, of course."

"What responsibility is that, Admiral?" Julian asked, ruing the limits of his powers of observation and deduction.

"Leading the dissatisfied and restless elements out of Iserlohn," said Murai simply.

A single drop of cold rain fell on Julian's heart. Had Murai given up on him? Decided that Julian was not worth cooperating with?

"Can't I change your mind, Admiral? You're the linchpin of the entire Yang Fleet."

For four years, in the shadow of Yang's magic and miracles, Murai had steadfastly fulfilled his duties as chief as staff. Now he solemnly shook his head.

"If anything, you'll be better off without me. I can't be of any more use to you here. Do I have your permission to retire?"

The years had left their mark on Murai's face. Julian noticed the streaks of white in his hair and was struck temporarily speechless.

"It's also the loss of Fischer and Patrichev," Murai said. "It's getting lonely around here, and I'm exhausted. Serving under Marshal Yang let me achieve a position far beyond my talents or achievements. I'm grateful for that."

Behind his plain, unembellished words, Julian caught a glimpse of his mental state.

"If I announce my departure now, the restless fringe elements will rally around me. They'll have the justification they want to leave: *Even Murai from headquarters is seceding!* I hope you understand what I'm aiming to achieve."

Julian felt that he understood Murai's feelings, to an extent. It was also clear that he did not have the capacity to keep the admiral at Iserlohn. The right thing to do was to thank him for his loyalty to Yang and send him off with his blessing.

"I trust you to do what you think best, Admiral. Thank you for everything. I mean that."

Julian bowed his head to Murai's departing form. The admiral was a coolheaded, meticulous man; a stickler for protocol and regulations who valued common sense and order. Had he always seemed so frail, though? When had that ramrod-straight back begun to develop a stoop? As Julian realized many things he had not noticed before, his head bowed again of its own accord.

In the corridor outside, Murai ran into Attenborough, and told the young man of his departure from Iserlohn.

"You'll be better off without me here. Finally give you a chance to spread your wings."

"No argument here. Of course, half the fun of drinking is breaking the rules against it."

Attenborough's voice had more feeling in it than the joke alone justified. He offered Murai his right hand.

"People are going to say terrible things about you. You're choosing to be the man everyone loves to hate."

"I can handle that. Compared to spending more time with you and your gang, it'll be a minor inconvenience."

With that, the two shook hands and parted ways.

Later that day, Julian was summoned by half a dozen members of the Revolutionary Government of El Facil, all wearing the same expression as he came in, and was presented with a painstakingly businesslike declaration.

"We have learned that Vice Admiral Murai is leaving Iserlohn. For unrelated reasons, we have decided to dissolve the revolutionary government.

We thought it best to let you know. Of course, we had no obligation to tell you, but…"

"I see," said Julian, with a lack of warmth that made the officials fidget uncomfortably.

"Don't think badly of us. The independence of El Facil was largely a pet project of Dr. Romsky's. He set the mood, and we were dragged along with his hopeless revolutionary activities."

Their obvious attempt to evade blame by placing it on the shoulders of one already dead rubbed Julian's sensibilities very strongly the wrong way.

"Was Dr. Romsky a dictator? Did you have no freedom to oppose him?"

The government officials had managed to lull their shame to sleep, but Julian's words shook it awake, and their struggle to keep it under control was evident in their voices.

"The point is that both Dr. Romsky and Marshal Yang are, tragically, dead. Our anti-imperial revolutionary activities have lost both their political and military leadership. What is the point in further confrontation and resistance?"

Julian had no reply.

"We must move past our attachment to a particular political system and take a broader view, working for the peace and unification of all humanity. Hate and hostility bear no fruit. You and your faction, too, would do well to drop the pose of martyrdom for the sake of a dead man's ideals."

Julian called on his full capacity for patience. "I will not stop you from leaving," he said. "But I hope you will allow us to part on good terms. There is no need to denounce what you yourselves were until only yesterday. I offer my thanks for all you have done for us. Now, if I may be excused?"

Haughtily, the officials granted permission for Julian to take his leave. He understood Murai's true intentions now—to take care of people like this. All those who lacked the bravery to succeed, fearing for their reputation or safety, Murai would gather together and lead away—knowing full well that he would bear the mark of deserter himself. Julian thanked the admiral silently, and marveled once more at Yang's insight in choosing a man like Murai for his staff.

Among the residents of Iserlohn who wavered were others who stood stone-still. One of these was Wiliabard Joachim Merkatz, former senior admiral with the Galactic Imperial Navy, now diligently following his strategic and tactical research plan even as he mourned Yang.

"I've thought about it often," he mused to his aide, Bernhard von Schneider. "Would it have been better to die at Lippstadt when Reinhard defeated me? But I don't feel that way anymore. I spent almost sixty years living in fear of failure, but then I finally came to understand that there was another way to live. I owe the ones who taught me that a debt of gratitude, and I intend to pay it."

Von Schneider nodded. It was he who had saved Merkatz's life three years before at Lippstadt. He, too, had agonized more than once over whether he had been right to do so, but now it seemed that the answer was clear. The way forward might be uphill, but it was the road he had chosen himself. He had no intention of straying from it.

On June 6, Iserlohn Fortress issued an announcement in the name of Julian Mintz, commander of the Revolutionary Reserves, announcing the death of Yang Wen-li and the formal funeral service to be held for him that day. At the same time, the Revolutionary Government of El Facil declared its dissolution, bringing its short history to an end.

CHAPTER 7:

HOLLOW VICTORY

I

ONE MAN'S DEATH brought despair to his allies and dejection to his enemies.

At 1910 on June 6, year 2 of the New Imperial Calendar, the Imperial Navy caught the transmission directed by Iserlohn Fortress at the entire galaxy. At 1925, the news of Yang Wen-li's death was brought to Reinhard on the bridge of the fleet flagship *Brünhild* by his new chief advisor Hildegard von Mariendorf.

Hilda's beautiful face, framed by her boyishly short hair, was dominated by uncertainty. Both her wisdom and the will that kept it under orderly control were drifting like thin ice on the waters of spring.

"Your Majesty, I must report something to you. Iserlohn Fortress just made a public announcement."

She spoke in a voice that did not suit her: hard, but with no edge. The kaiser's guarded gaze met her own across the room.

"Yang Wen-li is dead."

When Reinhard understood the meaning of his beautiful secretary's words, disappointment came down on him like lightning. He gripped the posts of his bed with both of his fair hands. This seemed partly to support his graceful form and partly to convey the violent emotions he felt even to inanimate objects. His ice-blue eyes were filled with something close to rage as he fixed them on the countess.

"Fräulein...Fräulein!"

His gorgeous golden hair was filled with the wind.

"You have brought me bad news many times, but this is the limit. Do you have the right to disappoint me so?"

Beneath skin like virgin snow, his blood vessels had become passageways for passions that now boiled over. He felt personally insulted. The man he had battled until that day, had anticipated matching strategies with again, had even hoped to get to know as a person through their upcoming talks, was suddenly gone. Did he truly have to accept such a senseless outcome? His rising fury suddenly escaped to the outside world in the form of a shout.

"Everyone leaves me! Enemies, friends, everyone! Why do they not live on for my sake?"

Hilda had never seen Reinhard reveal emotions so negative or express himself so violently. Forgetting even his unjustified attack on her, she gazed at the young kaiser. The golden-haired conqueror, wrenched by a boundless sense of loss, looked miserable and alone.

Reinhard had not been born with enemies, but it was undeniable that over the course of his life it had always been enemies who showed him the path he must take. The Goldenbaum Dynasty and its parasitic clique of nobles. The Free Planets Alliance and its admirals. How brightly his life had shone as he defeated them all in battle! But now he had lost the highest and greatest enemy of all of them, which meant he had also lost the opportunity to develop, to shine even brighter. His rage might have been connected to fear. Yang's death partly echoed the demise of Siegfried Kircheis. Reinhard had once more lost the presence he needed most.

"I need an enemy."

And yet Yang Wen-li had left him with everything still to be settled! He had stolen from Reinhard forever the chance to triumph over him. He had forced on Reinhard alone the duty of building their new age. He had set a course for another dimension, unaccompanied and unhesitating.

Had Reinhard not been sick in bed, he would have been pacing around his room. Disappointment turned to furious energy blazing within his porcelain cheeks.

"I do not recall granting that man permission to be slain by any hands other than my own. He denied me victory at Vermillion and at Iserlohn Corridor, he killed I know not how many of my precious commanders—and now he allows another man to murder him?!"

Reinhard's angry denunciation might have seemed illogical in the extreme to an outside observer, but Hilda understood that Reinhard himself felt it was perfectly fair. Eventually the fire of the kaiser's fury died down, but the gloom of his disappointment only deepened.

"Fräulein von Mariendorf."

"Yes, Your Majesty."

"I wish to send a representative to Iserlohn. An envoy to convey my condolences. Who do you feel might be suitable?"

"Shall I go, Your Majesty?"

"No, I need you here with me."

Startled, Hilda looked at the golden-haired conqueror's face before blushing internally. *Foolish! For an instant just now, what I was I thinking?*

"You are my chief advisor, after all," Reinhard added.

He did not notice the slight change in volume of the blood that flowed beneath Hilda's skin. He was intent on following the course of his own thoughts. This, Hilda knew, was simply the kind of person he was.

"Ah—I shall send Müller. I recall that he and Yang met face-to-face after the Vermillion War."

Informed by Hilda of the kaiser's will, Senior Admiral Neidhart Müller accepted the mission without complaint.

The life-or-death struggle he had waged against Yang Wen-li as second-in-command to Senior Admiral Karl Gustav Kempf was already two years in the past. After his defeat and failure to save Kempf's life, Müller had hoped to settle the score against Yang in a second battle, but that feeling had now sublimated to respect for his great enemy.

How many other comrades had he lost? Time of war or not, dwelling on the deaths of so many fine leaders, from Siegfried Kircheis to Lennenkamp,

Fahrenheit, and Steinmetz left Müller feeling a sense of desolation. But perhaps that list would now grow no longer. He tried to convince himself of this, but the winter clouds above his psyche showed no sign of allowing light through.

Yang's death came as a tremendous shock to the other imperial staff officers too. There were gasps and exchanged glances as they struggled to digest the ill-starred news.

Some were suspicious about whether they could truly be sure that Yang *was* dead, arguing that he might only have feigned his demise. But this was indeed mere suspicion, and none could offer any explanation for why Yang might resort to such a ruse. His startling battlefield strategies had made him famous, but faking his own death would have been out of character.

"Perhaps not, but we all know how wily he is," objected one officer. "Who knows what he might be planning?"

But neither Yang's admirers nor those who reviled him had ever imagined they would lose their greatest enemy in this way. The leaders of the Imperial Navy had always assumed that if Yang died, it would be in battle against them. And Reinhard, leader of those leaders, had believed this most strongly of all.

Oskar von Reuentahl had once told his chief of staff Hans Eduard Bergengrün, "Only one man in the galaxy has the right to slay Yang Wen-li: mein kaiser, Reinhard von Lohengramm. Even Odin All-father cannot usurp it." It is an open question, of course, whether von Reuentahl was sincere or simply commenting slyly on Reinhard's fixation on his opponent.

"Do you think he would die so easily?" some insisted. "It's some distasteful trap, mark my words. Yang is alive and in hiding." Perhaps it was precisely those who came to those conclusions based on no evidence who subconsciously hoped most fervently that Yang was still alive. It was fair to say that after the fall of the Free Planets Alliance, most of the mighty Galactic Imperial Navy's battles had been waged against Yang Wen-li alone. The unfortunate Dr. Romsky and his revolutionary government did not even draw comment from the Imperial Navy.

In any case, the imperial officers were unable to take any pleasure in the eradication of their enemy in this way. Even Wittenfeld, who seemed to nurture the strongest animosity of all toward Yang, paced the bridge of his flagship *Königs Tiger* in a thin haze of disappointment and discouragement, and his staff officers took care not to provide a catalyst that might turn their commander's disappointment into rage.

At the Battle of the Corridor, Wittenfeld had been the man responsible for the death of Vice Admiral Edwin Fischer, master of fleet operations for the Yang Fleet. It could even be said that Wittenfeld was the figure who had, if indirectly, set the course of Yang's fortunes from then on—but he himself had no way of knowing this, and no way of shaking off the feeling that Yang had taken his winnings and fled.

Enfolded in dull exhaustion, the Imperial Navy waited for new instructions from the kaiser.

II

In the first weeks of June, Julian Mintz was no more than a minor companion star to Yang Wen-li's dazzling sun. The imperial leadership had barely heard of him. The only admiral who had met the flaxen-haired youth was Wahlen, and that encounter had taken place under bizarre circumstances on Terra, with Julian using a false identity.

When Mittermeier raised the eminently reasonable question of who this Julian Mintz was who claimed to be Yang's representative, the intelligence division needed some time to respond. After an hour of combing through their data, they informed Mittermeier that Julian had been Yang's legal ward and was eighteen years old.

"I see. Poor kid. He's got hard times ahead."

This was not meant ironically. Mittermeier genuinely sympathized with the young man following in the footsteps of a predecessor who was simply too great to be equaled. He could foresee the difficulties that lay ahead for Julian, and knew that the more self-confident and competent he was, the deeper his missteps would be, and the more difficult to recover from.

The Imperial Navy was abuzz with opinions on the situation. "It doesn't matter who Yang's successor is—there's no way he'll be able to do as well as Yang did, let alone better," people said. "There's no guarantee that his troops will even follow him. The last redoubt of democracy proved impregnable to its enemies, but soon it'll be consumed from within." The troops' predictions of the decline and fall of Iserlohn as a democratic republic were an expression of their own excitement at the prospect of returning home. Regardless of the reasons, the day was near when they would finally put cursed, blood-soaked Iserlohn behind them and return to their homes and the families or lovers that awaited them there. Praise be to peace!

Shock and despondency changed slowly but surely into optimism and anticipation. It was already ten months since the troops of the Imperial Navy had left their homes to accompany the kaiser on his campaign. Those who served under Steinmetz had not seen the faces of their spouses or lovers or parents in over a year. Now that the great obstacle of the enemy was removed, their longing for home became stronger by the day.

One day after Müller departed as envoy, von Reuentahl paid a visit to Mittermeier. It had been some time since the two friends had enjoyed drinks and conversation together.

"It wouldn't surprise me if that multitalented minister of military affairs of ours had reached out and plunged the knife into Yang Wen-li's heart himself," said von Reuentahl. "Although I suppose even he can't be behind *every* intrigue in the galaxy."

"Not if I have anything to do with it," growled Mittermeier, and drained a glass of bitterness and dark beer.

How many times had the two of them gone drinking together since their first meeting on the front lines eleven years ago? Roaming the night streets with their arms around each other's shoulders, getting into fights but never getting the worse for them…Now they had both risen to the rank of marshal; they were senior imperial retainers, unable to carouse as freely as they had in those days. As commander in chief of the Imperial Space Armada, Wolfgang Mittermeier stood at the head of a hundred thousand ships; as secretary-general of Supreme Command Headquarters, Oskar von Reuentahl had a place by Reinhard's side and would one day rule the entire territory of the former alliance, the so-called Neue Land, as its governor-general.

That posting, however, would be effective only once the empire had defeated its immediate enemy, Yang Wen-li, and unified the entire galaxy. As a result, strange as it was, in those first weeks of June most of the Neue Land was not under the supervision of any imperial official at all. Admiral Alfred Grillparzer, the "Young Geographer," administered the imperial occupation of the planet Heinessen, former capital of the Free Planets Alliance, but who was responsible for the other alliance worlds, other stellar regions?

Nothing was decided, except perhaps within the breast of the young, unmarried, and childless kaiser. Presumably they would learn of his decisions on these political and military matters within the next few days, but the absence of any successor or heir to Reinhard made Mittermeier uneasy nonetheless.

Meanwhile, von Reuentahl nursed his own source of unease.

You grant me status and authority beyond what I deserve, mein Kaiser, but what is it you want in return? Is it enough to be a loyal and effective cog in your engine of conquest?

If that were all Reinhard desired, the bargain was one von Reuentahl could accept. A senior statesman and veteran admiral within the second galactic dynasty, respected as a capable and loyal official: such a life, and indeed death, was far from undesirable. If it was not quite in accord with his inborn essence, well, not all men could be guaranteed a life fully true to their nature.

Gazing into the reflection of his heterochromiac eyes in the mirror, von Reuentahl felt as if the *Ambivalenz* within him were fully exposed. If he could choose the path he wished, perhaps he would lead a life of both an incomparable liege and an incomparable friend, just like in a textbook. He found this idea endlessly tantalizing, although he knew that this was precisely because it was out of reach. This had been a bitter realization.

Soon the conversation moved on to military matters. How were they to dispose of Iserlohn Fortress now that Yang was gone?

"What do you think?" asked Mittermeier.

"An offensive operation is the only possible choice in both political and military terms. First we demand surrender, offering amnesty to the entire Yang Fleet. If they hold firm, we strike with the full power of the Imperial Navy. How would you approach it?"

"I feel the same way. With Yang Wen-li dead, Odin All-father grants the entire galaxy to the kaiser. To reject it would be to defy the will of the gods."

Was it not their lot now to plunge into the corridor with full force and smash the now-headless Iserlohn Fortress in fire and blood?

"However," Mittermeier added, "I doubt that the kaiser will deem it proper to attack an army in mourning."

Von Reuentahl looked at Mittermeier in silence. About to speak, he closed his mouth again to choose his words more carefully.

"And you feel that this is mere sentimentality? Until very recently, I would have agreed, but…"

"You have had a change of heart, then?"

"Everything depends on how you look at it, von Reuentahl. You and I both opposed entering the corridor initially, but the kaiser ignored our advice because of the presence of his great enemy, Yang Wen-li. Now that enemy is gone. Surely the most natural thing would be for the kaiser to return to his original strategy."

Von Reuentahl lowered his black-and-blue gaze to his glass. His pinched expression belied the alcohol on his breath as he exhaled.

"Surely you understand, Mittermeier, that yesterday's optimal strategy may be inappropriate today. The correct strategy while Yang Wen-li was alive may hold less value after his death. Of course, if the kaiser agrees with you, perhaps my thinking is wrong."

Between the two men, dark beer foamed.

"The character of the Imperial Navy will soon change. Where once it looked outward to conquer, it will turn inward to keep the peace within the empire. If everything is wrapped up according to plan, that is."

"Let it change, then. Most of our men will soon return home alive. The galaxy is all but unified. What objection can there be to that?"

"And you can return to your beloved wife, eh, Mittermeier?"

"Something for which I am very grateful," said the highest-ranking man in the Imperial Navy.

Von Reuentahl watched his old friend toss back another beer. They were very different by nature, but they had walked the paths of life and death together for years. The black of von Reuentahl's right eye was deep in shadow, but his blue left eye glinted sharply, as if signaling the two sides of his personality.

Mittermeier's lively gray eyes took this in and then, with some hesitation, he asked a question. "Whatever became of that woman who said she was pregnant with your child, by the way?"

All expression vanished from von Reuentahl's face as he answered. "She gave birth on the second of May. A boy, apparently."

Mittermeier grunted noncommittally. Neither congratulations nor condolences seemed entirely appropriate.

"It's mine," continued von Reuentahl. "Of that there is no doubt. Born in defiance of the gods, just like his father. If he makes it to adulthood, I'm sure he'll be quite the outcast. One red eye, one yellow, perhaps."

"Von Reuentahl, I don't expect you to be objective about the woman herself, but—"

"But the child is blameless?"

Mittermeier shrugged. "I'm not a father myself."

This counterattack was more effective than he had expected, wiping away the self-deprecating sneer of von Reuentahl, who almost seemed to recoil. Angels danced roguishly in the air between the two.

"You're better off that way," von Reuentahl said at last. "Less fear of betrayal. But enough about that. There's no reason for us to fight over a baby neither of us has even seen."

Mittermeier and von Reuentahl exchanged a slightly awkward handshake and parted. Of course, they had no way of knowing—knowing that this would be the final handshake between the Twin Ramparts of the Imperial Navy, and the final drinks they would ever share. It was June 8 in the second year of the New Imperial Calendar.

III

After parting ways with von Reuentahl, Mittermeier returned to the bridge of his flagship *Beowulf* to brood over the imperial ships on-screen. Bayerlein stood by his side, confusion and uncertainty in his usually spirited face.

"Does this mean it's all over, sir?" asked Bayerlein.

"An excellent question."

"It somehow feels as if…as if half the galaxy has turned to void. Yang Wen-li was a sworn enemy of mein Kaiser, but no one can deny that he was also a superb tactician. Just as day needs night to express its nature, I wonder if we didn't need him too."

For a moment, Mittermeier's heart beat faster as a kind of unease filled his breast. Then he firmly shook his head of unruly, honey-colored hair. Still unsure what had brought the feeling on, he changed the subject.

"When we get back to Phezzan, it'll be one funeral after another. Fahrenheit, Steinmetz, Minister von Silberberg…"

Bayerlein sighed. "What a year this has been!" he said. "It will surely go down in history as one of the Lohengramm Dynasty's worst."

"And it's only half-over."

"Please, Marshal, don't remind me! I only hope that I have already used up my annual allocation of bad luck."

Mittermeier chuckled at the utter sincerity on Bayerlein's face. If there really were such a thing as an allocation of bad luck and ill fortune, it would be much easier for people and states alike to draw up their plans for the future. Even his own wife Evangeline would no longer need to offer those devout, anxious prayers for his safety to Odin All-father every time he went out on campaign.

Suddenly something occurred to him. He turned to look at his subordinate. "Bayerlein, you have lady friends at home, surely?"

"No, sir."

"Not even one?"

"Er—well, no—that is, the service is my first love, sir."

Mittermeier was silent.

"Wait—no—I mean, I do hope to find someone as charming as your wife, sir, one day."

"Bayerlein."

"Yes, sir?"

"I've done my best to teach you how to lead men into battle. But when it comes to finding love and telling jokes, you'll have to figure it out yourself. Nothing wrong with a little independent study now and then."

Clapping his subordinate lightly on the shoulder, Mittermeier exited the bridge.

The kaiser was abandoning his campaign of conquest and turning back for home.

The news was announced to the entire Imperial Navy on June 7, just after Senior Admiral Müller departed for Iserlohn Fortress as funeral envoy. Mittermeier had been right: Reinhard could not bring himself to raise arms against an army in mourning. Although if the army in question had been Duke von Braunschweig and the rest of the nobility during the Lippstadt War, Mittermeier doubted that the kaiser would have had such compunctions.

Is this the flower of chivalry? Or has the kaiser simply lost his taste for conquest?

The question nagged at both Mittermeier and von Reuentahl as they diligently attended to their respective duties. Mittermeier was reorganizing the ranks of the entire navy for the journey back, while von Reuentahl was putting imperial headquarters in order, starting by sending wounded soldiers home.

The posthumous promotion of Fahrenheit and Steinmetz to imperial marshal had already been decided, but the kaiser had decided to further honor them with the Siegfried Kircheis Distinguished Service Award, named for his late friend. The state coffers would pay for their funerals as well as their gravestones, which was the highest honor a member of the imperial military could receive. However, in a Reinhardian touch—indeed, a Lohengrammian one—the only text carved on those gravestones would be their names, ranks, and dates of birth and death. When Reinhard's own gravestone was eventually put in place, it, too, bore nothing save the words "Kaiser Reinhard von Lohengramm" and his dates of birth, death, and accession to the throne.

Once Müller had returned from Iserlohn Fortress, the Imperial Navy's withdrawal began. There was no risk of enemy attack, but their professional military pride would not permit a disorderly departure. And so, in crisp, disciplined formation, the Imperial Navy left the region of Iserlohn Corridor.

Yang Wen-li is dead. He was the greatest defender of democratic republican governance and—excepting one other man—the greatest and best military leader in five centuries. Will his death mean the collapse of the republican faction? I once thought so myself, but I am no longer sure. Irrespective of his own desires in life, in death Yang Wen-li seems to have become an unimpeachable presence within the movement for democracy. Among those determined to continue his legacy and therefore his war, Iserlohn will surely become holy ground. Depending on the talent and capacity of that leadership, this meaningless fighting might not be over just yet. Of course, trapped on Iserlohn they will not be able to withstand the Imperial Navy for long, so what concerns me more is the possibility that other groups might seek to make use of them...In any case, let us give thanks for now to the kaiser and his staff for granting me the good fortune to return safely and see your face again...

The letter Mittermeier sent to his wife Evangeline contained a prophecy that escaped even him at the time.

IV

Though confined to his bed by illness, Reinhard had not ceased his work as emperor. Military affairs he left to marshals Mittermeier and von Reuentahl, but on the political side he dealt with all the day-to-day issues an autocrat must: building new structures of governance, reforming the legal and tax systems, establishing communication and transportation networks to organically merge existing territories with vast, newly acquired ones, and so on.

When his fever fell during the day, he ignored the protestations and prohibitions of his medical team, sat up in bed, and summoned to his sickroom the civilian officials he had brought on campaign with him. He approved paperwork by the ream, asked questions, offered admonishments when no answers were forthcoming, assigned new projects, and generally maintained vigorous and active.

These circumstances had arisen partly out of Reinhard's own energetic nature, but they were also a result of the death of von Silberberg, his trusted secretary of works, at the hands of terrorists. He had not been able to find anyone else who could do in the civilian realm what von Reuentahl and Mittermeier did in the military sphere. With each passing day, Reinhard's private regret for the loss of the inventive and diligent von Silberberg grew.

The head of Reinhard's cabinet, Minister of Domestic Affairs Count Franz von Mariendorf, was sincere in both his duties and in his personal dealings with the kaiser. He was a man of fairness and integrity, with sound judgment and a good eye for personnel in the context of imperial governance, but he was not the kind of politician who actively sought to build a new age.

Nor had Reinhard ever expected this of him. It was sufficient that the count faithfully carried out his orders and fulfilled his duties—or so Reinhard had thought. Now, however, with the burden of military affairs gradually falling from the kaiser's shoulders, he was beginning to feel that he did need someone to share the political burden with him after all. Von Silberberg might have been that man. If Siegfried Kircheis had still been alive, he would have complemented Reinhard's political abilities more than adequately. But both were now gone from this world.

He could have sought what he needed in Hilda, Count von Mariendorf's daughter. But by appointing her chief advisor at his imperial headquarters and strengthening her authority over military affairs, Reinhard had weakened her standing to speak politically. Even in an autocracy, the division between civilian and military officials had to be maintained. There were always exceptions, of course, but it would not do to declare someone exceptional right from the outset.

Hilda herself, understanding the position and authority vested in her, did her best not to respond to questions of governance. Reinhard would tease her for her evasiveness—"Oh, that's right—Fräulein von Mariendorf won't discuss such matters with the likes of me until I promote her to at least imperial prime minister"—and enjoy her momentary consternation. Reinhard had felt Yang Wen-li's death as the loss of a mind equal to his own, so it was natural that Hilda's significance as a source of intellectual stimulation should have increased.

Reinhard had never used the word "revolution," but the raft of political and social reforms he had initiated in his brief span as ruler were a revolution from above in all but name. Except, of course, for the fact that everything lay within the framework of imperial autocracy. Unlike his late rival Yang, Reinhard made no distinction between, for instance, his contempt for Job Trünicht as an individual and his assessment of democratic republicanism itself.

Reinhard had not sought to abolish the old titles, but neither had he created a new noble class. Even Mittermeier, whose military accomplishments were of the finest order, had not been made a duke or count. The Gale Wolf himself joked that this was because "Wolfgang von Mittermeier" would be too unwieldy, but he had also been heard to remark that the nobility were destined to be found only in historical museums, "as surely as the elderly are headed for the grave."

More speculatively, since he made no clear statement on the matter, Reinhard may have hoped to create a so-called liberal empire where the emperor and his subjects were directly connected, rather than separated by the wall of ceremonial dress that was the nobility. He may have had something even more novel in mind—but this must now remain forever unknown.

From his bed, Reinhard also made several decisions on internal affairs. Increased pensions for decommissioned soldiers, particularly the wounded. A better scholarship system for the families of those who died in battle. Financial compensation from the government for victims of crime. These were all the brainchild of his secretary of civil affairs, Karl Bracke, and then amended by Reinhard himself. Known since the previous dynasty as a reformist, Bracke had been strongly critical of Reinhard's autocratic leanings and militarism, but his policies as the new dynasty's first secretary of civil affairs had significantly contributed to realizing the Lohengramm Dynasty's characteristic approach best summed up as "social justice under autocratic control."

Even after two straight years of military expeditions, the empire's public coffers were still sufficient to ensure the welfare of the people. This demonstrated the sheer vastness of the wealth that had been usurped by the privileged classes during the previous dynasty's five-century reign. Now, the former nobility of the empire had been driven into penury by the confiscation of their property and holdings and were largely on the verge of starvation. As minister of domestic affairs, Count von Mariendorf had been generous enough to compensate them for the seizures, but the amounts involved were meager, and once the nobles, accustomed to spending freely, had frittered it away, there was nothing further the count could do.

"If one noble's death means the salvation of ten thousand commoners, I consider that justice," had been Reinhard's official comment on the matter. "If they object to starvation, let them work, just as the common people have for the past five hundred years." He shed no tears at the thought of the nobility facing the end of their days.

Reinhard's young bodyguard Emil von Selle bowed once and entered the room. His face fell when he saw the tray on the nightstand. Reinhard had not eaten a bite of his breakfast of beans, warm milk with honey, and a soft-boiled egg. Emil could not hide his concern over the kaiser's complete lack of appetite.

"Your Majesty, will you eat nothing at all?"

"I have no desire to."

"But, Your Majesty, you must eat if you are to recover your strength. I beg you, take at least some sustenance, however little it appeals, to fuel a swift return to health."

"You dare to issue orders to the emperor of all humanity, Emil? Must I partake of unwanted meals simply because my bodyguard wills it?"

Reinhard regretted his words before they were fully out. He saw the tears welling in Emil's eyes and knew that he had committed the most shameful act of all: lashing out in uncontrolled anger at a defenseless child. He had been on the verge of becoming a tyrant!

Despite his fever and exhaustion, Reinhard's fair features had remained as exquisite as ever, as if carved from pearl. Now, however, they glowed with shame. He reached out and stroked Emil's hair.

"My apologies, Emil," he said. "Sometimes my temper gets the better of me. Forgive me. I will eat, at least a little."

After his bodyguard left, Reinhard sipped two silver spoonfuls of soup. He might have taken a third, had not his chief aide Arthur von Streit sought an audience.

Von Streit's business concerned Steinmetz's bequest, such as it was. It seemed he had written a letter containing a kind of will in which he left everything he had to a certain woman. The will was neither legal nor formal, but von Streit requested the kaiser's permission to honor the departed man's wishes anyway.

"I have no objection," said Reinhard. "I am surprised, however. I thought Steinmetz was unmarried."

"He was, Your Majesty, but he did have a lover. Her name was Gretchen von Erfurt. It seems they had been together for five years."

"Why had they not wed?"

"As I am given to understand, the admiral used to say that until Your Majesty had unified the galaxy, as your subject he would not keep a household either."

"The fool…"

Reinhard's voice had a stunned ring to it.

"Mittermeier and von Eisenach are loyal retainers to me, but they both have families, do they not? Why did Steinmetz not marry this Gretchen, too? I would have sent them a gift in celebration."

"If I may, Your Majesty, when the kaiser himself will not take a bride, it is not surprising that his subjects follow his example. Do you not think so?"

"You are ordering me to marry, then? Is that your meaning?" Reinhard's elegant lips curved in a frown. It was as if some nature spirit had plucked the petals from a winter rose. "If I die—"

"Your Majesty!"

"Calm yourself. I am not Rudolf the Great. Emperor or nameless commoner, all grow old and die alike. I understand that much."

Von Streit was speechless. The golden-haired conqueror continued, a sardonic glitter in his ice-blue eyes.

"If I die leaving no issue, I expect someone of ability—retainer or not, it makes no difference—to install themselves as kaiser or king in my place. Such has always been my intention. I may have conquered the galaxy, but there is no reason my descendants should inherit it if they lack the ability and the renown to do so."

Von Streit met the young kaiser's gaze, directly and decisively. "I know that it is not my place to say this, but I beg Your Majesty not to delay in taking a bride and securing the line of succession. That is the devout wish of every subject in Your Majesty's empire."

"And father an heir like Sigismund the Foolish or August the Bloodletter? A fine legacy!"

"Maximilian Josef the Seer and Manfred the Fugitive were heirs too. The wise rule of the Lohengramm Dynasty can reveal its true value only if the dynasty itself survives. To guarantee that survival by legal means is fine. But to leave things to a succession of conquerors would not only cause needless bloodshed, it would also disrupt governance itself. Please, Your Majesty, reconsider the matter once more."

"Your point is well-made, and your counsel is keenly felt. I shall remember it."

Reinhard may not have been entirely insincere, but it cannot be denied that he luxuriated in the sense of freedom he felt as he dismissed von Streit from his room.

Once communications with Phezzan were possible again, Mittermeier contacted the Domestic Safety Security Bureau's office there to inquire about von Reuentahl's child.

"Elfriede von Kohlrausch has taken the baby she gave birth to late last month and disappeared," said the man who answered the call. "She has not been seen since."

Seeing the fury begin to fill the famed young marshal's face on his screen, the bureaucrat hurriedly transferred the call to his supervisor, who offered a superficial facsimile of apologetic sentiment bundled in self-justification.

"We don't have as much policing power as we need, and the bombing has been our main focus recently," he said.

"And yet the terrorist remains at large," said Mittermeier, disappointment curdling into rage. "So much for the Domestic Safety Security Bureau's powers of detection. Kessler's military police would have cracked the case long ago."

He cut the connection. He had never felt kindly disposed toward this woman Elfriede von Kohlrausch, who had temporarily driven his friend into a difficult position, but the thought of her wandering the streets with a babe in arms was unbearable. What sin, after all, had the infant committed?

"Just a baby…"

Thinking on his own marriage, still childless after eight years, even the highest-ranked admiral in the Imperial Navy could not exclude a degree of mild bitterness from his breast.

CHAPTER 8:

I

ON JULY 1, 800 SE—year 2 of the New Imperial Calendar—Reinhard von Lohengramm, first kaiser of the Lohengramm Dynasty, disembarked at Phezzan Spaceport. Because he had gone directly to Phezzan rather than via the old alliance capital of Heinessen, it had taken him less than a month to cross the entire former territory of the alliance, known now as the Neue Land.

Ten days earlier, on July 20, Marshal Oskar von Reuentahl had landed on Planet Heinessen as the newly appointed governor-general of the Neue Land, relieved of his post as secretary-general of Supreme Command Headquarters. With him in the territory remained 5.2 million officers and enlisted troops, and the imperial government dispatched ten thousand additional civilian officials to serve in his administration.

"Artist-Admiral" Ernest Mecklinger recorded his thoughts on the birth of this mighty new government for posterity:

"Von Reuentahl was an accomplished military man and an able civilian administrator. The newborn government was colossal in scale, dwarfing the high commission of the late Helmut Lennenkamp to effectively rule half of humanity. Kaiser Reinhard may have originally envisioned this structure of

governance with his dear friend Siegfried Kircheis at the helm, but Kircheis
had taken up residence in Valhalla, leaving only three men conceivably worthy
of this important office: von Oberstein, von Reuentahl, and Mittermeier. Von
Reuentahl was chosen, I imagine, partly because the dissolution of Supreme
Command Headquarters left its secretary-general without another role of his
own. In any case, it was not for some time that people began to ask why, of all
people, von Reuentahl had been appointed to the position..."

July 7, 800 SE, year 2 of the New Imperial Calendar. Afternoon.

The leadership of the Imperial Navy was gathered in the salon of the Baldanders, an exclusive Phezzanese hotel. Von Reuentahl and his staff officers were absent, having remained on Heinessen, but among those present were Marshal Mittermeier; Senior Admirals Müller, Wittenfeld, Wahlen, von Eisenach, and Lutz; and ten or so other full admirals. The state funerals for marshals Fahrenheit and Steinmetz and first secretary of works Bruno von Silberberg had been carried out that morning, and those three great servants of the empire had been interred in the presence of the kaiser.

Minister of Military Affairs Paul von Oberstein had been head of the funeral committee. No complaint could be leveled at his management of the event, but antipathy toward the man himself was evident, such as in Wittenfeld's cynical comment, "I wish he would stick to funerals—they suit him well, and cause no trouble for others."

The most urgent task of the leadership now assembled on Phezzan, from the kaiser down, was reorganizing the entire Imperial Navy. Major changes in the leadership structure would be required following the death in battle of the two commanders Fahrenheit and Steinmetz. Their fleets could not be left without leaders, and fleet sizes needed rebalancing across the board.

As minister of military affairs, von Oberstein had responsibility for such matters, but whether the commanders would fully welcome his interventions was a delicate question. The estrangement between the Ministry of Defense and the military itself may have been the distinguishing characteristic of the Imperial Navy in those early days of the Lohengramm Dynasty. Each recognized the other as fully capable, but they were separated by considerable psychological distance, and the visceral repulsion against von Oberstein in particular could not be dismissed—even if it had yet to reach a critical stage.

Senior Admiral Ernest Mecklinger, though not present for the meeting, would later write an extremely accurate account of the atmosphere among the participants.

Looking back on the first half of SE 800—year 2 of the New Imperial Calendar—the sheer scale of what was lost both in terms of human life and historical possibilities is overwhelming. On a personal level, the death of both Adalbert Fahrenheit and Karl Robert Steinmetz came as a great shock to me. Their bravery and ability as commanders were beyond reproach, and the solemn distinction they drew between loyalty and sycophancy also deserves to be remembered. Fahrenheit was taken prisoner after his valiant efforts could not prevent defeat in the Lippstadt War, but remained truly undaunted in spirit. When Steinmetz was made first captain of the warship Brünhild, *he admonished Reinhard von Lohengramm, his superior, for attempting to usurp his authority as captain. Having lost these two men, the other officers could only voicelessly observe the desolation in their ranks...Incidentally, in addition to these two, other first-class admirals like Karl Gustav Kempf and Helmut Lennenkamp had also been slain by the same enemy: Yang Wen-li. When knowledge of his death reached the admirals of the Imperial Navy, their sorrow deepened still further. Though they themselves might have been slain by this enemy commander had he lived longer, they still raised their glasses in respect at his passing.*

Neidhart Müller was surely the most representative example of this tendency, having served as Reinhard's envoy to Yang's funeral, but he had little to say after returning from Iserlohn. "His widow is a beautiful woman," was all he would say to anyone except the kaiser, and he drank in silence as if at a loss for what to do with the feeling of absence spreading within him.

Von Eisenach had always had a reputation as a taciturn man who used his mouth for nothing but eating and drinking, although Lutz allowed that he probably kissed his wife too. He was not given to merrymaking by nature, but on this day he seemed in good enough cheer.

Just a day earlier, Lutz had turned to his aide Holzbauer with a hint of purple in his blue eyes and said, "Oh, by the way—I'm getting married next year."

After 5.5 speechless seconds, Holzbauer finally managed to offer congratulations in the standard form.

"This year would be impossible," Lutz said, eyes still twinkling. "Too much mourning to do. Incidentally, do you know who my bride-to-be is?"

How could I possibly know that? thought Holzbauer. "Could it be the nurse with black hair who attended to Your Excellency during your hospitalization?" he asked.

Lutz was astonished. "That's right!" he said. "How did you know?"

Holzbauer was even more surprised. He had not expected to hit the mark. Lutz had saved his life, as well as his older brother's, and the love and respect he felt for his superior officer made him wish that Lutz had pursued a romance of a slightly more poetic nature. Did it not suggest a certain lack of effort for a senior admiral in the Imperial Navy to marry his nurse? Learning that Lutz was more than just a steadfast military man did bring him a certain joy, but still…

In the salon at the Baldanders hotel, the conversation eventually turned to the matter of terrorism.

"The Black Fox of Phezzan! What do we have to fear from him? He has abandoned his power and authority and become a miserable fugitive. The Black Mole, more like!"

"What do we have to fear from him, you say? Conspiracy. Terrorism. We never gave any thought to terrorists and their ilk, but von Silberberg and even Yang Wen-li both proved vulnerable to their attacks."

Senior Admiral August Samuel Wahlen grimaced bitterly at this. On the kaiser's orders, he had led the attack on the Church of Terra's headquarters the previous year. He had believed the organization to be obliterated then, and yet their squirming remnants had managed to murder Yang Wen-li. That the kaiser had not offered a single word of reproach only deepened the shame Wahlen felt. Silently, he resolved to take responsibility for eliminating the church for all eternity.

Heidrich Lang, chief of the Domestic Safety Security Bureau, had a formidable talent for exerting a negative influence on people and society. The loathing felt for him by Kaiser Reinhard's senior staff officers might not have been inevitable, but it was certainly understandable. Mittermeier referred to Lang as "a smear of filth on the sole of von Oberstein's shoe," and even warmhearted Müller had once described him as "an unlikable nobody with visible treachery behind his baby face." Oskar von Reuentahl eschewed words entirely: his only comment on the man was a cold sneer.

Lang's presence was tolerated as an unfortunate necessity. Any political system needed departments and people to do the kind of shadowy, unpleasant work he did. Even the Free Planets Alliance, for a time, had had a Bureau for the Protection of the Charter to put down anti-republican sentiment.

For his part, Lang was careful to do no injury to the common people, directing his surveillance and suppression at just three targets: nobles and bureaucrats of the former dynasty, republican extremists, and alliance spies. His survival in the Lohengramm Dynasty required considerable effort and staunch endurance of the cold treatment he received.

And yet, shortly after the kaiser arrived on Phezzan, the bureau achieved something that made even its critics sit up and take notice.

They captured the criminals behind the bombing that had killed von Silberberg and injured von Oberstein, Lutz, and Phezzan's acting secretary-general Nicolas Boltec. And Lang's role in the operation, as bureau chief, had been far from peripheral.

Osmayer, then secretary of the interior, despised Lang, even though the bureau chief should have been a capable subordinate. Not only did Lang position himself as an ally of von Oberstein, dismissing his actual superior—his designs on Osmayer's position were obvious if always deniable. As a result, Osmayer's first instinct was to ignore Lang's success, but rewarding good conduct and punishing wrongdoing were the foundation on which the Lohengramm Dynasty stood. If Osmayer did not recognize Lang for what he had done, he would run the risk of displeasing the kaiser.

With great reluctance, Osmayer reported the matter to the minister of domestic affairs, Count von Mariendorf. The news reached the kaiser's ears, and it was decided that Lang would be suitably rewarded.

Thus was Lang appointed to the post of junior minister of the interior, while retaining his position as chief of the Domestic Safety Security Bureau as well. He was also given a reward of one hundred thousand reichsmark, but he donated the entire sum to the Phezzanese Bureau of Welfare. This good deed was regarded with almost universal disgust as the rankest hypocrisy, but it was revealed after Lang's death that he had anonymously donated part of his salary to scholarship funds and welfare facilities since his time as a low-ranking bureaucrat. Hypocritical or not, his philanthropy had saved many. Utterly friendless, making no constructive contribution to the progress of history, Lang nevertheless led a life that provoked many in later ages to consider the way such different qualities could coexist within the same petty character.

The first message from the woman who claimed to be Dominique Saint-Pierre arrived at the Domestic Safety Security Bureau while Imperial Military Command Headquarters was still reeling from the sudden death of Yang Wen-li.

Lang kept a list at the back of his mind of the criminals he had already arrested and tried as well as those yet to face that treatment, and Saint-Pierre's name was on that list next to Adrian Rubinsky's, if in slightly smaller lettering. Saint-Pierre had been the lover of the so-called Black Fox, last landesherr of Phezzan and now a fugitive, and had acted as his accomplice in countless conspiracies. He should have had her found and brought into custody immediately, but after he read the letter, Lang instead incinerated it, flushed the ashes, and left the bureau by himself.

Thus began an unlovely arrangement between Rubinsky and Lang. Information about the terrorists behind the bombing was one of its fruits.

On July 9, the two of them spoke in Rubinsky's safe house.

"Welcome, Your Excellency," said Rubinsky.

The honorific tickled a part of Lang's pride pleasantly, but it did not satisfy his entire consciousness. This was not because Lang was above such things as titles and honors; rather, he believed that any expression of goodwill or welcome must conceal some kind of calculation or malice.

"Let us put aside those queasy formalities," he said pompously. "On what business have you called this loyal retainer to the Lohengramm Dynasty to speak with you today?"

If you were truly loyal, you would hardly establish clandestine arrangements with fugitives, thought Rubinsky, but he did not put the observation into words. He was not done with this villain yet. Rubinsky could be as obsequious in word and deed as necessary, as long as it was feigned. With the smile of a man-eating tiger, he urged a glass of the finest whiskey on his guest and explained that, although he was not requesting immediate action, it was his hope that Lang's influence as undersecretary might be able to repair his relations with the court.

Lang laughed right in his face. "Do not forget where you stand," he said. "If I were to say one word to the kaiser, he would soon relieve your shoulders of the heavy burden of your head. Do you think yourself in any position to make demands of me as an equal?"

Rubinsky did not bat an eyelash at the threat. "You wound me with your words, sir—my apologies, Your Excellency the Junior Minister. I was robbed of my authority on Phezzan for no crime at all. Why, you might even call me a victim!" His expression was not quite as chagrined as his tone of voice.

"And so you bear a grudge against the kaiser? You are a mouse defying a lion. Your presumption is simply outrageous."

"A grudge? Absolutely not! Kaiser Reinhard is a hero unequaled in history. He had only to ask, and I would have gladly surrendered my authority on Phezzan to him at any time. Instead, he followed where his conquering spirit led, ignoring such pebbles as myself that lay on the road. I find this a regrettable outcome—this is all I mean to say."

"Of course he ignored you. The kaiser has no need for goodwill from the likes of you. He holds the entire galaxy in the palm of his hand."

Rubinsky noticed that Lang often seemed to confuse the kaiser's authority with his own power. This tendency was absent in von Oberstein. Though both men were shunned by the Imperial Navy's admiralty, there was an enormous difference in psychological tenor between them.

"I am mortified by Your Excellency's observation," Rubinsky said. "However, I am sure that my sincerity has revealed itself to you at least to some degree. Were not the men I delivered to you truly the perpetrators of the bombing that took Secretary von Silberberg's life?"

"They came to my attention long ago. I simply lacked evidence. Unlike the dark ages of the former dynasty, in the reign of Kaiser Reinhard, no one can be convicted without proof."

Impressive, thought Rubinsky. This man known as a master fabricator of evidence had attempted brazen self-justification and naked sycophancy toward authority at the same time. Rubinsky offered a slanted smile thinner than paper, then casually let a small soligraph fall onto the rosewood table. Through the alcoholic haze, Lang's gaze fell to the object, then fixed itself on it. When he put down his glass, it was with a loud noise and a slosh of whiskey.

"Ah—does Your Excellency know this woman?" asked Rubinsky innocently.

Lang stared poisoned needles at him, but Rubinsky's deference was, it seemed, merely superficial. The face in the soligraph belonged to Elfriede von Kohlrausch—the former noble who had given birth to von Reuentahl's child just days prior.

"As far as I can tell, this woman is suffering from a tragic psychological imbalance," said Rubinsky. "A pity, especially in one so beautiful."

Lang was silent for a moment. "How do you know that?" he asked finally.

"First, she is convinced that she has a familial relationship with Duke Lichtenlade—a key retainer of the Goldenbaum Dynasty, and the author of an attempt on His Majesty Kaiser Reinhard's life! Surely none of his kin would dare to visit Phezzan."

"That is all?"

Lang appeared to believe that an arrogant demeanor would help him retain the upper hand. Rubinsky ignored his feeble attempt at bluffing.

"One more thing. The woman has a newborn babe—and she claims that he is the son of Marshal Oskar von Reuentahl, chief retainer to the *current* dynasty, and its most beloved admiral to boot."

Displeasure and hatred exploded soundlessly within Lang, sending odorless poison flying to every corner of the room. Rubinsky was liberally spattered, and considerable interest stirred beneath his blank expression as he regarded the rumbling of the active volcano now wearing Lang's skin. Naturally, Rubinsky knew more than he had let on. He knew that Lang had plotted to use charges against Elfriede to bring down von Reuentahl for high treason—and that he had failed. Lang had learned the hard way how deep the kaiser's faith was in von Reuentahl, a famed admiral undefeated in battle and a faithful retainer since the founding of the new dynasty. This had not failed to feed Lang's resentment.

"All right. There is no more profit in these coy insinuations," said Lang, a dark counterpoint of calculation and compromise in his voice. "You mean that you can see to it that von Reuentahl commits the crime of high treason. Are you quite sure you can destroy the man?"

Rubinsky nodded primly. "As you so ably discern, should Your Excellency so desire, I will exert every effort and see that those desires are met."

By now Lang had lost all capacity to feign arrogance.

"If you can do that," he said, "I can promise my assistance reconciling you to the kaiser. But—and listen carefully—*only after you succeed*. I am not fool enough to trust in the empty promises of a Phezzanese without proof."

"Quite correct, Your Excellency. No wonder they call you von Oberstein's right-hand man. For my part, I have no intention of seeking your trust with trickery. Allow me to make one additional proposal..."

Wiping off the whiskey that had spilled on his hand, Lang leaned forward in his chair. His eyes were those of a feverish invalid.

II

Before long, something happened that plunged the entire planet of Phezzan into astonishment: Nicolas Boltec, acting secretary-general, was taken into custody.

According to the announcement from Lang of the Ministry of the Interior, Boltec had been complicit in the bombing that had taken the life of former minister Bruno von Silberberg. His own injuries from that incident had been intentional—a way of averting suspicion. Boltec had harbored a smoldering resentment of von Silberberg because the latter had essentially usurped his position as chief administrator of the planet. This was the claim in the announcement from the ministry, and in due course Boltec ended the episode by committing suicide by poison in prison.

Naturally, Senior Admiral Kornelias Lutz was among those stunned by the development. "If getting injured in that bombing was cause for suspicion, I suppose Marshal von Oberstein and I are also suspects," he joked, but then, for a moment, his face froze. He was not among the conspirators, of course, but he had no way of proving that. What was to stop Lang arranging for his arrest as well?

The whole thing was suspicious. Lutz wondered if Lang had not simply fabricated evidence in order to arrest and then murder an innocent man. But there was no way to prove it, and Lutz did not see how it benefited Lang to bring down Boltec in any case. Of course, he had no way of knowing about the nefarious arrangement between Lang and Rubinsky.

Even so, unease and even fear made him unable to ignore the incident. If even a leading military figure and valued servant of the empire like Lutz was defenseless before Lang, what hope did anyone else have?

"If this goes on, our entire empire could be undermined by a single wicked official. Call it an overreaction, but I say poisonous weeds should be removed as soon as they send up shoots."

But Lutz had earned his fame on the battlefield, and was not comfortable with intrigues or information warfare. He decided to inform one of his most trusted and capable fellow senior admirals about the danger of Lang instead.

And so, in the early weeks of July, Senior Admiral Ulrich Kessler, commander of capital defenses and commissioner of military police, received an urgent warning from his fellow senior admiral. Through the lens of political history, this could be viewed as the military fighting back against an attempt by the domestic security bureaucracy to expand its authority. But this did not, of course, occur to Lutz himself.

As Lang's successes mounted, a woman watching them coldly turned to Adrian Rubinsky. "Surely you don't trust this man Lang?" she asked.

"How unlike you to ask a question like that, Dominique," said Rubinsky. There was no doubt that he expected to be repaid for the goodwill he had expended on Lang, but not even a hint of a smile showed on his face. "He's a nobody. Show him a looking glass that magnifies his reflection, and he is delighted. I simply directed him to the mirror he craved."

Unlike the stone-faced Rubinsky, the woman never stopped smiling, eyes and lips dripping with seemingly endless malice.

"And what does that make you? Didn't you make this nobody kill Boltec? I'm sure it must have been galling to see your former subordinate become Mr. Acting Secretary-General and strut around like the kaiser's most loyal retainer, but how can you relax with a drink after having an innocent man killed?"

Rubinsky put down his glass. The look in his eyes changed restlessly, but the rest of his face was entirely calm.

"You really don't see it? Or are you just pretending not to?"

"What are you talking about?"

"Fine," Rubinsky said after a brief pause. "Let me explain."

If she already understood, there was no reason not to tell her; and even if she didn't, there was still no harm in telling her.

"Boltec is nothing but a means to an end, and that end was having Lang kill an innocent man. With his own hands, Lang has tied the noose that will hang him."

"So if he tries to escape from your yoke, you can reveal the truth about Boltec to the kaiser, say, or the minister of military affairs?"

Rubinsky tilted his glass by way of reply. Casting a final glance at him, Dominique Saint-Pierre left the room, followed half a moment later by shadow and derision.

Dominique walked down a corridor and descended a staircase to another room deep within the building. After a cursory knock, she opened the door and light cut a rectangle from the gloom within. A young woman inside raised her head, but as soon as she met Dominique's gaze she looked away again, squeezing the baby in her arms more tightly.

"How are you feeling?" asked Dominique.

The woman declined to reply. Not out of fear, but pride. Still holding her baby, she looked back at Dominique, an afterimage of stubborn awareness of her station in life visible in her eyes.

"Marshal Oskar von Reuentahl will be arrested for treason before long," said Dominique. Rubinsky and Lang might not have what it takes to lead great armies and crush the enemy on the battlefield, but they are certainly capable of stabbing those who can in the back."

When the silence had flapped once around the room, a faint voice escaped the woman's lips. *Exactly what I am wanted*, it sounded like.

"But isn't he the father of that child you're holding?"

The woman said nothing.

"What have you named it, anyway?"

Once more, Dominique's question was met with a hostile silence. But it took more than that to upset the mistress of Adrian Rubinsky.

"There are so many types of people in the world," said Dominique. "Some couples want children but never conceive them. Some parents are killed by the children they do have. I suppose there is also room for children whose fathers are killed by their mothers."

The baby gurgled and waved its limbs.

"Do let me know if you need anything," said Dominique. "There's no point in letting the child die before you can even teach it to hate its father."

She turned to leave, and then the other woman spoke clearly for the first time. She wanted milk, she said, and clothing. She added a few more items to the list.

Dominique nodded generously. "All right. And I suppose we'd better find you a nurse as well."

Leaving mother and child in their room, Dominique looked back in on Rubinsky and saw him on the sofa, head in hands.

"What's wrong?" she said. "Another of your turns?"

"My head hurts. It feels like a dinosaur's battering the inside of my skull with its tail. Pass me those pills."

Dominique regarded her lover with an observer's eye as she handed him the bottle. Watching him swallow the pills, one meaty hand still pressed to his forehead, she reached out to pat him lightly on the back.

"The gaps between these episodes of yours are getting shorter and shorter," she said, coldly but correctly. "You must take better care of yourself. You'd look quite the fool if you took over the galaxy through plot and intrigue only to be brought down by a collapsing inner world. Why don't you see a doctor?"

"Doctors are useless."

"Oh? Well, it's your body—none of my concern. And I do agree that doctors would be no help here. If anything, you need a sorcerer."

"What's that supposed to mean?"

"I thought you knew already? Half of your problem is from a curse laid on you by the Church of Terra's grand bishop or whatever he calls himself, and the other half is from the vengeful spirit of your son Rupert Kesselring. No doctor can save you now."

This painful blow wounded his nerves, but Rubinsky showed no sign of it in his expression. Perhaps the pills had begun to exert their temporary power to heal, for the tension that bound his body like a thorny chain began to relax. He heaved a lengthy sigh.

"Vengeful spirits aside, you may be right about the curse. The archbishop seemed capable of that much."

"Oh, nonsense! If that man really had such powers, Kaiser Reinhard would be long dead. And yet he lives, in the fragrant flower of..."

Dominique trailed off in the middle of her sarcastic tirade. She had heard the recent whispered rumors that the kaiser was plagued by fever and often confined to bed. More than fifteen centuries since humanity's triumph over cancer, the human mind's vestigial reptilian tail was still vulnerable to being pulled into the swamp of superstition. Dominique shook her head in irritation and left the room. She had to order the milk for Elfriede's child, as well as the other items on her list. Apparently the mass of elementary particles that made up her character included a few electrons not of only one color.

III

On July 2 in SE 800—year 2 of the New Imperial Calendar—an imperial edict formally declared Planet Phezzan to be the new capital of the Galactic Empire and required the entire cabinet to relocate to Phezzan before the year was out. Senior Admiral Ulrich Kessler, commander of capital defenses and commissioner of military police, was also to move his headquarters to the new capital, leaving Odin's defense to Senior Admiral Ernest Mecklinger, rear supreme commander of the Imperial Navy.

From the minister of domestic affairs to the lowest-ranking bureaucrats and their families, over a million souls in all would make the journey of several thousand light-years. Countess Hildegard von Mariendorf, senior advisor to Reinhard at imperial headquarters, would see her father for the first time in a year. For Mittermeier's wife, Evangeline, traveling to her husband's new posting would be the first long journey she had ever experienced.

Amid the preparations for the move, Hilda found herself unable to maintain indifference to one question: the question of Reinhard's elder sister, Annerose von Grünewald, lover of the former emperor.

To the historians of later ages, the beautiful Annerose's influence on the formation of Reinhard's character was less academic theory than accepted wisdom, but at the time it had been nearly three years since she had gone into seclusion in her mountain villa in Freuden on the planet Odin. In all that time, brother and sister—likely the most beautiful pair of siblings in the galaxy—had not seen each other once. In losing that which should not have been lost, Reinhard had allowed past to be severed from present; the brilliance of that long-ago spring light, the melodies of those summer winds, were now far beyond his reach.

"Will Your Majesty be inviting the Gräfin von Grünewald to the new capital?" asked Hilda, knowing full well that she was overstepping her remit as chief advisor.

Reinhard's eyebrows moved slightly, as they always did when his hopes were disappointed or he was challenged on some sentiment he had yet to fully process.

"That, Fräulein von Mariendorf, has no connection with military affairs," he said. "Pray direct that remarkable intelligence of yours to the task of galactic conquest rather than palace trivialities."

This curt dismissal, however, was followed by a more personal reflection, as if Reinhard wanted his innermost thoughts to be heard. "Kircheis's grave is on Odin. To move my capital and headquarters to a location more convenient for me falls within my prerogative, but to do as I please with another's place of eternal rest is not."

Realizing that Reinhard was indirectly revealing the reason he would not invite his sister to Phezzan, Hilda remained silent. She had known the question would only make things awkward for her, and brooded, as usual, over her inability to rationally explain the emotions that had driven her to ask it anyway.

"I shall return to Odin one day," Reinhard continued, "but when that day will come is not yet within my power to discern. So many things remain to be put in order first."

Hilda did not, of course, ask what these were.

Reinhard stood on the banks of recollection, gazing down at the waters of the past. The clock's hands reversed direction, and night and day alternated with increasing speed until finally the former won out, and a scene from the past appeared before the kaiser's eyes.

"Annerose! It's dark! It's dark!"

He was a small child—four years old? five?—waking one night to smothering darkness and crying out desperately for help. He pressed the switch of the lamp by his bedside again and again, but no light came to drive the dark away. Later he would learn that their power had been cut off because his father had not paid the bill. "Protector of the Imperial Household!" A fine standard of living for a noble!

Hearing her brother's screams, Annerose came running from the next room. Later Reinhard would wonder how she could have been so fleet of foot through the pitch-blackness in her nightgown. But when he called, she always came.

"Reinhard, Reinhard, it's all right. I'm sorry I left you alone."

"It's dark, Annerose!"

"It is dark, but I can see your golden hair so clearly! How beautifully it shines!"

"That gold lights up the darkness, Reinhard. You must be the light yourself, for then nothing will frighten you, nothing will hurt you, no matter how dark it is. Become the light, Reinhard..."

With melancholy mien, Reinhard raised his fair hand to sweep back the cascade of golden locks that had fallen onto his brow. As a child, when he wanted his sister, he only had to call and she would come. Indeed, on the day she'd stopped coming to him, had she not been in need of his assistance for the first time?

And had he not been powerless to help her?

He knew that he owed her an infinite debt.

As the busy days continued, a piece of information both surprising and unpleasant made its way to Reinhard: Job Trünicht had petitioned the kaiser for entry into government service.

As chairman of both the Defense Committee and the High Council for the former Free Planets Alliance, Trünicht bore grave and inescapable responsibility for his fatherland's demise. He had fled to the imperial capital of Odin pleading the danger he faced from radical elements of the former alliance seeking revenge, but at forty-five years of age, he had still been young for a politician, and soon turned his personal and financial resources to the task of seeking, or rather hunting down, a position within the government.

The news sparked a flicker of displeasure in Reinhard's expression, like the sight of something unclean. After a few moments of silence, however, he bared his white teeth in a malicious grin and nodded, almost as if in recollection.

"If Trünicht so badly craves a government post, I shall grant him one. Von Reuentahl was asking for assistance from an administrator familiar with conditions in the former alliance, I believe?"

The surprise on Hilda's face quickly changed to exasperation.

"Your Majesty, surely you do not..."

"High counselor to the governorate of the Neue Land—the perfect post for Trünicht, is it not? If the citizens of the former alliance should happen to make him the target of their rock flinging, well, that also would be welcomed by von Reuentahl."

"Your Majesty, I see no need for this. Surely assigning him to oversee the development of some far-flung world would be sufficient."

Reinhard laughed and waved his graceful hand.

The offer was clearly outrageous, but Trünicht—despite having claimed refuge in the imperial capital for his own safety—accepted it the following day.

"He *accepted*?"

His own responsibility for this outcome notwithstanding, Reinhard could not help feeling deeply displeased by it. He had assumed that Trünicht would never accept such a position, and intended to bar the former alliance leader permanently from public service on the basis of that refusal. Clearly, he had misjudged Trünicht's sense of shame in both qualitative and quantitative terms.

"How dare he show his face among the very people he betrayed? The man's gall could power my largest warship's main cannon!"

"It was Your Majesty's decision," said Hilda tartly. Reinhard made a noise of irritation.

If he had denied Trünicht's request outright, that would have been the end of it. If Trünicht had declined the post, the result would have been eloquent proof of Reinhard's convictions, if acquired in a somewhat mean-spirited way. But Trünicht's acceptance of the offer made Reinhard's gambit nothing but a simple, childish mistake. The kaiser had made many personnel choices since appointing the late Helmut Lennenkamp high commissioner on Heinessen, but this was the first he had felt dissatisfied with.

Naturally, the military had their own opinions on the appointment.

"Trünicht is taking up an official position in the Neue Land governorate, you say?" said Mittermeier. "Von Reuentahl won't be happy about that!"

He found the matter grimly amusing at first, recognizing what the kaiser had intended to do. But his amusement faded as he began to suspect that, however brazen-faced Trünicht might be, he must be concealing something that he expected would make such a position tenable.

At times like these, Mittermeier was wont to confide not in the young and forthright Bayerlein but rather Büro, rich in the wisdom and experience of years. Büro was also old friends with von Reuentahl's chief of staff, Bergengrün, meaning that he took personal interest in the matter.

The idea that Trünicht might be conspiring with von Oberstein to bring down von Reuentahl seemed to Büro rather a leap, but it was too grave a question to dismiss with a laugh.

"I do realize that it betrays my own prejudice to see von Oberstein's shadow behind every event in the galaxy, but still," said Mittermeier, his voice almost a lament as he ran an agitated hand through his honey-colored hair. He was thirty-two this year, and looked even younger. Usually, he did not meddle in matters he considered improper for military personnel to be involved with, but he could not be sanguine where his friends were concerned. Büro promised that he would privately warn Bergengrün to be careful, and with this Mittermeier had to be satisfied.

On July 31, a message was delivered to the office used by Minister of Military Affairs Paul von Oberstein. The bearer was Commodore Anton Ferner.

Marshal von Oberstein read the letter alone in his chambers. His face always remained expressionless regardless of the grave concerns that weighed on his mind, and this was no exception. After reading the message, he made sure to completely incinerate it.

Ferner came back into the office on other business and, after receiving his orders, suddenly retrieved from memory a matter from some days previous.

"By the way, Minister, I hear that Job Trünicht will be returning to the fatherland he abandoned in grand style—as high counselor to its governorate."

"And this surprises you?" von Oberstein said.

"I never expected His Majesty to actually follow through on the idea. Trünicht himself must be utterly without shame to accept such a posting, but I wonder if there is not also someone pulling his strings."

Von Oberstein did not respond directly. "Phezzan will soon become the official capital of the Galactic Empire," he said. "The center of the galaxy in every way."

"Indeed, sir."

"Even an ordinary citizen cleans a new house before moving in. Do you not think it best to cleanse not only Phezzan but the empire's entire territory for the sake of His Majesty?"

This was quite loquacious for von Oberstein. He was not usually the type to explain things to his subordinates until they accepted his point of view.

"I see. You mean to smoke out the Black Fox and the other bogeymen who have gone to ground. With Trünicht as your tool..."

Ferner was sincerely moved. He knew that his superior the minister of military affairs was a man of no private interests, and felt great respect for von Oberstein's diligence in advancing the goals of the state and the emperor himself. In that respect, von Oberstein was an unimpeachable public servant.

But von Oberstein's ideas for stabilizing imperial rule always revolved around the elimination of harmful elements. Ferner wondered how long it would be before the imperial leadership began to resist such purges.

Even a pillar riddled with termites might still be the only thing keeping the house up. Once he eliminates everyone who poses the slightest danger, what will be left? The minister of military affairs might find himself trapped under a pillar toppled by his own hand.

But Ferner had no intention of sharing these thoughts with von Oberstein. This may have been because the minister of military affairs had clearly already anticipated such objections, and was proceeding with his plans anyway.

CHAPTER 9:
NEW GOVERNMENT IN AUGUST

I

ON JUNE 12, before the imperial capital's move to Phezzan had been officially decided, Senior Admiral Neidhart Müller of the Imperial Navy arrived at Iserlohn Fortress as Kaiser Reinhard's funeral envoy. His flagship *Parzival* had made the voyage alone, and the only officers with him were Rear Admiral Orlau and Captain Ratzel.

Müller's visit naturally struck the people of Iserlohn as odd. There was even some suspicion that he might be a "dead agent," but for the kaiser to sacrifice a man of such importance to his military was inconceivable. Nor, Julian thought, would such treachery be in accordance with his nature.

Walter von Schönkopf agreed, although the comment he offered was less than direct. "Kaiser Reinhard loves to put on airs," he said. "He didn't resort to tricks like that when Marshal Yang was alive, and he's certainly not going to now that only us small fry are left."

"Wen-li often spoke highly of Admiral Müller," said Frederica. "I'm sure he would be happy about this visit. I say we let them meet one last time."

And so it was decided. Müller was invited inside the fortress.

Müller was exactly thirty years of age, with hair and eyes both the color of sand. He greeted the representatives of Iserlohn with a solemnity bordering on reverence. He was no great orator, but his sincerity was obvious in his words of condolence and in his attitude when paying his respects to Yang's remains in their ceramic case.

"I am delighted to meet you," he said to Frederica. "Your husband was our greatest, mightiest enemy."

Julian had met Siegfried Kircheis three years earlier, when the imperial commander had visited Iserlohn to represent the empire at a prisoner exchange. Kircheis had impressed Julian deeply. He was not the type of man to argue forcefully for his positions, but he had burned an unforgettable memory into Julian's head before departing. When he had heard the news of Kircheis's death, he had been struck by the distinct feeling that a star had sunk below the horizon.

Thinking back also on his meeting with August Samuel Wahlen while in disguise on Terra, Julian realized that none of the highest admirals of the Imperial Navy he had met in person had seemed to him unpleasant people. He was moved anew by the depth of Kaiser Reinhard's wisdom in selecting and appointing such leaders.

Müller did not prolong his visit, largely to forestall any suspicion that he was there to spy on the situation inside the fortress. During the brief period before his departure, he spoke with Julian over coffee in a room overlooking the port.

"Herr Mintz," he began, showing respect for the boy twelve years his junior with his choice of honorific. No doubt he would have observed protocol in dealing with any representative of Yang Wan-li, regardless of age, but kindness toward those below him in the hierarchy seemed to be in his nature. This did not imply a lack of courage on the battlefield: despite his own relative youth, Müller had changed flagships three times during the Vermillion War as he struggled to frustrate Yang's designs.

"Herr Mintz, I was not granted any political authority by the kaiser, but if you should wish to discuss peace with His Majesty, or offer your allegiance, I would be happy to act as messenger."

If the words had been spoken in the superior tone of a victor, Julian might have replied with violent outrage. The fact that they were not left him without an immediate reply. After climbing the slope of thought for a few moments, he said, "Commander Müller, I hope you will forgive my making this analogy, but—if the kaiser you love and respect were to pass on, would you change the flag you salute?"

"Iron Wall Müller" understood the import of the question at once. "Herr Mintz, it is just as you say. I spoke foolishly. I am the one who should ask your forgiveness." He bowed his head in apology before a slightly embarrassed Julian.

Internally, Julian was considering another hypothetical. If he himself had been born in the Galactic Empire, he mused, he probably would have wanted to become a military man like Müller. He recalled something Yang had once said in connection with his meeting with Kircheis: "Even the finest human beings have to kill each other if they're on opposite sides." As that memory played behind his retinas, Julian bid Müller farewell.

"I suppose our next meeting will be on the battlefield," said Müller. "Be well until then."

"And the same to you."

The smile in Müller's eyes was so gentle it was hard to believe he was Julian's enemy, but this warmth was soon replaced by the shadow of confusion. The port was full of freighters busily preparing for departure, and long lines had formed of men and women waiting to board with luggage in tow. They wore clothing of all kinds, but those dressed carelessly in former alliance uniforms stood out.

"Who are they?" asked Müller. "If I may ask, of course."

"They are the ones who have given up on Iserlohn's future and have decided to put it behind them," said Julian. "Commander Müller, I know I have no standing to ask such a favor, but if the Imperial Navy could guarantee them safe passage back to Heinessen, I would be very grateful."

Müller was not the only one surprised by how these departures had played out. When Julian had decided to throw open the fortress's stores so that those leaving Iserlohn could take supplies with them, von Schönkopf had argued against it. Even if they could produce enough to replenish those stores eventually, he said, there was no need to hand over their purse to bandits.

"We can't store more than we need in any case," Julian had replied. "Far better that they should take and freely use what they need to. They aren't getting any salaries or pensions, after all."

"You're too accommodating for your own good," had been von Schönkopf's assessment, delivered through a rueful smile.

Now it seemed that Müller was just as taken aback by Julian's magnanimity, enemy or not.

"Regarding the guarantee, you have my word," he said. "But, if you will pardon the question, will you not face trouble in later days if some of those departing choose to cooperate with our forces?"

"Yes," said Julian. "A great deal of trouble. But that is something we will simply have to endure. Some may be compelled by force, and it would be wrong to criticize them for that."

Müller studied Julian with his sandy-colored eyes, as if truly seeing for the first time how much the apprentice had learned from the master. And then, with a final smile of goodwill, Müller departed Iserlohn.

After seeing Müller off, Julian spoke with Caselnes.

"Putting the future aside, it seems that right now Kaiser Reinhard is able to process the Iserlohn problem within the limits of individual sentiment," said Julian, sipping a cup of tea he had brewed himself. "It seems to me that the kaiser lost his will to fight the moment Marshal Yang disappeared, on a level much deeper than mere politics or war."

"You have a point," said Caselnes. "I suppose that, without Yang Wen-li, Iserlohn Fortress is just some pebble on the periphery to him."

"But that isn't actually the case." Julian began to retrace his own thoughts. "The kaiser will relocate his capital to Phezzan. That will make Phezzan Corridor an artery joining the newly unified empire and uniting its influence. Development of the peripheral sectors will begin, starting from the direction of the Phezzan Corridor, and the expansion of human society itself will have Phezzan at its center. History and society will move on without Iserlohn. These, I think, are the kaiser's intentions."

"A logical idea, I suppose, given his position. What surprises me is that you were able to tease it out. Your feel for strategy is remarkable."

Julian nodded at Caselnes's praise, but it was a reflexive gesture rather than a sign of agreement. He was desperately trying to re-create the strategic map that Yang had had in mind before his death. There were some things that only he could decide as best he could, but in the end he had nothing else to rely on.

"The kaiser's attempt to conquer Iserlohn was rooted in emotion. He was fixated on Iserlohn Corridor not because the fortress was there but because Marshal Yang was."

"I suppose so. So the moment Yang died, he reverted to his cold-blooded strategist side, then? What do you suppose comes next?"

"This is a hope, not a prediction, but…"

"You're sounding like Yang already," Caselnes teased. Julian laughed. It sounded to Caselnes like the most adult laugh he had heard from Julian yet, but this may have been his fondness for the boy at work.

"Marshal Yang always said that Iserlohn Fortress's strategic value was predicated on Iserlohn Corridor having a different political and military power at each end."

"Yes, he told me that too."

"The reason we enjoy peace and security now is, ironically enough, because we no longer have that value. But if that value were to be restored—in other words, if the empire were to fracture—a turning point would come to Iserlohn."

"Hmm."

"In any case, I don't think the situation will change too suddenly. Ahle Heinessen, founding father of the alliance, took fifty years to complete his Long March. We should be prepared to endure at least that long."

"In fifty years, I'll be almost ninety—If I'm still living at all." Caselnes rubbed his chin with a rueful smile. He was thirty-nine and still in his prime, but the only remaining member of the leadership older than him was Merkatz. "You know, I'm still impressed by the way you and Mrs. Yang took on such unrewarding roles. People are bound to criticize her, saying that she leveraged her husband's name into political power for herself. As for you, when you get it wrong, you'll face a storm of criticism, and when you get it right, people will say you just stole Yang's ideas or that some of his luck rubbed off on you."

"As long as I do get it right, people can say what they like," Julian replied simply.

By the end of July, everyone who wanted to leave Iserlohn Fortress had done so. Those who remained were finally able to begin the task of creating a new organization.

There were 944,087 of them in all—612,906 men and 331,181 women. Most of those women were married or related to one of the men, and few lived alone. The gender imbalance, though unavoidable, was sure to cause problems before long.

"Oh, absolutely," Olivier Poplin said. "Almost half the men in here have no prospects at all, and frankly I'm not interested in helping out the losers either."

This grand declaration was made in a voice faintly redolent of alcohol, and Julian realized with quiet happiness that Poplin was recovering from his psychological slump.

"In the end, though," Poplin continued, "We have to keep an organized military. Which means we're not going to just suddenly establish a new state."

What *would* they do, then? Julian needed new ideas.

II

Amid the turbulence caused by Yang Wen-li's death and Kaiser Reinhard's order to move the capital, the war appeared to subside to an extent, giving way to a season of peace. It could be said that Yang's assassins had opened the curtain on that season, but not one of them had lived to enjoy the fruits of what they had wrought.

The two imperial destroyers used in the assassination had been found in early July, one as a burned-out husk drifting in a sector near *Leda II*, and the other intercepted by a cruiser group commanded by Senior Admiral Büro as it fled the scene of the crime. The second destroyer had ignored Büro's orders to halt, opening fire on its pursuers instead, but it had never had a chance. Under the concentrated glare of a dozen energy beams, it had blossomed into a fireball that consumed everyone aboard.

Thus were the men who had carried out the assassination of Yang "martyred" to the last. The one whose blaster had fired the killing shot was never even identified by name.

An investigation was, of course, immediately opened regarding the circumstances under which the assassins had posed as imperial troops, but the suicide of ten officers of the Imperial Navy made progress extremely difficult, if not quite impossible. It was clear that these men had encouraged the martyrs in their self-satisfied intoxication.

As governor-general of the Neue Land, Oskar von Reuentahl ranked alongside the various ministry secretaries, and his military and political authority extended across the entire territory that the Free Planets Alliance had occupied until the previous year, with 35,800 ships and 5,226,500 troops under his direct command. This fleet was officially named the Neue Land Security Force, but it was known informally as the Reuentahl Fleet.

As his base of operations and the home of his administration, von Reuentahl chose the Euphonia, a luxury hotel that had often hosted receptions and conferences for the alliance government in the past.

The Neue Land Security Force had five million officers and enlisted troops, making it larger even than the alliance military in its final period. Perhaps it was simply too much physical power to be commanded by one man. Five million souls, stationed in what had been enemy territory until yesterday, all longing for home—and it was von Reuentahl's responsibility to keep them together. The pressure would have crushed an ordinary man.

But von Reuentahl accepted the position without betraying a hint of concern. Within days, he had proved himself an effective leader and administrator even off the battlefield. By the end of July, the former citizens of the Free Planets Alliance had come to accept, if not welcome, the governor-general's rule. Their consumer lifestyles had not sunk below the levels reached in the last days of the alliance, and public safety had been maintained. Despite the millions of imperial troops among them who enjoyed extraterritoriality, military discipline was strict and no atrocities occurred. If anything, crimes committed by those who had fled the former alliance fleet after the death of Yang were a greater problem.

Von Reuentahl divided his official authority into two domains—military affairs and public safety, and civic administration—each overseen by a deputy. For the first domain, he appointed to the post of inspector general of the military his faithful and long-serving lieutenant Admiral Hans Eduard Bergengrün.

Some, including Grillparzer and von Knapfstein, were dissatisfied with this decision. They were full admirals as much as Bergengrün, and resented being under his authority, even if only formally. In fact, because they had moved from being subordinates of Lennenkamp to the being under the direct control of the kaiser, they actually felt somewhat superior to the new inspector general.

As deputy inspector general, von Reuentahl chose Vice Admiral Ritschel, who had served as secretary-general of the outpost in Gandharva under Senior Admiral Steinmetz and was recognized for his practical ability and knowledge of domestic conditions in the former alliance. Ritschel was less warrior than home-front military official, and so he had not fought in the Battle of the Corridor and had been spared the fate of dying alongside his commanding officer. This was a lower position in the hierarchy, and so did not arouse the ire of the full admirals.

Aware of Grillparzer and von Knapfstein's grumbling, von Reuentahl eventually summoned them to the governor-general's office and set them straight in his acid-tongued way.

"So, you have issues with my choice of inspector general. Were you aware that Bergengrün is older than you and has been a full admiral for longer? And tell me: If I had made one of *you* inspector general instead of Bergengrün, how exactly would the other have reacted?"

Both left without another word, never to voice such dissatisfaction again—at least not in public.

On the civic front, von Reuentahl accepted Kaiser Reinhard's recommendation and chose the technocrat Julius Elsheimer as his deputy. Elsheimer had served ably if briefly as undersecretary of works and of civil affairs for the empire, making him a suitable director general of civil affairs in the Neue Land. Coincidentally, he was also the brother-in-law of Senior Admiral Kornelias Lutz, as the husband of Lutz's younger sister.

And then there was Trünicht, high counselor to the governorate. Elsheimer was a capable official, but unfamiliar with the internal affairs of the former alliance. An advisor was what he needed, but he doubted he could expect useful service from a man who had abandoned his responsibility to his nation and his people in favor of securing his own personal security.

"I confess I find this appointment curious," said Bergengrün. "After the unfortunate death of Yang Wen-li, the kaiser sends the former head of the alliance back home as an imperial official? Is this His Majesty's way of making a cynical joke at democracy's expense?"

Von Reuentahl, however, understood the kaiser's feeling at least in part. No doubt his aim was to embarrass this brazen-faced former alliance official. Trünicht may have had the talent and dedication to become head of state and chief executive of an entire nation, but what drove him was the exact opposite of Reinhard's aesthetic consciousness.

"Well, it doesn't matter. Trünicht's abilities and knowledge might be useful, but the man himself needn't have any influence on decision-making."

"We will use him, but not trust him," was von Reuentahl's comment, retained for posterity in the official records. The heterochromiac governor-general intended to dispose of Trünicht at the first hint of suspicious or subversive behavior. Making a point of accepting the man, unpleasant as he was, would help create that pretext for eliminating him.

Another problem von Reuentahl faced around this time was the people who had left Iserlohn Fortress and sought to return to Heinessen.

When news of this first reached him, von Reuentahl's eyes filled with thought. For Ritschel, however, the memory of having lost his commanding officer in a battle with these people only days ago was too fresh for him to feel positively inclined toward them.

"What do you intend to do, sir?" he asked. "They may have left the Yang Fleet, but can we really offer an unconditional pardon to the bandits who seized Iserlohn Fortress and resisted the kaiser?"

His views were not unreasonable, but no purely military solution was available. "Realistically, we can't arrest over a million people," said von Reuentahl. "We also have to consider the hearts and minds of the former alliance itself. It would be foolish to give their unease room to grow."

In the end, von Reuentahl's instructions were as follows: The transports carrying the so-called seceders would be permitted to land at Heinessen Military Spaceport No. 2. The civilians and noncombat personnel among the seceders would be given full freedom and would be recognized as subjects of the empire within the year. Enlisted troops and lower-ranking officers would be allowed to return home as well, but would have their names recorded first as a precaution.

Finally, higher-ranking officers and officials of the Revolutionary Government of El Facil would be added to a registry containing names, addresses, and fingerprints, and be required to present themselves once a month to the authorities to renew their registration card until the empire had formally carried out their punishment.

After deciding on these measures, a new discovery made von Reuentahl sink back into deep thought: there on the list of senior officers was the name of Vice Admiral Murai.

This was a man who, in his role as Yang Wen-li's chief of staff, had earned high praise for his leadership both on the battlefield and back at headquarters—and yet now he had left Iserlohn entirely. What was more, reports indicated that he had volunteered to lead the seceders, and that his actions had been the deciding factor convincing many to join their ranks.

"Do you suppose he gave up on Iserlohn after the death of Yang?" said Bergengrün. "I'm not naive enough to believe that human sentiment is eternal, but it makes me uncomfortable to see it change this dramatically, even in another."

"Do I suppose he gave up?" replied von Reuentahl. "Recall the end of the Lippstadt War, Bergengrün. Why did the kaiser knowingly allow an assassin to enter his presence? There's an example worth keeping in mind, wouldn't you say?"

Bergengrün had no reply.

Three years earlier, upon the death of Duke von Braunschweig, leader of the confederated aristocratic forces, von Braunschweig's confidant Ansbach had dragged his remains before Reinhard. This apparent act of disloyalty to the duke had in fact been part of an attempt on Reinhard's life—one which ultimately led to Siegfried Kircheis throwing himself between Reinhard and his would-be assassin, martyring himself for his friend's future.

"Should we take this Murai fellow into custody, then?"

"We don't need to go that far. Just put him under surveillance as a precaution."

In any case, von Reuentahl was not inclined to punish the seceders too heavily. On the contrary, his calculation at that time was that praise for Yang Wen-li would sharpen the criticism among the former alliance citizens against those who had deserted the cause after Yang's death.

Among the seceders who poured into Heinessen was a certain man claiming to be an upstanding civilian from Phezzan. He was young, perhaps thirty years of age, with an active air and a cynical expression.

This was Boris Konev, proud independent Phezzanese merchant and old acquaintance of the late Yang Wen-li. He was flanked by his administrative officer Marinesk on one side and his astrogator Wilock on the other. The Domestic Safety Security Bureau could have hung the three men up like rugs and beaten a good two or three miles of mischief out of them.

"So, the free merchant planet of Phezzan is going to become the empire's home base, under the direct control of His Majesty the Kaiser. This is why it doesn't do to live too long," said Konev, although he was more circumspect regarding Heinessen, whose soil they were treading on at the time.

"Still, Captain," Marinesk replied with apparent thoughtfulness, "that means Phezzan's going to be the center of military operations and hooked up to the galactic economy and transportation networks too. That Kaiser Reinhard's more than just another warlord to think that far ahead."

"That's what's so annoying. A man as handsome as that should be satisfied with looking good. Leave a little brains and bravery for the rest of us." As he spoke, Konev's hostile gaze was directed toward a poster for a memorial ceremony for Yang sponsored by the governorate. "I don't care for our new governor-general much either. He's aiming for at least two or three levels of political effect here—"

Suddenly Konev shut his mouth. His eyes were now following four or five men in gray uniforms who had just passed in front of the poster.

Marinesk looked back and forth between Konev and the men. "What is it, Captain?" he asked.

"What is it? You were on that worthless rock Terra with me last year, weren't you? I saw one of those men in that creepy underground temple. They called him the bishop or archbishop or something."

Wilock's black eyes shone. "Which means they might be the ones who ordered Yang Wen-li's assassination," he said.

"Exactly. The men who actually did the deed were just a bunch of living weapons. Whoever set events in motion is off toasting their success somewhere as we speak, I bet." Konev stamped his foot with anger.

The three Terraists transported to Iserlohn had never talked, although it was unlikely that men like them, fringe figures within the church, had been trusted with any great secrets in the first place. *Yang Wen-li was an enemy of the faith and we eliminated him in accordance with divine will*, they had insisted, demanding only martyrdom. Extremely harsh questioning by Captain Bagdash had revealed nothing more, and the question of what to do with the men had become a topic of some debate among Iserlohn's leadership.

After discovering Yang's body, Julian had let his fury explode, hacking at the assassins in a mire of gore. When it came time to formally sentence them to death, however, he hesitated, and as the days passed with the matter still undecided, the Terraists killed themselves one by one. Two bit off their own tongues, and the third beat his head in against the wall of his cell.

"That Julian's got a good head on his shoulders, but he needs to loosen up a bit," said Konev. "He won't beat the kaiser with ideals and good sense."

"You always say that, Captain. But he's doing a good job for a youngster. Just trying to complete what Marshal Yang began is impressive enough."

"He can't use Yang as his manual forever. Yang's dead. And, frankly, he didn't choose the best way to die, either. If he'd fallen in battle with the kaiser, that'd be one thing, but…"

"It's hardly his fault. Blame the Church of Terra."

"I do! That's exactly why we're following these guys."

The gray-clad group entered the back streets, and Konev and his crew followed them through the winding lanes for a good twenty minutes. Finally the men vanished into the rear entrance of a private home.

After waiting for what seemed like long enough, Boris approached the high stone walls. Running his gaze across the nameplate, he let out a low chuckle.

Job Trünicht.

This sprawling building had once served as the official residence of the alliance's High Council chairman. It had been waiting here quietly since, and now its master had returned with a new position

"Looks like we can expect a pretty good show here on Heinessen. I think I'll stay awhile to watch."

III

Julian Mintz knew all too well how unprepared he was for his new position, and how undeserving of it. He fell far short of Yang Wen-li not only in the obvious area of experience but also in terms of talent and capacity. All he could do was keep asking himself "What would Marshal Yang do?" and muster all his powers of memory and understanding in search of the answers. Yang had left him so unexpectedly and so soon.

"Good people, fine people, killed for no reason. That's war. That's terrorism. That's where the sin of both ultimately lies, Julian."

Julian understood this. No—he thought he understood it. But it was still hard to accept. It was hard to bear the knowledge that Yang Wen-li had been pointlessly murdered by ignorant, reactionary terrorists. Was his own longing to find meaning in that death a tacit recognition of the efficacy of terror? Was it just another example of how the living co-opt the dignity of the dead for political ends?

But, Julian thought. *We need Yang. If we are to protect the tender shoots of democracy he left to us, we need his help, even from beyond the grave.*

A democracy, but one forced to rely on loyalty to individuals. This paradox had bedeviled Yang during his life, and following his death it was stronger than ever. Both Frederica, his wife, and Julian, heir to his military and political thought, saw no way to ensure that his ideals took root in the real world except by projecting a false image of Yang's own life. With all but a fraction of the galaxy unified under the autocratic rule of Kaiser Reinhard, the only way the ideals of democratic governance could withstand the triumphant march of the empire was to become the ideals of Yang Wen-li, Hero, Champion of Democracy.

The "individual as personification of democracy" that Yang had sought urgently but ultimately unsuccessfully in life had been found by his inheritors. It was the late Yang Wen-li himself.

A historian of a later age wrote:

"Alexandor Bucock and Yang Wen-li were both renowned admirals who had supported the Free Planets Alliance in its final age, but the meanings of their deaths were entirely different. Bucock's demise was the end of democracy, as symbolized by the collapse of the political entity that was the Free Planets Alliance. Yang's death was the rebirth of democracy's spirit—a new democracy not bound by the framework of the old alliance. Or, at least, his successors thought this a real possibility. Indeed, if they had not thought so, they could hardly have withstood the situation in which they found themselves. Yang Wen-li was to them not only undefeated but immortal…"

Amid his grief for Yang and his hatred for Yang's assassins, Julian realized something.

When Marshal Yang left us, he was still undefeated. No one ever beat him. Not even Kaiser Reinhard…

Would that be some small comfort? Julian recalled Frederica's words, and felt a small but barbed thorn within his breast. *"I wanted him to live. Even if he lost every battle he fought!"*

Yang Wen-li now existed only in records and recollection. But, conversely, despite his death, those recollections remained a rich harvest, those records eternal. His trajectory of undefeated victory, from El Facil to Astarte, Iserlohn, Amritsar, and finally Vermillion, would stand forever. Perhaps the inheritors of the Lohengramm Dynasty, oppressing the entire galaxy, would seek to mythologize their founder by eliminating the historical facts that impinged on his divinity. But not even the Goldenbaum Dynasty had been able to hide the monstrous deeds of Rudolf I. Whatever victories the sword enjoyed over the pen were temporary at best.

Julian had once suggested to Yang that he draw on his battlefield experience to write a book on military tactics.

Yang shook his head vigorously. "Absolutely not," he said. "In strategy, there are rules and approaches that are more correct than others, but tactics go well beyond theory. The right strategy leads to victory, but it's only victory that lets us see, in retrospect, that a tactic was right. No military leader with any brains would pin their hopes on tactical victories to win back strategic advantage. More to the point, they wouldn't include the hopes of those victories in their prewar calculations at all."

"Why don't you put *that* in the book, then?"

"Who can be bothered? You can write it if you like. Make sure you add plenty of praise for me—that'd be nice. How about 'He was a quiet man of intelligence and charm'?"

Yang had always deflected the conversation with jokes when it turned toward him.

Julian also recalled something Yang had told him about revolutionary strategy the day after they'd reoccupied Iserlohn.

"We chose the path of occupying Iserlohn Fortress, but that wasn't the only choice we had."

Instead, Yang explained, they could have kept the Revolutionary Reserve Force on the move, building democratic structures of governance wherever they went. Instead of relying on a single base of operations, they could have made the entire galaxy one giant mobile outpost, and swum in a "sea of the people."

"That might even have been better. Perhaps *I* was the one obsessed with the fantasy of Iserlohn, not the Imperial Navy."

It was not strong enough to be called regret, but Yang did seem wistful over the idea. Placing before his guardian what must be the nth-thousandth cup of tea he had made since joining the Yang household, Julian asked the almost too obvious question: "What stopped you from doing that?"

He was sure that Yang would have chosen the best option possible, so the question was what had forced Yang to abandon this strategic philosophy and take the next-best path.

"Money," said Yang with a rueful smile. "You have to laugh, eh? As long as we stay in Iserlohn Fortress, we can make our own rations, weapons, ammunition, whatever. But…"

But if they left Iserlohn and began to wander, supplies would be a regular, unavoidable necessity. They had been able to make use of an alliance supply base during the Vermillion War, but that option was no longer available. Whatever they received from now on would have to be paid for—and they had no capital. Simply seizing what they needed was not an option. They had no choice but to fortify themselves somewhere they could be self-sufficient. If their military resources had been sufficient, they could have stormed the Imperial Navy base at Gandharva, taken its supplies, and then changed course, but the Yang Fleet had not obtained resources like that until it had taken Iserlohn.

"Tactics are subordinate to strategy, strategy to policy, policy to economics. That's just how it is."

Whatever strategy Julian and the residents of Iserlohn took now had to be long-term. Kaiser Reinhard, the Lohengramm Dynasty, and the Galactic Empire had merged into a single threat. Constant awareness of the direction of Reinhard's political and military strategy would be their first task.

But if the situation did not change for the better during Reinhard's reign, any nascent republic would have to face down and negotiate with his successor. What that entailed would, of course, depend on whether Reinhard married and produced an heir or not; and in the latter case, a different response would be needed depending on whether a new unifying leader emerged following a short struggle for supremacy, or whether chaos and division were prolonged.

A computer could simply output INSUFFICIENT DATA—PREDICTION NOT POSSIBLE and abandon its responsibility, but a human did not have that luxury. It was vital to gather more information, which was one reason Julian had sent Boris Konev to Heinessen.

On one of his regular visits to Frederica's office bearing a pile of reports and approval requests, he found her drinking tea. Something about her color worried him.

"You must be tired, Frederica."

"Oh, a little. But at least I understand now. Working on a project based on your own ideas and taking care of matters within the authority granted to you are two very different things…"

She took a sip of her tea and sighed heavily.

"I'll just have to craft my own principles for action as I go. And so will you, Julian."

"Yes. That's absolutely right."

A tremendous realization riding in a tiny boat of recollection came to Julian. He felt something akin to awe at the sheer amount of mental work Yang Wen-li had gotten done in his life, between napping and drinking tea and breaking his record losing streaks in 3-D chess.

Julian's memories of Yang's words and deeds were vast, but they would never be added to again. He himself would have to put them in order, systematize them, and guide himself by the results as he strove to fulfill the responsibilities that had come to rest on his shoulders.

On another day when youthful vitality and exhaustion struggled within both his spirit and flesh for dominance, he had just finished mechanically consuming his meal in the cafeteria when a paper cup was placed before him.

"Drink this."

Julian blinked. He could not immediately credit the favor he had been shown. Standing before him was Katerose "Karin" von Kreutzer. The paper cup was full of a liquid of a color somewhere between black and brown. Its pungent smell declared it to be neither coffee nor tea.

"Thank you," he said.

The mysterious drink's flavor also defied his expectations. The change in his expression seemed to melt the thin layer of ice encasing Karin as she watched.

"It's not supposed to taste good," she informed him. "It's medicine. An old Kreutzer family remedy for fatigue. Ingredients and preparation method strictly kept secret. For the comfort of the person drinking it."

Karin's indigo eyes moved to the side, away from Julian's gaze. The population of Iserlohn Fortress was only a fifth of what it had been during its heyday three years ago. Those who lived there rarely found themselves faced directly with another person.

"This place sure feels empty now that everyone with any sense has left, doesn't it?" said Karin.

"You didn't leave."

"Unfortunately for you, I don't like moving house. And I respect Frederica too much anyway. I want to help her."

Julian was warmed by her determination. It was these words, rather than the Kreutzer family remedy, that melted his fatigue like frost in the sun.

"Obviously," Karin continued. "Any woman who could look at her and not want to help is barely a woman at all."

"The same goes for men, too."

Julian immediately wondered if this was a misstep, but rather than reacting with indignation, Karin apparently chose to ignore him. She put one finger to her well-formed chin.

"Frederica lived with her chosen man for one year, and my mother for just three days," she said. She seemed uninterested in discussing her mother's "chosen man," and so the topic tended the other way. "I once asked Frederica an impolite question. 'What do you see in Marshal Yang?' I said. But you should have seen how proud she looked when I did! This is what she told me: 'Why don't you look at the man right in front of your eyes who's trying his best to do his duty, and tell me what you see?'"

As she spoke, Karin studied Julian like an appraiser scrutinizing a potential forgery.

Julian's shoulders sagged. "If I could avoid doing my duty, I would!" he said. "But I can't ask anyone else to do it for me."

Perhaps calling himself "immature" was giving himself far too much credit. Perhaps his abilities had already ripened, and these were their limits.

"I understand you think you're not ready for your responsibilities yet," said Karin. "Maybe you're right. But there's nothing shameful in that. I've made immaturity one of my strengths, and I've been doing quite well."

Karin's hair, the color of weakly brewed tea, swayed slightly. Her indigo eyes shone as if cut from a rainbow. *She really is von Schönkopf's daughter*, thought Julian. He found the realization oddly moving, but did not give it voice. Could he trust the feelings of affinity she was revealing to last forever? But, no, "affinity" wasn't even the right word. "Compromise," perhaps, or simply "caprice."

"Frederica's inspiring," said Karin. "But maybe that's what makes men want to take advantage of her. I don't mean Marshal Yang, of course—but irresponsible men who exploit women who show any generosity are disgusting!"

It was clear that this accusation was not directed at Julian, but he couldn't help cringing on behalf of its actual target. Of course, that target himself would probably brush it aside with a scornful laugh: *Get a dozen or so men under your thumb before you start to complain about them.*

Behind Karin and Julian was a large and decorative potted plant, and beyond that was a table at which two men sat, their coffee cups long since empty, with nothing better to do than listen to the fragments of conversation brought their way by the breeze from the ventilation system.

"Well, it looks like before father and daughter could be reconciled, those two managed to mend their half-baked relationship," said Olivier Poplin, with a smile that wasn't even entirely cynical. "Imagine just sitting around and still having beautiful women come your way. Julian has Yang's luck there."

"Women? I only see one."

"You mustn't let your envy show, Admiral Attenborough. That's one more than none. There's no 'one point whatever' when it comes to women."

"Who's envious? Not everyone in the world shares your warped values."

"Yes, I understand that some men save all their foppery and whim for the revolution."

The two master troublemakers exchanged smiles like young carnivores and then, without any signal passing between them, turned their gazes back to where Julian and Karin had been—but were no longer.

"In any case, it's good to see our younger contingent show some psychological development instead of just locking horns all the time," proclaimed Attenborough gravely, though hardly a senior statesman himself.

"Indeed," said Poplin, matching his friend's pomposity. "One's youth can hardly be spent on revolution alone."

And so, riding the twin rails of solemnity and humor, the Iserlohn Express continued its daily advance.

"We must decide on our name," said Frederica at one of the meetings of the leadership. "If we declare ourselves an independent republican state, we will be abandoning all hope of compromising and repairing our relations with the empire. It would also muddy the relationship between state, government, and military. Is there something more suitable for a small organization like ourselves?"

Even von Schönkopf, Attenborough, and Poplin, the standard-bearers for frivolity, began thinking deeply on Frederica's question. This, perhaps, was the main reason she had been made their leader.

Finally Poplin's green eyes twinkled. "'Iserlohn Commune,'" he said. "Not bad, eh? It almost rhymes."

"Vetoed!" said Attenborough at once.

"Vetoed? But why? Surely you can't expect to judge my ideas with your awful taste."

"In the entire history of revolutions, no organization calling itself a commune has succeeded. I don't want to turn Iserlohn into democracy's grave."

In the face of Attenborough's surprisingly serious objection, Poplin seemed to decide not to argue the point.

The silence returned, but before long it was broken by the gruff voice of Captain Kasper Rinz.

"There's no point in a flashy, attention-grabbing name," he said. "Marshal Yang didn't care for such things either. We aren't naming something that'll last forever, so why not just use 'Iserlohn Republic'?"

Not so much by popular acclamation as through lack of objections, this carefully unprovocative and artless name was accepted. How brightly and bewitchingly it would shine forth from the pages of history was yet to be decided.

However, from that moment on, to make it easier to distinguish them from the Revolutionary Government of El Facil, their organization became known as the "New Government in August," or just "August Government."

Frederica stayed on as leader, but a bureaucracy was needed to support her. Echoing the early organization of the Free Planets Alliance, three additional conferences in all were held to decide on its structure.

In the end, they decided on a secretariat plus six other bureaus: foreign relations and intelligence, defense, finance and economy, works, law, and internal affairs. Any more than this, everyone agreed, would only complicate things unnecessarily.

The Bureau of Works was in name and mission based on the imperial Ministry of Works, but there was no shame in borrowing what had been proved effective. All nonmilitary hardware and energy sources within the base were placed under its control.

All the newly created bureaus would obviously need leaders. Caselnes's experience in military administration and supply made him the obvious choice for head of the Bureau of Defense, but the other bureaus were left leaderless for now. Still, Julian was far from pessimistic.

When Ahle Heinessen, founding father of the alliance, had embarked on his Long March, he had not been accompanied by a single noble, wealthy man, or person of social distinction. His companions had been the nameless masses, whose resistance to authoritarianism had brought them nothing but abuse and oppression. Together, they suffered through a journey lasting half a century, and together they accomplished the momentous task of founding a nation. Frederica and Julian were not unique in their position. No one *began* their journey as a person of renown and dazzling achievement.

"We shall put statues of Ahle Heinessen and Yang Wen-li side by side at the General Meeting Hall, the Central Committee, the Chairperson's Office, and the Revolutionary Reserve Force Headquarters—those four places only, and forbidden at all other public locations. We don't want to slip into hero worship…"

Frederica's explanation reminded Julian of Yang's stiff expression at their wedding, bringing a smile to Julian's lips. "Marshal Yang would have been embarrassed to stand beside the father of the alliance. He'd say he didn't deserve it."

"Oh, I'm sure he'd rather just lie around napping in Valhalla or wherever he's gone, but I'm afraid we're going to need him with us at least until the fate of his creations is decided," said Frederica.

Before long it was August 8, 800 SE, year 2 of the New Imperial Calendar. It was the sixty-ninth day since Yang's death. This was the day they had chosen for the formal founding of the Iserlohn Republic.

After paying her respects to Yang's remains in their ceramic case, Frederica Greenhill Yang was accompanied by Julian to the ceremonial venue.

You will watch, won't you? Frederica silently asked the man who had left her alone, who had changed her life not once but twice, as she approached the podium. The venue was a vast, open floor of the base filled with thousands upon thousands of spectators, their eyes and fervor all focused intently on Frederica. Amplified by the microphone, her voice declared to all of humanity that, in one corner of the galaxy, democracy was still putting forth green shoots, however tiny.

"I, Frederica Greenhill Yang, in accordance with the will of all those who support democratic republican governance, hereby declare the founding of the Iserlohn Republic. Our struggle to realize the freedom, equality, and democratic ideals that began with Ahle Heinessen will continue..."

Her voice was neither strong nor loud. In reality, Frederica's audience was just one person. She knew that she was only here because another could not be.

"I offer my gratitude to everyone determined to nurture the shoots of democracy even in these unfavorable and unfortunate circumstances. Thank you. When this is all over, I hope to be able to thank you again..."

As her voice trailed off, for a moment the hall was filled with tens of thousands of individual silences. But soon, led by Julian, Attenborough, and Poplin, these dissolved into cries of acclamation.

"Long live the Iserlohn Republic!"

"Damn Kaiser Reinhard!"

The air filled with cheers and thrown berets, and countless fists were thrust high.

And so the Iserlohn Republic was born. Its population was just 940,000 to the empire's forty billion, making it a mere 1/42,500 of humanity, but it kept the standard of democracy high.

The Galactic Empire and the Lohengramm Dynasty had yet to complete their program of galactic unification. Whether the unexpected death of Yang Wen-li would serve to hasten or retard their efforts, no being alive could say.

ABOUT THE AUTHOR

Yoshiki Tanaka was born in 1952 in Kumamoto Prefecture and completed a doctorate in literature at Gakushuin University. Tanaka won the Gen'eijo (a mystery magazine) New Writer Award with his debut story "Midori no Sogen ni..." (On the green field...) in 1978, then started his career as a science fiction and fantasy writer. Legend of the Galactic Heroes, which translates the European wars of the nineteenth century to an interstellar setting, won the Seiun Award for best science fiction novel in 1987. Tanaka's other works include the fantasy series The Heroic Legend of Arslan and many other science fiction, fantasy, historical, and mystery novels and stories.

HAIKASORU
THE FUTURE IS JAPANESE

TRAVEL SPACE AND TIME WITH HAIKASORU!

USURPER OF THE SUN—HOUSUKE NOJIRI

Aki Shiraishi is a high school student working in the astronomy club and one of the few witnesses to an amazing event—someone is building a tower on the planet Mercury. Soon, the Builders have constructed a ring around the sun, threatening the ecology of Earth with an immense shadow. Aki is inspired to pursue a career in science, and the truth. She must determine the purpose of the ring and the plans of its creators, as the survival of both species—humanity and the alien Builders—hangs in the balance.

THE OUROBOROS WAVE—JYOUJI HAYASHI

Ninety years from now, a satellite detects a nearby black hole scientists dub Kali for the Hindu goddess of destruction. Humanity embarks on a generations-long project to tap the energy of the black hole and establish colonies on planets across the solar system. Earth and Mars and the moons Europa (Jupiter) and Titania (Uranus) develop radically different societies, with only Kali, that swirling vortex of destruction and creation, and the hated but crucial Artificial Accretion Disk Development association (AADD) in common.

TEN BILLION DAYS AND ONE HUNDRED BILLION NIGHTS—RYU MITSUSE

Ten billion days—that is how long it will take the philosopher Plato to determine the true systems of the world. One hundred billion nights—that is how far into the future Jesus of Nazareth, Siddhartha, and the demigod Asura will travel to witness the end of all worlds. Named the greatest Japanese science fiction novel of all time, *Ten Billion Days and One Hundred Billion Nights* is an epic eons in the making. Originally published in 1967, the novel was revised by the author in later years and republished in 1973.

WWW.HAIKASORU.COM